Destiny: 0422

Alex Conway

www.newgeneration-publishing.com

 New Generation Publishing

For Emma, the tonic to my gin..

Joel Lundy

1.

Five minutes past six. Joel Lundy sat at the kitchen table sipping a cup of coffee and watching the second hand on the clock slowly tick and stutter around the dial. As ever, the kitchen was untidy. The rubbish bin needed emptying. The worktop was littered with bread crumbs and coffee granules. A stack of food tins - baked beans, tinned salmon, sweet-corn and cans of fruit cocktails – awaited attention. In the fading light, the tins reminded him vaguely of a cityscape. A riot of shape and colour. The labels like billboards - Welcome to Food Land.

But this wasn't Food Land. This was the kitchen of 85 Reigate Terrace, his home for the past two years. One of many during his eighteen years of life.

He took his eyes from the clock and gazed out of the kitchen window at the dusk sky, a darkened rich blue with clouds looking like giant waves. The clouds looked familiar but he couldn't recall from where. For most of his life he'd been watching them, fascinated by their amorphousness, awed by their splendour, and occasionally amused by the random forms that rose and fell and vanished into the horizon. Did nature have a sense of humour? At times it seemed so. He put the china cup on the table and was about to get up and clear away some of the mess when there came a tremendous thud from behind. The front porch. His father, no doubt. He flinched at the sound of Alfred Lundy's return, maybe flinching a little too much at the mere thought of him.

Seconds later, the kitchen door banged open and his father walked into the kitchen, proud as a peacock but considerably less colourful. Joel regarded Alfred Lundy as an average-sized man, five feet nine inches maybe, with a body like a bullfrog and chiselled looks that occasionally startled old ladies in the street. His face was a dull grey, the highlight of which was an immaculately trimmed moustache that extended with perfect symmetry distances from the centre of a slightly crooked nose.

His hands were big and workmanlike. On his forearms were dark blue tattoos depicting symbols and mottos of the mighty King's Hampshire Regiment. The ink had faded long ago, leaving spots like ink spillages dripping into his wrinkled skin. He wore a perfectly ironed white shirt and a pair of starched black trousers. The trousers were too tight and exacerbated the sag around his hips. He hitched at them occasionally, but they always slipped back to where he wore them most comfortably. "Joel," he said, nodding at his son. Joel nodded back, but said nothing and glanced down at Food Land, no longer a cityscape but a pile of cans that needed sorting out.

"What's been going on today then?" The timbre of his father's voice fluctuated between rough and smooth, like a barber's razor lashing a strop.

Joel paused for thought. "The usual… y'know…"

"That's it? The usual?"

Joel shrugged.

"Place looks a mess."

"I guess. I'll deal with it."

Alfred Lundy regarded his son for a moment, then shrugged and strode over to the sink. There were some plates and cups and cutlery waiting there, but not too much. He spun the tap and reached for a bar of soap and washed meticulously, clearly savouring the feeling of cleanliness before rinsing his hands and forearms under the flow.

Joel watched his father thoughtfully, gauging his mood, exploring the vibe in the room which was as chilly as ever. Was now the best time to broach the subject? He wasn't sure. But sooner or later he knew he had to. Or was he simply going to bottle it up again? No, the time was now. He cleared his throat and straightened his back.

"Actually," he said, aware his voice was thin and reedy. "There was something I wanted to ask you, Dad."

"Go on…" said Alfred, letting the water pour over his hands.

Joel swallowed and searched his mind for words but they were all jumbled up: a kaleidoscope of hopes and feelings and needs and intentions.

"C'mon then. Out with it."

Joel's mind was in meltdown. He couldn't think straight. He looked out of the kitchen window, noticing for the first time black spots appearing on the varnished window frame. Finally he found a thread of his idea and pulled on it.

"I… I'm thinking of doing something else after I get my exam results, Dad."

Alfred turned off the tap and shook his hands into the sink.

"How's that again?" he said, not looking round.

"Y'know, outside of the army."

Now that wasn't so hard was it? said a voice in his head.

Shut up, Joel told the voice.

The old man turned slowly, a condescending smirk spreading across his face. He gazed at Joel, eyes glittering, lips pressed tightly closed, then walked over to the kettle.

"Something else, huh? Such as what?"

Joel glanced out of the window as time seemed to stand still. Birds were hanging in mid-air. A cat was frozen on top of a fence panel. The clouds had crashed to a halt.

"Not sure yet," he tried to get the old man's attention back. "I went to the job centre yesterday, they said go back tomorrow… apparently some positions were coming up… but something issss going to commmeee up… I promise, Dad I… juuuuusst," he slurred his words incoherently.

His father appeared quite calm, staring despondently out of the large rectangular window and focusing on a vacant space. Joel sensed the calm before the storm. With a rub of his moustache he turned around. "You do realise who you are don't you, Joel? Your name and your family history? You are aware of such trivial things I take it?" he questioned sarcastically.

"Of course I do, Dad."

"Well?"

"Well what?"

He cleared his throat, his block-of-a-head dead still from behind. His voice changed abruptly, like a calm breeze in the ocean quickly turning into a storm. "Your grandfather and your great grandfather all did their bit. True men. Warriors they were! Serving their country so we could have freedom today, and now you're saying it's not for you. Is that correct, son?"

"I'm bloody aware what they went through. Had enough of it in our history classes!" Joel bit back.

Alfred turned around. Yellow stained molars shone through as he widened his lips. "And you stand there with your scraggy clothes and your floppy hair telling me everything this family has done in the course of history, for the sake of their country, means nothing to you? Dear God! What is it with you lot today? You've no idea of the sacrifices your fathers have gone through to make this world a better place…"

Joel shifted his stare into a pan of water sitting on the kitchen stove. Small ripples appeared.

"…Ridding the world of the scum that blights this planet, making sure we can have the life you all take for granted…" His father carried on for another five minutes, the same old self-righteous, jingoistic and gung-ho rhetoric that Joel had heard a thousand times before.

Finally Alfred finished and wiped a hand across the beads of sweat that had popped out on his forehead. The right words had left his mouth, but he looked perplexed and shaken. He walked over to his son and placed his meaty fingers on Joel's skinny arm.

"Son, I'm not asking for much." His breath was dehydrated, and foul smelling. "I was in your boots twenty-three years ago and now it's gone I wish…" he paused and took a chipped mug out of a cupboard. "…I really wish I was your age starting off on the great adventure once again, y'know?" His brow loosened and shoulders slumped. Turning his back on his son he placed a tea bag in the mug. Joel could see how much it meant to him, emotion was seeping through the guarded face of the old soldier, while masking a true expression underneath.

Joel felt guilty; he always did. Living up to his father was not an easy task.

With a sudden turn of the ankles Alfred marched upstairs, rattling a framed photo on the wall. Twenty-five young men in pristine parade uniform, noses turned up, mouths glued shut. A pride emanating from the collective soul of 1 PLATOON – C COMPANY – 1ST BATTALION KINGS HAMPSHIRE REGIMENT.

An ominous brown bottle and a lottery ticket hung out of his jacket pocket as he traipsed up the stairs. The ticket would probably have the same numbers selected. A combination of 0, 4 and 22. Three digits that would have real significance for both Joel and Alfred.

2.

The sky was overcast; a dull, murky colour with a filthy smog clinging to the air. A cooling breeze hugged the air as the sun tried to punch through the barriers of cloud, while over the horizon jet-black fumes pumped into the atmosphere from two gigantic chimneys. The fumes spiralled like mini tornadoes.

Across the industrial park a flock of pigeons nestled into the cracks of vacated buildings, competing for nest space and looking out for scraps of food. Amongst the grey feathers and incessant squawking dashes of bright incandescent yellow flittered between the buildings.

Joel gingerly got to his knees, surprised by the bright flashes lighting up the drab park. He was sitting in grassy wasteland that encircled the tin factory, eastwards of the pigeon nests. He squinted and made out what appeared to be two canaries enjoying the afternoon's flight. The birds casually darted around the pre-fabricated buildings in a circular motion, out-flying the cumbersome pigeons with relative ease.

Joel brushed his fringe away from his forehead, fixated by the yellow flashes weaving in and out of the industrial park like heat-seeking missiles. "See that?" he said.

Ivan lay on the grass beside him, his

hands casually linked behind his head, gripping his auburn ponytail in a delicate embrace.

"The canaries? Old news. They've been hanging around here for weeks," Ivan replied, picking a clump of yellow grass from the turf.

Joel reached into his jacket pocket and pulled out a packet of Golden Virginia tobacco and a pack of Rizla papers. He rolled two cigarettes and lit them both, still enthralled by the bright flickers of gold buzzing around the buildings. "Where did they come from?" he turned to Ivan's motionless body.

"Not sure. Escaped pets, I guess."

The flight of the birds was muted, completely silent like in a dream. "Where do you think they're going?" Joel asked. Ivan sat up and raised his left eyebrow. He looked at his friend: innocent, infantile eyes the colour of chocolate, a birthmark on his neck just under his chin, lips that stayed in two perfect straight lines.

"How am I supposed to know where they're going? Didn't bring my bird migration maps with me today!"

Joel shook his head. "Well it's nice to look at."

"C'mon let's go! Should have gone by now," said Ivan.

"How long have we been here?"

"Pushing on three hours I reckon."

Joel suddenly broke his gaze away from the canaries flight "Three hours? Ok, let's face the world again."

Joel heaved his wiry frame off of the dry, sandy earth.

They left the industrial wasteland of Brookbank Park. Once a thriving centrepiece of industry, Brookbank Park was now nothing more than a museum piece slowly sinking into a dry, sparse piece of Hampshire. They took a canal path that snaked under Westhamton High Street, past mounds of black refuse bags and disused jerrycans that lined the bank. "Satan's long toilet leading to nowhere," Joel would often say. The concrete path was cracked, as if an earthquake had torn the ground apart. Ivan peered into the canal where perch and catfish were rumoured to have swum years ago. A flow of dull brown sludgy water trickled along the canal duct, trying to find its way towards the English Channel. Water markings had stained the sides of the canal structure, highlighting what was once a healthy water level. Syringes, plastic toys and dumped electrical goods littered the path. Ivan kicked a rusting toaster out of the way. "I thought waterways were supposed to be nice places to walk along?" he said.

"The source of life!" Joel mockingly replied. They continued along the path until they reached North Bridge where their paths would always alter at this time in the afternoon. Joel moved towards the bridge, away from Ivan. "I'm gonna head home and try out this new CD, *Modest Mouse* think they're called," he said.

"Modest who?" Ivan replied.

"Mouse."

"Can't say I've heard them."

"I'll let you know if it's any good."

Ivan stood at the bottom of the bridge, hands in his jean pockets, glancing at Joel. "Are you confident about tomorrow?"

Joel shrugged, veering from the path into a muddy incline, humming 'Maggie's Farm'.

"See you on results day then!" Ivan shouted.

"What will be, my friend!" Joel replied. He kicked an empty can of Lilt into a patch of stinging nettles then turned and looked at Ivan from above. Ivan strolled down the canal path, shoulders relaxed, ponytail blowing in the wind, with a confident expression shining from his face. Right now Ivan was everything Joel wanted to be. He looked down at his right hand, which had been trembling since yesterday. His other hand clamped down on the shaking, redden fingers to try and suffocate the tension. It was no good. Nothing could compete with the angst gnawing away at his insides. Watching his friend gliding along the worn path that would lead past the town centre joining the A314 into the Copthorne estate he felt sad. That was the nicer part of Westhamton: greener grass, smoother roads, with house extensions painted pristinely white. Even the air tasted nicer.

He realised, that his own crossroads were now very close.

3.

I am the lone soul roaming this wilderness. Always in a crowd, yet always alone.

The words crawled along the paper, burning the back of Joel's retinas. He placed the poetry book in his jacket pocket as the engine of the bus growled from outside.

Drops of condensation appeared as he looked despondently out of a steamy window and caught a blurred glimpse of his own reflection: flush white skin, a messy fringe of grease and loose ends and a neck appearing ravished.

It was an unusually early start for Joel today, for he had decided to visit the Westhamton job centre. The bus was quiet, a few pensioners sat at the front staring into the unknown while the driver chewed on a packet of peanuts. At the back of the bus two girls dressed in school uniform buried their heads in a copy of Smash Hits, deciding when they would do the next bunk from school. Joel sat in an aisle seat biting his thumbnails waiting for the departure; last night's argument between his father and mother still ringing in his eardrums.

As soon as he had boarded the no. 76 bus this morning, something felt strange, like he was being watched within. It felt eerie and quiet, the chatter from the school-girls a minor hum in the background. He quickly flexed his neck behind to scan the interior. Low and behold! There it was. He had sensed it. The great symbol of hope, placed strategically on a board above the automatic swing doors, all freshly printed, watching him intently like a hawk. "*You can't escape me. This is your destiny! This will convert the boy to man, you'll see!*" it said.

Joel moved seats and stared out towards Copthorne Park, trying to ignore the young impressionable face and the bold lettering. An elderly lady was walking two spaniels around a playground. The lady let the dogs off the leash and watched them chase each other around a set of swings with boundless enthusiasm. 'Yap! Yap!' he could hear the dog's piercing bark through the glass. 'Yap! Yap!' The lady sat down on a bench, observing the joviality on the dog's faces.

Joel's father had a thing for dogs. *Bielefeld, Germany about six years ago, that's it!* His memory kicked in, reading like a film script… *Father and son walking in a park (a park not known to the squaddies) a few miles out of the city centre. A Brown Labrador approaches with a stick in its jaw. His father takes the stick, throwing it high into the sky. The dog chases, tail wagging, legs motoring. He looks up at his father: a smile creeps out from the side of his mouth and looks away before his father turns his head.*

"Go on, your turn!" his father says. He takes the stick from the dog's jaw and flicks his wrist, launching the stick into the air. "Ha ha!" He smirks. Father and son glance into each other's tired eyes; a rare moment of empathy.

Joel's eyes felt heavy. It had after all been an early start. His eyes felt heavy as the bus pulled away.

He suddenly felt a tap on his shoulder. It was the silver-haired driver with an inflamed gut. "This is us young man!" the driver said.

"Oh…" Joel said. "Thanks."

"This is us as well!" the poster above the doors added. *"What else are you going to do, Joel, sit around all day daydreaming about Picasso and Dali? This is the real world, my friend, now do the right thing!"*

The voice sounded more fervent than before, as if the sticky gloss was starting to peel with every venomous word. Joel took one glance at the board before dropping down onto the pavement: **'BE THE BEST!'** printed in white bold. **"BE DEPRESSED!"** Ivan's tongue in cheek remark had made him laugh that day. Ivan always had a way of adding levity to a serious situation with a cutting remark.

The morning was damp, with a drizzle blowing in his face. He left the bus and took a left turn down the Old Mews which always smelt of freshly cut grass. Past an Italian restaurant where a man was sitting outside eating a bowl of linguine. His mind raced back to the bus journey; the authoritarian voice in the poster, spaniels yapping in the park. It felt like doors were closing all around him, shutting him off in a strange, unearthly world.

Shop shutters opened, the steel panes crashing the roller housing like a signal for the new day of trading. He strolled past a sports retailer in a constant state of **CLOSING DOWN,** some charity shops with piles of clothes dumped by the entrance, a hair salon in need of a floor sweep and JoJo's Music Store: his one source of salvation during the summer term.

The shop front appeared to be concealed away from the adjoining shops, hidden in an alcove between an alleyway and the high street. Joel could spend hours browsing the dusty CD racks of JoJo's, discovering a whole new world from Stereolab to Siouxsie & the Banshees from Leonard Cohen to Low. Each record unique, talking to him in a different way, whether it was screamed vocals, plucked guitar strings or richly textured synthesiser tones. JoJo's always seemed like an exciting, fervent arena. Full of brashness and exuberance while the humdrum existence of life waited quietly outside: taking children to school, sweeping the pavements, begging for change. Joel peered through the shop window and realised it was 9 o' clock. *Ha! JoJo's doesn't live by the rules. Always opening at ten rather than nine.*

He was already thinking about the next visit.

He then recalled his task of the day, in the real world: looking for work. The Westhamton job centre foyer was a hive of activity. Faces all seemed to blur into one. He climbed a chilly flight of stairs where teenage girls loitered, smoking Lambert & Butler cigarettes and young men (who could have been school boys) argued down mobile phone handsets. Joel followed a sign, the one he always hoped would take him to some kind of Promised Land: **LOOKING FOR WORK?**

Current Vacancies… Manual Labour… Factory Work… Office Admin… Retail… he scanned through the pieces of card hanging from a velvet notice board:

Retail:

Cashier - Supermarket… Security Guard - Toy Store… Warehouse Operative - Supermarket… Shop Assistant - Local Art Shop…

He picked the card up and went to the waiting area:

Shop assistant

Local art shop

9-6 four days a week

Competitive wages, please apply

This could be the one! A voice in his head appeared. *Calm down will you? It's probably already been filled…* Another voice countered. He snapped a ticket from the machine.

The waiting area had a stale, fetid aroma to it: a musty concoction of tobacco smoke, body odour and un-hoovered carpet. Peeling yellow paint flaked from the walls, exposing crumbling plaster and hints of breeze block. Joel looked down at his feet, at the darkened cream carpet. The fabric looked to have once been a pristine white radiating around the office. Now, dark patches were ubiquitous; spreading like a virus.

He took a seat and waited for his number to appear. A middle-aged man sat to his left, slightly overweight with jowls hanging off his cheeks like lead weights. The man fidgeted restlessly; biting his nails and combing his parched hairline. Joel noticed a murky tattoo on the man's forearm, vaguely resembling a crown draped in a union jack. **2 LI NI** was printed underneath the crown.

68 flashed across the LED screen, his number. Joel arose and headed towards a plump woman behind a pine desk. The woman glared at Joel like a suspicious police officer, with hoggish pupils peering over a pair of white rimmed glasses. With trepidation he handed over the card.

The woman's podgy fingers thudded against a keyboard. "Let's see… What qualifications do you currently have?" she asked.

Joel sighed, glancing at a stain on the carpet: "Still waiting for my A level results. I should get them by next week."

"Next week?" The woman curled her lips and arched her wispy eyebrows.

"Tuesday, I believe."

"Well I'm afraid that is not much good! The criteria clearly says three A levels, grade C or above."

He felt like he was back at school, explaining a poor essay. "But I am really keen, and think my results will be a match for the position."

"But you don't have them now, do you?"

He paused, thinking about telling a white lie. "No… No I don't."

"Hmmm…" she stared into a monitor screen. Joel looked at the back of the clunky monitor, wishing it would swallow up the old bird, whole.

"Come back next week. Then we can talk some more." She reached for a biscuit in a drawer.

"But won't the position be filled by next week?" Joel protested.

"Possibly… I cannot…" She paused, her molars crunching and grinding on the biscuit. "70!" she barked, staring blankly into the monitor perched at the edge of the desk. Joel sensed a cue to leave.

As he turned out of the corridor the poster appeared again, this time on a chipboard wall up a smaller flight of stairs. It watched the despondent figure of Joel walking down the steps like a higher being, paving the steps of the Westhamton job centre towards a foregone destiny; a destiny filled with hopes, dreams and aspirations.

He took one final look at the motivated soldier, crawling under a cargo net. A mere kid… trapped in a caged destiny.

4

Joel awoke suddenly, the thump fizzing in his veins. Results day had finally arrived.

He grabbed a stained dressing gown and waltzed down the carpet steps. The radio had been left on his parents room.

"The Labour government of Tony Blair sets out ambitious reforms for education. Tony Blair states that every child should have a pathway to higher education, no matter your social standing"

He was too young to cast the vote back in May, missing out by a few weeks. He remembered his father being excited by the bright dawn of New Labour, Tony Blair being the new JFK of UK politics. Gone were the days of council house's sold to the highest bidder, bankers bellies growing while the working man struggled to find a paycheck. The working man, the military man, felt a brief sense of empowerment again when Blair waved to the crowds outside No. 10, that grin projecting out to a New Britain. Or so he was told.

The stairway was a narrow passage with no natural light. Bright yellow wallpaper adorned the walls and the carpet was an egg yolk shade, revealing a slight radiance to the dark passage. He entered the living room, a smell of last night's sausage and chips still hovering in the air, past unpacked boxes and a black wall unit made from recycled chipboard.

Entering the front porch, he looked down at his feet where four envelopes laid on a doormat. Rifling through the post he picked out the letter marked: **SOUTHERN COUNTIES EXAMINATION BOARD** and fumbled with the tight seal around the brown envelope. This was it, the day of reckoning. His eyeballs slumped to the pit of their sockets:

B - English Literature

C — History (Modern)

F - Business Studies

"Good old business studies…" He stared at the letter F. "…The most non-descript generic useless piece of shit subject ever invented!" His countenance resembled a blank piece of canvas, emotions hitting a brick wall. The magic letter F did as expected, confirming the confirmed.

A TV remote beckoned him from the scratched leather sofa in the living room. He slid down amongst the roughened textures and fiddled with the shiny buttons, snuggling in his robes. Channel 5 was showing a black and white B-movie, with tin-pot sound effects and horrid, cardboard acting:

"I tried, I tried but there is nothing here. Either I join them or I face an eternity of solitude and starvation," *the American lead grumbled, quivering in*

the corner of the cheap studio. "But they are robots. They are all programmed the same. Before I know it all of humanity will be lost. Lord, please tell me the answer!" he yelled to the heavens.

Around midday Joel's mother, Belinda came home, with an excitable expression dancing off her face. Joel glanced at his mother; she was wearing the same stonewash jeans and red cotton jumper from yesterday. "So what's the scores? Come on!" She took out a hairpin, and scanned the floor like she was looking for something.

"B, C and an F." He looked straight into his mother's serene, ageing hazel eyes.

As she took off her trainers her height descended further into the carpet. She sat on the sofa next to her son, a carefully planned answer brewing in her head. He glanced at the scuff marks rippling around the rims of her trainers.

"Well that's better than was predicted…" She stroked his back. "I'm sure there are plenty of universities who'll take you on, love."

"You serious, Mum?…" He became agitated. "What would Dad say to that? I can just see it now: you want to waste our money, taxpayer's money, dossing around for three years while I'm here grafting."

"Why… why do you think he would say that?"

"I just know, Mum…" he sighed. "Just

know."

"Don't put yourself down love; you have talent, remember that. I want you to have a good think about it."

Joel stood up. "Think about what, though? You know where I'm headed!" His socks trawled along the yellow carpet like a hobo killing time on a cold afternoon.

"But it's… it's not a complete lost cause!"

He exhaled through his nose. "I don't know what is going on any more, Mum, part of me thinks it's going to be an adventure, that this is going to turn me into this big strong man Dad hopes for. The other part of me can't help wondering what it's like on the other side."

Belinda looked deep into her son's chestnut eyes. A lost wilderness gazed back at her.

"Let me talk to him, cook him a nice gammon steak." She rubbed his shoulder in that comforting, maternal way, dusting off all of life's great problems in one careful swoop. He recognised the exact pitch in her voice, the same resignation drawling every word on that car journey years ago, when they had visited a housebound Aunty Caroline who had glandular fever:

"You still alive back there?"

"Yeeeeaah."

"You're very quiet, Joel."

"Just looking out the window."

Belinda turned her attention away from the rear-view mirror towards the road ahead.

"Half an hour I reckon."

Joel gazed out of the Escort window, watching fields upon fields of emptiness. He wondered who or what had occupied the fields; one, two, five hundred years ago: horses on carts, peasants sowing the land, a small village with one tiny shop and a population of twenty folk.

"Mum."

"Yep."

"Where are we going again?"

"Aunty Caroline's remember?"

"But what for?"

"You're making a habit of not listening, aren't you?" Her tone implied a telling off was around the corner. "We're staying a couple of days, help her out."

"Because she's not well?"

"Because she's not well."

Joel's eyebrows flattened into a submissive line. He looked at the back of his mother's tightly formed ponytail. It was always there, ever since he could remember; flapping side to side like a pendulum made of mousey brown hair.

"Mum."

"Yeah."

"Why is your hair always tied up?"

Joel could see a smirk from her left cheek in the rear-view mirror.

"It's easy that's why."

He turned back towards the window, no further questions needed. He fiddled with the seatbelt that was digging into his abdomen. "I thought Dad was going to fix this seatbelt, Mum. It's hurting!"

"I did tell him before he left, is it pulling too tight?" She tightened her grip on the steering wheel, her knuckles turning a light purple.

"Yeah it is."

"He should have bloody fixed… never mind… never mind." She let out a frustrated sigh.

"When is he back, Mum?"

"Couple of months, remember?"

"Why?"

"You know why, Joel, he has to keep the peace in Northern Ireland. That place you've been talking about in school."

"The one with the guys in balaclavas?"

"That's the one."

Joel glanced out of the window. A tractor was pulling two fertiliser jets across a field of crops with two seagulls hovering. "I still don't understand why he is over there, Mum. Why isn't he here with us?"

Belinda quickly turned. Joel's eyes innocently gazed out of the windscreen. She wanted to explain the complicated facets of history, politics, and religion and why the British Army were away spending months, years away from their loved ones. And why Joel's father felt the need to join the army in the first place. "It's complicated love. He will be back soon."

"Then where are we moving to, Mum?"

"Moving to? What do you mean?

"George in my class asked if I wanted to go round his in the summer holidays to play some Nintendo."

"Oh, ok," Belinda's tone dropped to the bottom of the car floor. "I'm not sure yet, love. We'll see what Dad says when he's home. Where would you like to go you if you had the choice?"

He looked out of the window at the clouds and the faded white moon; the sky always there when he looked up, changing colours but always present, a ceiling protecting the little beings on Earth.

"I don't know."

"Must be somewhere, c'mon!"

"Maybe some place where I made a friend? Find a place where we could find a den to hang out, hide from the adults and look at those funny shapes in the clouds."

"Sounds like a nice, quiet place."

"Maybe we could kick a football around and look for worms in the soil as well."

"Worms eh? Aren't they a bit wriggly?"

Joel lifted his cheeks. It was nice to talk about another place, secluded, far from the adults.

Belinda tweaked the rear-view mirror to look at her son longingly watching the world go by. The look on his face wishful, accepting of his fate as a creature born in the army machine. How hard could it be to make a friend at school? A friend known for several years, to grow up with, and then go their separate adult ways?

She realigned the rear-view mirror to the empty road left behind; a road already gone, left in the far distance of memory.

Mother and son sat in the car interior, silent, waiting for the next set of orders to be issued when the soldier returned.

Joel couldn't get angry with his mother for long, no matter how hard he tried. He always thought in a previous life she would have been a peace broker, or some kind of diplomat. Calmness personified. Shrugging his shoulders he sat back on the sofa.

"I won't hold my breath," he continued. "I don't know what else to do. Ninety percent of our class will probably find work straight away; the thought of further education frightens them…" A defeated look washed over his face. "I think me also."

She moved along the sofa next to her son, carefully scanning the bewildered shades etched on his visage.

"Maybe the old man is right. Least I'll have food, shelter and some money coming in. It wasn't so bad in Cyprus was it? Maybe I can get a permanent posting out there. Least they've got some sun. Never did Pablo any harm! My sketchbook isn't going anywhere is it?"

She looked deep into the darkness of his pupils. Two little dots conceived in her own blood, looking for an answer. Her mouth opened slightly, waiting to speak. She tried to give the most precious thing in her life the right answer, but her vocal cords were muzzled, pulling a muted string in space.

Joel hesitantly pulled his gangly legs off the leather and skulked upstairs into his bedroom. Belinda stayed on the sofa, shoulders compressed from the massive weight pushing down on her small frame. "Oh Alfie!" she sighed.

Joel's bedroom was small in diameter, approximately eight by six foot with a low ceiling. A boiler creaked and groaned in the corner of the room, radiating a warmness for which he would be grateful on cold winter nights. Wood-chipped wallpaper draped every inch of the rendered plaster walls; posters, drawings, and paper cuttings covered large swathes of the white woodchip. The largest wall had sketchings of pre-historic mammals dressed in green suits, juxtaposed against scrawled quotes of Keats, Bob Dylan, Nick Drake. He shut the MDF door and kicked a bunch of clothes lying on the carpet.

A double-glazed window shone from the south-facing wall, piercing the drab net curtains hanging from a thread. The lunchtime sun lit the room like the orange from a furnace. He jumped onto his bed and peered out of the net.

Pre-fabricated townhouses hung around the skyline like unwelcome aliens, varying in size, a sea of grey. Breaking up the rendered plaster and breeze block walls telephone wires drooped over his line of sight, criss-crossing between streets like spider web trails. To the east stood the two chimneys, towering over Hampshire like something out of *The War of the Worlds*.

Mustering inspiration was proving difficult. He shifted through a pile of CD's stacked in the corner of the room, next to some paint tins. "That's it!" he triumphantly declared, and loaded a disc into a stereo on the floor. The warm baritone of Nick Drake began to float around the room: "Saw it written and I saw it say, pink moon is on its way…"

The bristles of a thick brush lightly touched a small canvas, propped up on a chair.

"We're nearly there, nearly there…" he said.

"Pink moon, on its way…"

The sun broke through the net curtains the next morning, little rays of light bounced off Joel's forehead; warming his head until his eyes opened to the bedroom ceiling. He then turned towards the canvas.

There it stood on the wooden chair; the paint still wet, gleaming iridescent. The painting stood out like a beacon on an ocean night sitting on the navy-blue chair, proud, waiting to speak. He longingly gazed at his creation: Red lines mingled with green blocks, bird shadows hung in the distance, a figure waved in the near distance to a dot in the sky. He gaped at the canvas, trying to de-cipher his own raw viscera. It was like trying to recall the fragments of a dream, dots connected somehow.

The mattress springs squeaked as he arose and grabbed a cigarette from the side of the bed. His legs swung wide, knocking a can of Coke over the carpet. He stared at the dark sticky mess; with the black liquid fizzing on the yellow carpet. *Cocaine they used to put in this stuff*, he thought.

Quickly he gathered a pair of jeans and a woollen jumper and slung the clothes around his body, tied his trainers together and dashed towards the front porch. The front door slammed shut, the thud hitting him straight in the chest like it had when he last saw his father.

He took a deep breath and wandered down Reigate Terrace, noticing little characteristics of the street he hadn't noticed before. Reigate Terrace, like much of Westhamton, had been moulded into one homogenous lump: little characteristics one street from the next; thin townhouses, gravel drives, wood panel fencing, orange brick walls. The town a good example of post war architecture trying to solve a housing crisis with a ruthless, efficient architecture that looked like it could blow over with a sudden gust of wind. Garrison towns like Westhamton where all part of the norm for the Lundy family, like many other families attached to the Kings Regiment's umbilical cord; Bulford, Londonderry, Dover, Stafford. All enclosed in an insular military bubble. Then there were the children of the King's Hampshire Regiment: the 'pad-brats', always trying to outdo one another with daddy's inflamed anecdotes. The recollection brought a fading smile.

He passed through a playing field, somewhat overgrown, that backed onto the A314. The field was soggy and clinging to the soles of Joel's trainers. He ran through the field, ignoring the splash-back of mud on his jeans.

Johnny Crummock in Londonderry was the best one. His father had apparently taken out an entire platoon in the Falklands using only a bayonet and a black belt in Taekwondo. "Argies didn't know what hit them once they ended up in Dad's bunker!" Crummock would boast.

His trainer soles brushed along the grass. The field seemed bigger, extra square feet poured out of each side of the goalposts housed on either side. The soles of his battered trainers ploughed through the dampened blades of grass until he reached a hedge at the top of the field. A gap in the hedge appeared; he angled his chest through the hedge to avoid the bramble bushes, and headed onto Westway.

The Westway newsagent appeared around the corner of the hedgerow. He bought a packet of Golden Virginia and a pack of ibuprofen pills from the shop, rolled the tobacco and lit a cigarette. The tobacco smoke encroached into his lungs and lingered on his red raw gums, making him feel human again.

He knew Johnny Crummock was destined for the army, it was written in his own DNA. As for his own father, he was not sure; hazy memories of his grandfather Herbert lingered. He strolled back through the playing field, smoking his cigarette and trying to remember conversations with his father about the army. Racking his brain over and over he couldn't actually think what they had actually spoken about for eighteen years.

5

09:20 - DPT WESTHAMTON / 11:51 - ARR CHIPPING BURSE

Joel sat on a bench in the train station foyer, staring at a timetable of acronyms and digits.

The compressed voice of Cliff Richard hung around the station, echoing. He looked around at a man in the corner of the station, the key-maker, polishing a pair of leather shoes humming 'We don't talk anymore'. A vacuum cleaner buzzed in the opposite corner of the station, near the newspaper kiosk.

He turned back to the timetable. *"So. Joel Lundy. This is it…"* The voice in his head again. *"New life. Career. Adventure into the unknown eh?"* Tobacco smoke blew across his face. He took a deep drag on his cigarette.

Thoughts and lamentations and digressions pounded the walls inside his skull: The last conversation with his father, the poster, the woman at the job centre, Ivan, treading a road towards a normal life. Different forces pushing Joel towards this new life, new destiny, with Her Majesty sitting on her throne. Soon he would be a new cog on a giant machine.

A red Cavalier appeared out of the corner of his eye, pulling up in the taxi rank at the station entrance. The passenger

door swung open and an overweight woman
tumbled out, munching on a breakfast bar.
He looked beyond the car, at the
townhouses painted chocolate with pebble
dash render. Two solitary figures sloped
across the road looking for a direction:
One man was carrying a copy of *The Sun*.
Under the other man's arm a copy of *The
Racing Post*. Joel's focus then turned to
the lustreless grey sky cursing
Westhamton. Maybe he would see the inner
beauty of the town when he returned on
leave? He was not so sure.

He threw the cigarette on the floor and
turned, with his footsteps echoing
around the tiled floor of the station
foyer; the last steps of a civilian in
Westhamton. Was he supposed to memorise
his surroundings? Take a snapshot of this
moment in time? Keep the cigarette butt
in his pocket? He boarded the train,
still unsure.

The train arrived at Chipping Burse just
after 11:52 to a blue sky. Peering out
of a carriage window he peered at the
passengers hurriedly moving from
platform to platform, shuffling like
ants in a colony. The soldiers stood out
from the civilians; lugging camouflage
printed rucksacks, a suspecting look in
their angst-ridden, pubescent eyes.

ATR CHIPPING BURSE – FOLLOW THE RED ARROW

A sign had been erected in the middle of
the platform in bold red lettering. Joel
grabbed his holdall bag from an overhead
shelf; the bag smelt stale and musty from

years in the loft. Swinging the bag over his shoulder he left the train carriage. The first few steps on the platform floor felt cold and icy on the soles of his trainers. He could smell diesel in the air from exhaust fumes pouring from the back of the train. As he passed the sign he glimpsed a smiley face scrawled on the white background. The intrepid strings in his chest pulled tight - *"No going back. Where are you? Where are you?"* Green and black suddenly appeared, a kaleidoscope of forests beaming around the small station. There were three men in khaki uniform. One had three stripes embezzled onto an olive-green jumper; his acquaintances each had two stripes and appeared more youthful stood next to him. The only way to distinguish the two soldiers appeared to be cheek shades: One silky white with no blemishes, the other red with shaving sores. All three soldiers stood perfectly upright, chests puffed out impeccably, pinkish chins pointing upwards.

Joel approached his new hosts nervously, touching his scraggy hair. The soldier's scalps were shaved fine, exposing pink stubbly flesh around their ears that led to a dark green beret. Joel glanced at the headwear, the shape of a beret was critical to a squaddie's status he had heard. Each beret was shaped differently, with pointed edges and creases marking one from another. He admired the neatness of the mouldings and the way the material looped around their foreheads like a tree snake hugging a branch before angling tightly below the right eye.

He followed the lines of Three Stripe's jumper, passing two razor-sharp creases that blazed a path down the soldier's trousers, to a twinkle of boot-caps that were so highly polished Joel could see his face appear in the black leather. The turnout was impressive, much smarter and a lot cleaner than the ones he had seen growing up.

"Name?" Three Stripes asked in a quick, authoritative manner.

"Joel." The response spat out of his mouth like a rocket.

"Kind of a name is Joel? Only do surnames here, sonny."

"Ohhh, ssssorry Lundy," Joel stuttered.

"Ok Lundy pick up your shit and follow us down to that Lanny over there." Three Stripes pointed to a darkened green Land Rover parked in the drop-off area of the station. Joel trudged towards the vehicle, feeling like a frightened rabbit who had just heard the crack of a shotgun. Two boys who looked the same age as Joel had gone ahead and as he approached the Land Rover they both turned in unison, masking an intimidation that lurked somewhere beneath. The recruits' baggage was thrown into a side door of the Land Rover. Joel entered the other side, quickly followed by the two recruits who seemed to look at Joel for correct etiquette tips.

The soldier with whiter cheeks yanked at a gearstick and revved the Land Rover into life. He threw a piece of chewing gum from a side window and signalled to Three Stripes from inside. Three Stripes and the soldier with redder cheeks threw their bodies into the passenger side of the vehicle. A shriek of tyres burning on tarmac pierced Joel's eardrums as the Land Rover left the station.

Joel gazed out of the window, at trees and lampposts rushing past - Chipping Burse a haze of green and grey, colliding with the odd car or groups of sparrows. Within minutes the Land Rover approached the barrack gates. A steel barricade painted a harsh black, with a red line streamed through the middle of the giant steel pane. The gate was intimidating to look at, standing ten feet tall with barbed wire, trickling around the edges. Joel had seen many gates like this, the great barrier between military and civilian life cutting off two worlds instantly. He tried to peer over the gate from inside the Land Rover but all he could see were the clouds of a new day. Two recruits with oversized camouflage jackets peered through the open window and signalled to the driver. A third recruit, with a rifle slung over his back appeared and pushed at the gate and a flood of light blazed through the Land Rover. "Welcome to the real world!" said Three Stripes. The steel gate swung open and the Land Rover parked up next to the guard room.

Joel and the two recruits quickly jumped out of the Land Rover. "Right, pick your shit up and follow Corporal James," bellowed Three Stripes. All three picked up their bags and followed the corporal towards the guard room complex. "*The mouth of the barracks*" Joel had heard somewhere. Little snippets of information popped up in his head, titbits he had heard from his father and the garrison kids:

"*Always salute officers.*"

"*Never look instructors in the eye.*"

"*Don't slouch.*"

"*BEASTINGS!!!*"

He caught a quick glance at Corporal James, the whiter-cheeked instructor with two stripes: over six feet tall, with a toned torso ripping through the rough fabric of his shirt. The corporal said few words, preferring to flitter between the recruits and project ice from his battle-hardened pupils. The corporal raised a hand in the air, signalling for the recruits to gather next to a lowered brick wall. "C'mon, haven't got all day!" His posture remained rigid and upright throughout the introductions.

"Ok, stop here runts!" the corporal shouted. His chin was pointy, ears pokey and the blue in his eyes furtive. "Over there, fill out those forms. Sign it. Simple." The three recruits filled out next of kin forms in the guard room, Joel was unsure which parent to write down.

Surroundings of men and icy testosterone swayed it towards his father. He finished the forms and turned around to see four sets of inquisitive eyeballs suddenly luring on the other side of the guard room.

"What you lot looking at!" barked Corporal James. The other recruits quickly scattered, like pigeons scavenging breadcrumbs. "Right… this way to B-Block."

Deft rattles punctuated the airwaves as they moved speedily through the ATR barracks, Corporal James leading from the front. Joel looked down. The tarmac felt even colder than the train platform. Suddenly, fifty metres in front he caught sight of a green swarm quickly marching his way. The swarm of arms, boots and berets quickly reached Corporal James, who signalled to move off the road.

"Deft! Ight! Deft! Ight!" the instructors bellowed. "Swing those arms! I SAID SWING!"

Thirty pairs of boots clattered along the road, consuming the tarmac. Joel looked down: his scuffed trainers looked pathetic amongst the glistening boots parading past. "Deft! Ight! Deft! Ight!" The platoon of recruits passed swiftly through – one body of mass training for war. He dared not look into the eyes of the platoon.

"This way!" Corporal Jones signalled to a long, single-storey building. The three recruits followed the hefty bulk of the corporal; past neatly trimmed patches of grass and slim paths of sandstone tile that appeared to lead into a wood. The corporal approached an alleyway which led into the building. Suddenly he stiffened his back and raised his right arm in a salute.

"Sir!" he bellowed.

"Corporal!" the fresh-faced instructor replied. Joel caught a glimpse of silver badges on the instructor's epilates, gleaming in the face of the corporal.

A red brick building appeared through a chink of light on the other side of the alleyway. It blazed an orange glimmer against the darkness of the alley. Joel again looked down at the floor, admiring the cleanliness of bins not overflowing and pavements that had been scrubbed clean. Even the loose leaves of a baby elm tree had been swept up. The orange glow faded as the recruits re-joined the open air and B-Block appeared twenty metres ahead.

The corporal signalled towards the entrance, a door frame painted dark green with an MDF door ajar. The corporal rushed into a dark corridor with Joel the first to follow. Cargo nets hung from the walls, peering down at the new bodies. The poster back in Westhamton sprung to mind. He marched into another corridor, which was brighter and reeked of bleach, then turned right into a large open-planned room with a partition dividing the room into two.

"Welcome to paradise…" Corporal James said with a mocking sneer. "Sleeping arrangements are on the notice board over there. Get a good night's rest." A smirk appeared on his chalky face. "The fun starts tomorrow. Seven AM outside the block. DO NOT I repeat DO NOT be late." He left the room, playful smirk still engrained.

Joel's attentive stare looked up at a white clock next to the notice board. It was the same model as the one back home, without the dust. He looked at the clock: 1 o'clock. The two recruits unpacked their bags on the other side of the room. He could hear canisters, possibly deodorant, being placed on shelves and a squeak of holdalls being dragged along the linoleum floor. His holdall dropped to the floor, and he looked at the notice board to find his name.

LUNDY – BED 7

He sat on his allocated bed and reached for a tobacco packet from his jeans. While he rolled a Rizla paper he surveyed the new environment.

Linoleum was curling around the skirting boards and wooden window panes were starting to flake. His eyes were drawn to the magnolia walls covered with posters, placards and notes written on orange placards. He looked at a wall opposite his bed-space:

RIFLE PRINCIPLES
SECTION COMMANDER ORDERS

LIKELY ENEMIES

RULES OF THE FIELD

Like I need to be reminded where I am!
he thought.

Each part of the room had eight single
beds, with a locker parked next to each
bed. The chipboard lockers stood around
six feet tall, painted a mahogany colour
that clashed with the bright walls and
linoleum floor. He gently tapped one of
the locker doors. "Masking tape?" he
muttered. "Consumers wouldn't put up
with this cheap chipboard shit, would
they?" He noticed dents and scratches on
the outside of the locker door,
shuddering to think from what exactly.

The general condition of the room was
shabby around the edges but clean and
liveable. With a quick step he moved
towards the notice board.

**07:00 ROLL CALL OUTSIDE BLOCK - CIVILIAN
DRESS**

He walked back to his bed-space, feeling
the strings of his chest pulling tighter.
He visualised an old man inside his chest
dressing a young boy and polishing his
shoes, getting ready for the big day
tomorrow; the day the boy becomes a man.
A bar mitzvah of sorts. The two recruits
chatted in the adjacent half of the room
while Joel was amongst his thoughts. They
conversed with each other like they went
to the same school, knew each other's
families and supported the same football
team. Des and Dick, he would call them,
in his head.

He sat on his allocated bed, the chatter of the other recruits briefly filling the empty space. The chatter began to make him feel empty and numb, like his emotions were falling away into a dark vortex. He rested his head against a pillow and stared up at the ceiling, away from the flashing cards.

"Another day, all it is," he said.

6.

With a sudden jerk Joel leapt up off the bed, with sweat dripping from his forehead. He hit the light button on a watch he had found in the toilet block: 06:29. Steam gushed out of an iron in the other section of the room. He yawned and scratched the light stubble patch on his chin. As he turned in the bed and looked around the room a disorientating sensation pulsed inside his head.

Bright orange screamed from the other side of the room, waking him from his slumber. One of the recruits suddenly appeared from the adjacent room and walked into the corridor. He leapt out of the bed, dressed in a t-shirt and pants and followed the recruit - Des or Dick? He couldn't remember which.

A sharp breeze swung through the corridor, catching him on his bare toes. An observation he had not noticed before was the slick paint job on the walls of the corridor. The magnolia paint covered every corner immaculately, without cracks, lumpy plaster or mould. The ceiling even had perfectly painted coving blending into the edges of the wall.

The washrooms had a clean overpowering aroma like a swimming pool. The sterile smell hung in the corridor, eroding the faint whiff of boot polish and soap. He turned into the washrooms, noticing splash-back tiles missing, taps caked with lime-scale, cracked mirrors hanging from the walls. A stark contrast to the pristine corridor.

A tap gently oozed cold water into a basin. He splashed water on his face and closed his eyes, imagining he was in his bedroom staring at the ceiling ready to waste another day. Recruits came and went into the washrooms sporadically. Joel looked at their panic-stricken faces in the mirrors; reflections of little boys with toothbrushes hanging from their gums and stray hairs sticking out of their temples. They ghosted in and out of the washrooms, avoiding contact with one another. He looked at his own reflection. His face looked more like his father today, of all days. He didn't bother washing his face, brushing his teeth or dampening his hair. The other recruits hurriedly pushed past him as he left the washrooms.

"What to wear?" he pondered, opting for a pair of navy-blue jeans, black T-shirt with an Aphex Twin logo and the same shabby trainers he had worn yesterday. It felt strange wearing the clothes of 'Joel the civvy' on barracks, like the last rights of a civilian before the machine took over. Suddenly a voice morphing into a gruff bark erupted through the corridor and into the room:

"You have one minute to get outside. One minute you hear me!" Panic gripped the room. Des and Dick sprinted from their bed-spaces into the pristine corridor.

*Six to seven now, the note said seven –
one minute to walk outside…* the
mathematics processed. He closed the
locker door and wandered casually down
the corridor, nerves tingling with
dread. As he turned the corner of the
corridor it felt like a wind was pushing
his body into the jaws of an abyss. "Just
another day…" he muttered.

About twenty recruits stood outside the
block entrance in perfectly straight
lines, three men deep, fear gripping
their facial muscles, the smell of
anxiety in the fresh, morning air.

A pair of rusty brown eyes shaped like a
bird of prey glared at Joel as he passed
through the doorway. The eyes belonged
to Sergeant Jasper. Three stripes, the
platoon sergeant. The glaring eyes
followed him to the second row.

Every recruit had been told to stand in
a certain position, chest puffed out,
legs approximately thirty centimetres
apart and head tilted towards the sky,
away from the glaring staff.

"You lot who've just casually turned up
better start standing in the right
position!" boomed the Sergeant "NOW!"

Chin up, legs apart, chest out. They
tried to force their bodies into the
unnaturally stoic position.

"My name is Sergeant Jasper and I am your
platoon sergeant. In case you are blind,
dumb or plain stupid this is 2 Platoon
and your company is B Company…" The

sergeant pointed at a sign on the side of the building. He then strolled from the first recruit in the front row to the last; intently watching each strand of hair, flicker of the eye and puff of the chest.

"When you signed your papers you were given an eight digit number, your service number. This number is your own passport to army life. Memorise this. It will stay with you throughout your career…" Joel's brain tried to scramble the eight digits: *a number, so I am now just a number now? 2406? Or was it 2407? 24060422, I think.*

"…To my right are Corporal James," the sergeant continued, "Corporal McAllister, Corporal Van Giesling and Corporal Black; they will be your section commanders throughout your basic training."

The sergeant looked at a recruit in the second row wearing an oversized hooded top and scruffy jeans. "Haircuts you lot! Haircuts! That…" he pointed at the recruit's wavy fair hair covering his ears "…is not acceptable. You will find the camp barbers opposite the cookhouse. By tomorrow morning I expect to see nice shaved swedes. Nothing hanging from the sides, this is no hippie commune!" The sergeant's eyes suddenly veered off to the left. "Everyone, feet together… ATTENTION!"

In walked a baby-faced instructor with a boxed chin and blonde wavy hair poking out of his beret. Two gold diamonds were stitched onto his lapels, the metal shone in the morning sun. He walked up to the sergeant and the corporals exuding confidence and hubris. "At ease!" he said.

"Gentlemen, welcome to ATR Chipping Burse. Your new home for the next six months…" The instructor sounded like an excitable child about to go on holiday. Joel glanced at a bulge resembling a plum jutting out of the instructor's throat.

"My name is Lieutenant Cuthbert Smythe; I am your platoon commander." He spoke like a hunter just back from a big expedition to the wilds of Africa. Joel marvelled at the lieutenant's bronzed complexion, exacerbating an athletic figure; an Adonis next to the pasty minions.

"Six months gentlemen and you will no longer crave civilian life…" he continued. "You will have changed from nobody on the street to having a purpose. A purpose in your life…" The lieutenant's tone was less forceful than the other instructors, calmer and more diplomatic. "The great mission to free the world from misery and tyranny. All in the great name of Her Majesty the queen…" he stopped to clear his throat.

"Your lives will change forever. You will be part of a family – forget about Mummy, Daddy and the dog. This will now be your family. Each one of you will have a part to play in serving Her Majesty's forces, showing the world that the British Army IS the best fighting force in the world."

He stopped next to the sergeant, clearing his throat again. "The Kings Hampshire Regiment is the finest infantry regiment."

The lieutenant casually strolled up and down the front row, always keeping a distance from the recruits in front and the instructors to his left.

"However, not all of you will come through the challenges that await you." He glanced at the sergeant.

"The weak, the insipid, the cantankerous and the whimsical will suffer," the lieutenant moved his hands together. "The true warriors will prevail. Ready to fight a new day."

"Legs together. ATTENTION!" screamed the sergeant, and the bronzed lieutenant disappeared, leaving five sets of indomitable eyes peering down at the students. Joel looked skywards.

7.

The next morning Joel stood by his bed-space. His right foot was quivering and a foul, metallic taste lingered at the back of his throat. Fear cast into a flavour. He glanced around the room at the other recruits by their bed-spaces awaiting the entrance of Corporal James. A strange look of apathetical resignation cast a shadow across their faces.

The mirror in Joel's locker shone into the corner of his left eye at his oddly shaped cranium; reflecting a bump at the back of his head and a small scar from a biking accident above his left ear. His face looked older, wiser, with a higher sense of gravitas. The hazelnut camouflage had disappeared, cut to a fine length of five millimetres. It looked peculiar, unrecognisable. Dark rogue strands flaked onto his shoulders as he rubbed his hand through the fine hair.

"Can I just have it shorter on the sides but longer on top?" he had asked the barber.

"Numbers 1 to 4, all we do," the barber hastily replied. Sitting back in the barber's chair he felt completely sucked in, no way out: the transformation was beginning. The razor hummed and buzzed, releasing the greasy locks from his head as they floated to the floor then lay dead on the cold tiled floor. Looking at the hazelnut clumps littering the floor he felt an attachment, a bond that had broken. His head suddenly felt cold, numb.

Each recruit had ironed their barrack dress, ensuring a crease as sharp as a knife glided along the middle of each trouser leg. Green covered each recruit like a walking jungle, dark green jumpers, with olive-green shirts poking out, lighter green combat trousers and black leather boots sparkling like diamonds.

The door to the block suddenly opened, reverberating along the slim corridor. Within seconds the stocky frame of Corporal James appeared in the doorway. Corporal James hadn't introduced himself yet, he had just floated amongst the shadows waiting for the right moment. The shadowy figure casually strolled into the room with a scowl on his pink, unattractive face. His DPM sleeves were rolled to his elbows exposing scrawls on his muscular forearms. Joel had a quick look out of the corner of his right eye as he strutted into the room: two, three Kings regimental cap badges, a naked woman and an angry looking British bulldog all intertwined on his forearm.

"So… the new batch has arrived," the corporal mumbled, eyeballing every recruit while passing each bed-space. The bulky corporal's nose stuck out like a raven's beak and his chin curved upwards like a fresh banana. He sloped past Joel's bed-space, his DPM combats smelling like the interior of a new car. "Welcome… Actually, fuck welcome!" he said. Joel marvelled at the unjust aesthetics of the corporal's face.

"The new batch… this is always exciting for me. And it can be for you gents! My section. Four section!" He stopped in the middle of the room facing a pin-board adorned with the King's Hampshire Regimental honours. "My only advice to all of you is simple: DON'T FUCK UP! More times you fuck up; more chance you've got of being back-squadded, and no one in this section is getting back-squadded!" his voice turned up a notch as he glared at a short recruit in the corner of the room. "If that happens… I WILL take it personally!" He menacingly eyeballed the recruit and sauntered out of the room. The recruit nervously wiped the spittle from his forehead, using the corporal's dot of spit to shine his boots, a trail of fear and uncertainty hanging in the air.

The living quarters juxtaposed from messiness to cleanliness, rotating from weekends to weekdays. Block inspections on a Monday would bring about frenzied cleaning action around the block while the whiff of stale beer and soggy chips was eradicated. Any signs of un-cleanliness on a Monday would be punished by Corporal James accordingly, depending on his flaky whim. One day a fragment of a Pringle crisp had fallen into one of the urinals, causing Corporal James to go volcanic with rage. Four section were locked in the freezing bathrooms on

Monday night with white air exhaling from their lungs. Eventually the corporal unlocked the bathroom at three in the morning, letting half the section go to sleep. A rotation was supposed to let the latter half get to bed at half-past four. They never emerged to relieve their frozen comrade's, causing a riff in the section. Joel eventually hauled his achingly blue body onto his mattress at five o'clock.

He closed his heavy eyelids… "Six AM revile!"

He felt the flash of light spray across his face and heard a bellowing husky voice but a resistance hauled his exhausted mind back into the enchanted woods of his dream. Silver birches were reflecting off the sun, turning the bark from muddy white to polar sharpness. Butterflies flicked around the delicate branches, resting on the fresh shoots which poked out like mole snouts on a grazing field.

His body rolled sideways, arms locked into his side as his cranium collided with the wooden edge of the skirting board. He looked up at the ceiling, the collision dulling his senses. Corporal McAllister's dark blue beret came into focus slowly. "You think you can sleep in on me, runt? Get the fuck up now!" Joel quickly glanced left to right: SA80 rifle pictures and the King's Hampshire Regimental flag flickered from eyeball to eyeball. The mildew from the window pane hit his nostrils as the enchanted woods quickly faded away. He grabbed his wash bag and rushed to the washroom, shivering all the way down the corridor.

Dick nearly bumped into him. The steam from the showers poured into the corridor as he sprinted into the washroom and threw the wash bag above the nearest sink. The rest of the platoon swarmed around the washrooms, like bees around a nest, lubricating the cogs ready for the day ahead. He stood motionless at the fuzzy image in the mirror as the swarm flittered in and out of the washroom. Steam had clogged up the vision of the square mirrors. His skull throbbed, body shivering with nervous tension.

The recruits busied themselves with block tasks: sweeping, dusting, mopping while Joel hopelessly stared at patches of skin poking out underneath the steamy mirrors.

"C'mon Lundy, we've got to get this cleaned up in ten minutes!" Des shouted at his upright corpse. Joel wiped the surface of the mirror with his palm, ready for the next chapter of face lacerations. His neck burned from yesterday's shave. With a lethargic flick of his wrist he reached inside the wash bag and pulled out a disposable razor. The razor scraped against the parched skin of his neck as he winced in pain. Blood spots flowed into the sink, dripping in a blotchy pattern. He hurriedly wiped the mirror again looking for stubble growth amongst the clouds of steam masking the mirror.

It was over in a minute. He rushed to the toilet and unrolled some paper to stop the blood dribbling down his chest. "Outside the block, ten minutes. Let's go, runts!" a gruff voice bellowed down the corridor. Joel ran back to his bed-space and quickly donned a starched shirt, wriggled into a pair of combat trousers, tied his boots and attempted to mould his beret around his skull. He looked in the mirror: no matter how hard he tried the material wouldn't mould into a neat crease around his head. The fabric jutted out like the sideways profile of a cap. As he gawped at the monstrosity sitting on his head, he let out a quiet snigger. Here he was about to attend drill lessons and he looked like Benny Hill. He sniggered again.

"Let's go! Let's go!" Sergeant Jasper's tones echoed around the corridor. Joel joined the rest of the platoon outside. It was a warm day, not a cloud could be seen in the sky. Sergeant Jasper prowled the outside of the block flanked by Corporal Black and Corporal Van Giesling, all three instructors decked out in parade caps, sandy-coloured shirts and dark green trousers.

The recruits lined up outside the block with noses projected skywards, exposing puerile pupils to the deft brightness of the sun. Ten men wide, three men deep; a perfect rectangle ready to lose its rigid shape.

"At ease," Sergeant Jasper calmly ordered. The point of his drill cap sparkled with a quick flash. In perfect symmetry thirty pairs of boots stomped onto the paving slabs with each recruit widening their leg span accordingly.

"Today is your first day of drill…" said the sergeant. "Drill, as you may or may not know, is the organisation of a body of soldiers into battle, forming a solid disciplined unit." A metallic clink bounced off the paving every time the sergeant's steel toe cap connected with the ground. The corporals stood motionless, peering at every recruit from under their cap visors. The pack haphazardly moved to the parade square.

For the next hour Sergeant Jasper instructed the platoon on how to turn their feet, march and respond to orders on the parade square. "Left turn! Right turn! Quuuuuick March!" The platoon stumbled, heels and toes bustling with one another until the sergeant had gone blue in the face.

"Clumsy idiots! It's not hard! Turn on your heel, stamp your left foot down and away you go!" Joel tried to grasp the commands mechanically spraying from the sergeant's thick lips, but the brooding eyes of the corporals panicked him.

"Lundy move your left heel not the other way around, you muppet! And swing your arms in rhythm with your footstep!" The sergeant's gravelly voice echoed mysteriously in the open space. Joel focused on the heels of the recruit in front of him, equally in a state of flux with which limb to swing in what direction.

Rat-a-tat! Rat-a-tat! Boots collided against the paving, sounding like sporadic gunfire.

"C'mon, it's supposed to be a smooth march. Left! Right! Timed to perfection, not this clusterfuck I can hear!" Each time a recruit was caught out of step it cascaded down the line, causing stumbling fits and disturbing the whole pace of the platoon.

Eventually the platoon managed to march around the parade square, arms swinging, boots tapping in one motion. The rhythm of the footsteps sounding more fluid, robotic.

Joel looked around at the sea of green before him. He thought about historical video tapes at school: a Nazi parade, a Soviet parade, a Japanese parade, thousands of men stomping the roads of Leningrad, Peking or Prague carrying huge flags and saluting the man. The main image engrained in his memory was the look on every soldier's face as they passed the camera: focused, fixated and intent. He'd had nightmares about them.

As the pace grew and the rhythm became tighter, he felt more enclosed trapped in the 'body of men'.

The genesis had begun. A new machine was taking form which he was now firmly part of; no longer on the periphery of his father's stories on the outside looking in. Thirty boys clunking their boots together. A giant centipede with no brain of its own.

The platoon marched off the parade square. "Left! Right! Left! That's better, platoon!"

8.

"Hands off cocks! Hands on socks!" the duty corporal bellowed through the corridor walls - sounding like a drill sergeant from a Vietnam movie. Joel kicked himself from his slumber, feeling dizzy as he tumbled from the mattress.

The platoon looked groggy. Joel looked at his cohorts as he lined up ready to jump onto an eight tonne Bedford truck for range day. Sleep tissue clinging to eye-lashes, sporadic yawning, shoulders bent inwards.

The truck roared into life, past the guard room, out of the main gate into 'Civvy Street'.

The breeze of the morning simmered against Joel's cheeks - it felt coolly refreshing. The truck sped through a country lane, brushing against bramble bushes and overgrown elm trees and sweeping over dark patches in the tarmac that once resembled game birds. Joel looked at the pile of decomposition in the lane - soon to vanish into the tarmac leaving just a few dried-up feathers and bits of a crushed beak.

The truck took a sharp right turn into an empty car park and down a narrow lane that led into a row of trees.

"Right! That's us. Let's go!" shouted Corporal McAllister. The recruits jumped off the tailgate and assembled in three rows while a baby-faced officer gave a safety brief. Joel looked at the officer reading procedures from a ring-bind folder wondering how meticulous safety standards would have been during range training for the Crimean War… *All the "tallyho!" and bombast, with inexperienced officers sending grunts towards an enemy in a foreign land… Stumbling over each other's arc of fire until a leg was blown. Fast forward sixty years to the Great War. Improved technology – same problems. Casualties from friendly fire nothing new.*

"The shooting ranges of Chipping Burse are located approximately ten miles from your barracks on disused farmland the MOD purchased post 1945…" As the young lieutenant gave his safety drool Joel looked out past the two hundred metre range to the vast expanse of blanketed green. The ground was lush emerald, damp, with little foliage breaking up the landscape. Either side of the range lanes varieties of trees and shrubbery had been newly pruned by the head grounds-man; Henry Boddington's great grandson according to the officer. Two pheasants appeared in the distance, scouring the ground for seeds. He then noticed a group of rabbits hopping on the open ground and wood pigeons clinging to the skyline. The pigeons hung in the air then glided into blooming elm trees at the back of the range. The scene was like a Nintendo game.

"Lane one, Private Bailey. Lane two, O'Dowd. Three, Mace. Four, Jilks," bellowed Sergeant Jasper. "Five, Private Clark. Six, Lance Corporal Jennings. Seven, Jones Eighty-one. Eight, Dodson. Collect your rounds and await further instructions."

Private Jones stood nearest the lanes, acknowledging the lieutenant. Jones not being the most uncommon surname meant members of the platoon could end up as numbers to differentiate. The last two digits of the recruit's military number would attach themselves like a leech to the respective surname, a digit soon replacing a name. Joel glanced over at Jones holding his SA80 tight to his chest. Jones didn't care; he was another new kid on the block who would have responded to potato-head or knob-chops if addressed that way.

Day-sacks and webbing dropped in unison on the gravel. Joel retired with the rest of the platoon to a wooden shelter. He went to sit in the corner of the hut as the other recruits gathered in their respective cliques to clean rifles. Corporal Black and Corporal Van Giesling stood outside of the hut smoking and sniggering.

"Dirty bastard!" said Van Giesling.

The smoke drifted into the hut as the first shots commenced. A crack vibrated around Joel's eardrums like a pinball machine with a wave of drones immediately following, thundering through the English countryside unabated.

"She said twenty, but I've got my

doubts!" Corporal Black said.

"Sure she was outta kindergarten?" Van Giesling suggested, snorting like an overexcited pig. Joel sat back against an oak bench; his thoughts recalled Londonderry and the stolen milk money that his father had gone ballistic about. He never did find the culprit.

Corporal Van Giesling and Black wrapped ear-defenders around their berets and headed for the shooting lanes. The next batch fixed the straps to their cumbersome helmets and clipped their heavy webbing around their waists. Joel looked at his big hunk of a helmet and wondered why they were necessary on a range with rifles pointing in the opposite direction. Corporal James strolled off the range towards the wooden hut with McAllister following behind. James's footsteps were large and lumpy like an elephant running across the desert. He approached Joel, glaring suspiciously.

Joel took off his helmet and scratched his head. He felt around in his smock pocket for a pack of Marlboros attained from last night. The pocket was a velvety felt texture, soft. He grabbed the cigarette box. It had been crushed during the journey, fabricating the cigarettes into slight bends. He tried to straighten a cigarette out, his fingers carefully guiding the tobacco inside the paper, giving it a stiff backbone like a guard at Buckingham Palace.

James trotted towards Joel. "Fucking hell, Lundy, your fags bendy again! Maybe they're trying to be like you. Bent and out of shape eh?" Two recruits next to Joel chortled at the cheap jibe. The corporal grinned, feline-like, exposing black fillings and gums the colour of ripe beetroot. James then proceeded into the hut and took a swig of a water bottle while eyeing Joel. Joel lit a bent cigarette and wiped a sweat bead from his forehead. He could hear the corporal making monkey noises in the hut.

The next set of targets shot up out of the ground, the bullets pinging off the metal sensors when the tin targets appeared. "Next position against the post!" shouted the lieutenant. The drone ceased and the batch of shooters squatted, supported by a wooden post on each lane.

Each time the targets flipped over the shots fired off in synchronisation to the nanosecond. Most were successful, some not so. The synchronised wave of gunfire echoed around the range, from the north then the east: a thunder effect rolling through the trees and the meadows and the bushes. It kept coming, no targets safe from the gunpowder tsunami precipitated by eight rifles.

"Next batch, you're up!" Sergeant Jasper shouted.

Joel strolled to the first lane and loaded a magazine into the chamber of his rifle. It locked into place, cosy.

"You will have four sets. Firstly in the standing position, secondly unsupported squat, third the supported squat and lastly on your belt buckle." The lieutenant's tonsils sounded like they were being sliced by razor blades.

Joel pushed his left knee forward leaning his body into a forward position and raised the weapon into his right armpit. His left hand caressed the plastic handguard like a new-born baby. Then the fingers of his right hand curled around the trigger, awaiting the signal to squeeze the life out of the trigger.

He jilted his head down and looked through the SUSAT lens at the lane magnified: a different world. Fruit worms crawled over un-ripened raspberries in the bushes, rabbit droppings formed curly patterns in the mud, blades of grass swayed in the wind. He quickly glanced over the SUSAT lens at the calm of the English countryside juxtaposed against angry young men wanting to bring hellfire down the range.

It's what we are paid to do... shoot at things... innocent metal things now... not so innocent in the future... boys the same age trying to kill us... just because some fucking colonel told them to. He digressed.

The springs squeaked as the targets lifted fifty metres ahead. Each target was imprinted with a nightmarish face depicting the enemy: teeth snarling, devilish eyes, hunched shoulders with an oversized helmet. The resemblance to an American GI uncanny.

He took a deep breath, closed his left eye and peered through the magnified tunnel. The top end of the crosshair was aligned with the tip of the GI's nose. He squeezed the trigger. An initial reaction sent a jerk up his spine which turned his shoulders to jelly, GI missed. Steadying his palm on the hand guard he adopted the stance again and set up the crosshair to collide with the GI's right cheekbone. Exhaling he squeezed the kill lever.

Time halted. Lifting the heavy Kevlar helmet away from his forehead he looked down the range while the wind blew against his eyebrows. Down went the GI, falling backwards. He aimed at the next targets.

The index finger on his right hand was morphing into his trigger finger. He felt it possessing the flesh. The finger suddenly became stiff. A strange hesitance started to grip his hand every time he went to take another shot. Corporal Van Giesling ordered him to hurry up. "Lundy there's taking your time and there's ripping the arse. The enemy would have seen and killed you by now. Mong!"

He changed positions, going through the routine the same way he had been taught: get in a comfortable body position. Line up the target. Breathe out and gently squeeze the trigger 'POW!'

The session finished. "14/20 target succession rate," the lieutenant said. A relatively successful shoot, but he left the range feeling unsatisfied. He could feel his stomach holding the excitement down and nullifying the adrenalin. As he left the lane he noticed the rest of the platoon nestled in the hut playing a game orchestrated by Corporal James.

"Come on then, who's next? Jones Eighty-one let's see it. If it helps imagine Carmen Electra is riding you up 'n' down!" Joel stopped short of the hut and lit a cigarette.

"I'll try!" Jones replied.

Joel peered through the front window of the hut. All eyes were on Jones 81. The Yorkshire lad's face looked like it was sucking on a fresh lime. His eyebrows then lifted and his mouth opened "Aaaaaaahhhhhh!" An orgasmic groan purred from his mouth.

"What you reckon, Mac, that was a pretty good one. Best so far I reckon."

"Haven't seen O'Dowd yet," replied Corporal McAllister. "He's got the look of a cum face king."

"Tuh! Half these lot probably haven't left first base yet," James insinuated. The rest of the platoon longingly gazed servant-like at Corporal James. The absurdity of the exercise perplexed him.

"Hate to see your bird, Eighty-one!" The recruits chortled and grinned like a pack of wild dogs. Joel then realised it was just a game; a game amongst the section commanders to see who could pull the best cum face. He turned away from the homo-erotic scene, took a drag on his Marlboro and stamped it out on the gravel.

Clenching his right fist he looked down at the defective tool attached to his wrist; his fingers were stiff, the skin on his knuckles had gone a dark red "You'd better not do that again!" he whispered and walked towards the Bedford truck.

A clatter of rifles collided with the metal floor of the truck as the platoon mounted and disappeared from the range. As the truck sped off the range's rabbits returned to the grassy lanes and the pheasants timidly poked their beaks back around the blackberry bushes. Hellfire would be back another day.

9.

"WHAT'S THE BAYONET FOR!?"

"TO KILL!" the recruits screamed. "TO KILL!"

"What?"

"TO KILL!" The war cries grew in intensity, raging, bubbling like a volcano ready to blow. Joel's jaw was shivering. His skin a pale blue. The soaking wet recruits lined up in banks of six, forced into press-up repetitions and ready to run at sandbags on a hill.

The platoon had been kicked out of their beds at five o' clock on a chilly October morning. Bins were strewn across the floor of their bed-spaces, lockers trashed, mattresses upturned while the spiteful corporals embarked on their own payback after being pushed to death eight years previous.

"Get up! Out of bed, you piece of shit wankers!" the words bumped around Joel's head until he felt dizzy. Corporal James had the biggest spring in his step, smacking the recruits around the head and shouting in their cowering faces until his spittle was evenly sprayed. With sleep lines still creased onto their jaded faces the recruits were then herded up like an inferior race and marched around the barracks: "Press-up. Sprint with rifle above head. Squat thrust. Sprint with your buddy over your shoulders. Leg raises!" The repetition continued for two sweaty miles until they reached a dirty pool at the back of the barrack perimeter and were wading in filthy water up to their chests. Each recruit was prodded, poked and humiliated so that by the time the bayonet was fixed to the end of their rifles the inner animal was ready to be unleashed.

They ran at the sandbags. Boys acting like desperate soldiers with bodies shivering and howling and adrenaline crackling their nerve endings, while the corporals bellowed the same obvious question:

"WHAT'S THE BAYONET FOR? WHAT'S IT FOR?"

Joel looked down at the mud caking his chin. *'To dice onions? Cut string?'*

His bank quickly got to their feet and ran at the evil sandbag enemy. He held back, watching the two recruits ahead of him screeching and hollering like they were about to assault the killer of their parents. "Get up there, Lundy, now!" Corporal James salivated furiously.

He ran towards the sandbags lying on the wet grass while maddening bedlam flanked his shoulders. Suddenly the muscles in his thighs seized up, like he was caught in an ice block. The other recruits charged at the sandbags, stabbing at the hessian material.

"Aaahh! Aaahh!" The instructors looked on, watching their own creations beginning to flower with a mixture of glee and madness plastered on their war-dog faces.

Joel jogged at the sandbags half-baked. It felt like his adrenaline gland was refusing to play ball. He approached the raging recruits stabbing at the sandbags then slipped in the mud, narrowly missing the tip of his bayonet with his nose. The melee continued around him as he lay face down in the mud.

"TO KILL!" the recruits screamed in unison like a group of programmed robots. "TO KILL!" Boots squelched, the instructors shrieked, panting airways exhaled into the morning sky. Before Joel could get to his feet the next bank was shovelling past with bloodshot eyes, eager to stick the knife in. Joel ran to the back of the platoon, assuming the press-up position away from Corporal James's dead-eye stare.

The next bank postured and yelled, ready to exhale all their pent-up aggression into the world, which had now changed into a cauldron of seething rage.

Suddenly a realisation manifested: the soldier was now taking over the human being. He peered at the neat lines of boys waiting for the death order. Months of training had led the boy onto a path that would lead here, a transformation from boy to man, man to soldier. The prerogative of the brigadier sitting in his ivory tower clear:

"Make these boys hate. Pump up their

testosterone. Fill their blood with poison. Flood their brains with orders to kill another boy on the other side. Simple!"

The same theory used for many years. "*Best Army in the world"* Joel had been told. As he looked past the sandbags and overgrown ferns over the barrack perimeter he saw a strange sight: a river flowing from a hill in the distance; the colour sharp, incandescent red. A red so bright it made him blink. It looked to be flowing downstream into the barracks.

By the time the 'beastings' had ceased and the corporals had taken off their devil masks it was a bright, warmer autumnal morning. Starlings shrilled from the trees. A cooling breeze descended amongst the ranks. The look on their faces one of wild excitement and relief at a job well done, mission accomplished, with the transformation now complete. The river then vanished.

10.

Joel put the pencil to one side and read the piece of paper in his hand: **"I ride the bus. But where will it take me? The gates of hell neither here nor there…"** The air on the minibus was filled with cigarette smoke. Joel looked around to seek the smoking culprit; having a suspicion the burly driver was to blame.

The noisy windscreen wipers went to and fro… to and fro… clearing lumpy raindrops from the windscreen. As the rain cleared from the windscreen Joel imagined he was on a ship on the high seas looking for lost treasure. Sooner or later the ship would run into a lagoon with turquoise water, tall palm trees, sand as white as snow. Paradise close by.

The silence in the bus was tetchy and uncomfortable. Every time the wiper cycle went round felt like a heartbeat fading away. Nine recruits sat in silence on the minibus with heads readily shaved, tattoos newly painted and physiques nicely toned. Joel turned his shoulders, trying to alleviate a dulling tension pulling at his muscles. Deep amongst his scattered thoughts he thought about the advert on the bus back in Westhamton and that word: 'destiny'. Flashbacks of Bulford and Londonderry suddenly appeared. *"Why are road journeys always the best thinking time?"* he mused. *"Is it the world passing by innocently out of a glass window that brings clarity?*

Always an A and a B. I just wish I could be stuck in the middle somewhere. Let the wind take me to utopia please!" He glanced out of the window at a giant factory on the outskirts of Dortmund, towering over the city like an unwelcome shadow. The factory not dissimilar to the chimneys of the Westhamton skyline. *"At least Dad will be happy. But is he happy? Proud? Relieved…? Ah well, he got his way…"*

Each recruit stared ahead, solemnly focusing on a non-existent target. As if their brains were programmed to bail out and take an ambush position. Joel sat at the back of the cramped minibus with his hands curled up into tight balls like they were grasping at an imaginary rope. A grey holdall sat on his lap, watching the flat German land whizz past. He turned his head around the stuffy interior, contemplating the Allied soldiers in 1944 crossing the English Channel - heading for Normandy and to death.

Signs on the autobahn suddenly appeared for Ziegborn. The minibus took a slip road off the autobahn, descending into a street with unusually bright coloured shops. A cathedral with wooden slats painted white and black, top to bottom, stood out in the parade. Ziegborn: Centrum. Joel gazed at the sign. He again thought of his father, about to rendezvous with his new home on a barracks when James Callaghan was prime minister during the Winter of Discontent. He would often talk about this time; reminiscing about rubbish left on the streets, power cuts, inflation, a fog that stubbornly refused to lift. Bodies piling up in the morgue as gravediggers went on strike. A time when joining the army seemed like a utopia away from the mess on Civvy Street.

The recruits shuffled around the minibus, packing bags and picking crumbs off the floor. A large steel gate suddenly appeared in the distance, painted jet black with the king's crown painted in the middle: **1st Battalion The Kings Hampshire Regiment.** A shiny, bronze crown with fern leaves poking out of the sides. It had a folky, medieval feel about it.

Two soldiers stood at the gate; dressed in khaki waterproofs and soaking helmets, looking disinterested. One of the soldiers waved the driver through the gate. As the minibus passed through Joel could feel the eyes of the two soldiers like two heat-seeking missiles. *"Gallipoli barracks?"* the irony brought a wry smile.

A chill flashed across Joel's cheeks as the recruits jumped out of a side door of the minibus into the Germanic air. The air was blustery and damp, shivering the marrow of his bones. He wiped the raindrops from his forehead and grabbed a Bergen rucksack from the back of the minibus.

Gallipoli barracks. As he picked up the

hefty rucksack he looked around at this town within a town; like a market square of a provincial town the parade square was the focal point of the barracks. Around the square three-storey asbestos buildings hugged the perimeter. The ugly buildings resembling port-a-cabins dumped on top of each other. Another grin crept across his face. The buildings were painted a dark blue regimental paint that was fading. The paint looked to be covering up dark patches that were spuriously splattered over every exterior wall.

The recruits were ordered off the minibus and taken to their respective company headquarters. Joel would be joining 3 Platoon, A Company a lance corporal informed him. Summers and Boyd would be joining him, two recruits he had passed basic training with. A grey-haired corporal with a slight limp showed the three boys to the temporary accommodation in HQ Block, just across the parade square. "The battalion are on exercise in Poland, before you ask," the corporal informed them. The corporal's appearance looked beaten and worn out, of a soldier on his last legs. The corporal reminded him of someone.

HQ Block acted as a transit block for new recruits and attaches. It was also the home for battalion HQ staff and other members of the battalion left behind; commonly known as rear party. Joel looked at a section of felt roofing flapping in the wind, slapping against dark red brickwork as they entered the building through a swing door.

Foam tiles hung from a low ceiling. The block seemed quiet, with a dust coating the skirting boards and coving. A cosiness warmed his lungs. It felt snug. The corporal limped through the main door of HQ Block and into a musty smelling corridor. "Follow me," he said and opened another door. The next door swung back quickly hitting Boyd flush in the forehead. "Might want to watch that, cock," the corporal muttered and turned onto a flight of stairs. A dark orange carpet snaked its way around the floor, changing shades the further it appeared from the windows. Joel was intrigued by this quirky, mysterious hunk of a building. It felt worn and withered just like his grandmother's house in Eastbourne.

Summers, Boyd and Joel were shown to a room on the first floor. Joel entered the room. It was poky and claustrophobic, with an aroma reminiscent of the family dwelling in Gutersloh ten years previous: putrid carpets, dried-up fruit, stale tobacco. That same lived-in smell from garrison to garrison. Six dusty bed frames occupied the room, standing like statues from the apocalypse. Joel grabbed a stained mattress from the corner of the room and threw it on one of the wire frames. "What's that smell?" said Boyd.

"Smells like a dead mouse or something," Summers replied.

"It's just old," Joel added.

Boyd rubbed his forehead. "Hope we're not stuck here for too long, eh?"

Joel dropped his Bergen on the bed and went into the corridor where muddy footprints had stained the orange carpet. He climbed another flight of stairs, poking around the vacant rooms. The rooms in HQ Block looked to have originally been planned to house four to six soldiers. Six bed frames clogged up the limited floor space pointing in different directions room to room. Joel wandered into a darkened room, noticing fixtures which could have been lifted from the austere 1970's: chipboard cream cupboards, spiralled wallpaper, curved yellow light fittings. He turned to the windows. Each room had two windows placed in the middle of the back wall; circular nautical windows which projected little natural light into the rooms.

He wandered into the washrooms. Beige tiles covered the floor up to the ceiling with square mirrors in the middle held on by rusty screws. He passed two large bath-tubs and four corroded steel sinks. Then he turned a corner to a shower room with modern shower heads and shower curtains which moths had been feasting upon. Out of the washrooms he ventured back down the stairs until he was in the corridor where Boyd had been whacked by the swing door.

The corridor led outside, with steps also leading into a basement. He turned his head outside, checking uniform. A bold sign faintly glimmered from the basement: **1 KINGS HQ NO ENTRY**.

He glanced along the corridor then quickly dashed down the stairs into the basement.

A steel door as thick as breezeblocks guarded the basement. On the door appeared to be a missing lock. He pushed at the door and it opened. A light switch on the wall was the first object he saw in the dark. He flicked the switch and an orange caliginous glow lit up a dusty corridor. The appearance of the corridor seemed misty, like a swamp. Spider webs covered the ceiling and small odd shaped granules covered the floor. He picked a handful up; their texture was like sand, a dark black colour, the smell not pleasant. Quickly ejecting the granules from his palm he moved down the corridor.

The basement was small and suffocating, similar to the rooms upstairs. He let out a dusty cough and gingerly wandered down a cold passage as the orange glow faded. The walls appeared to curve inwards, towards wooden slats in the ceiling. Along each wall were hundreds of metal cages, a rusty brown colour. He approached the end of the corridor to another thick steel door, which appeared to be locked. He kicked at the door and a padlock dropped to the floor. By now his curiosity could not be reasoned with. He pushed at the door and saw a faded light shining beyond a pitch-black corridor ahead. He rubbed his arms. A squeaking noise was audible. He reached for a lighter in his jeans pocket, flicked the flint and slowly creeped down the corridor. The steps echoed around the subterranean dungeon and kicked up vapour trails around his feet.

As he slowly paced down the corridor towards the faint light he thought about his comeuppance. What would happen? It was exciting, terrifying. The same intoxicating mix of paranoia and excitement had consumed his reasoning in the summer of '91. "What would our Australian cousins think… ha!" he laughed.

The Lundy family found themselves stationed in Bulford, Wiltshire. Barely two months into the posting and Joel was bored on the summer school break. He had found solace in a forested hideaway a mile from their cramped little house that he was trying to keep secret from the world. He closed his eyes:

Willow trees lined the path to the enchanted woods, a path that ascended for twenty-two metres (he had counted it exact), then descended into thick thorny shrubbery. He felt around the bush, trying to find the break in the thorny cloud. Popping his milky-skinned face through the gap he yanked the rest of his body into the wet, muddy entrance. Little brown rabbits ran for cover, rouge sparks flicked through the trees. He squelched through the mud and surveyed the unknown treasure trove of Bulford. He liked this place, no irritating humans invading his space.

Taking the path that led westwards he went past two small ash trees. "West, always best!" his teachers would always say. The earth was dry around the ash trees, sucking up moisture that the other trees and shrubs were competing for. A cool breeze swept across his hair, awakening the bracken lining the path. He continued along past a badger's den and past a solitary hogweed plant perched on a mound until the old chestnut tree was within sight. Circling the chestnut tree, with remnants of decomposed conkers on the ground he kept a look out for spies hiding in the undergrowth. Suddenly he leapt into a bracken community near the tree. His hands began pulling away at the dead twigs on the forest floor. A green plastic shovel appeared (a tenth birthday present from Aunty Caroline) he continued removing the twigs until a gaping hole appeared in the soil.

Joel surveyed his work: a perfect square-shaped hole in the soil was starting to disfigure into an alien circle. "This is unacceptable," he said. "What would the Australians think of their new guest when I drop through the hole?" and continued to re-adjust the borders of his pristine getaway.

His eyes opened. Each step gave off a tinny echo. He was now in the basement's basement; the core of the Earth would be in sight soon. Counting twenty steps he stopped ahead of a sprawling store area and moved the lighter towards a cage. He peered through a wire metal entrance and squinted to try and compensate for the lack of light. Through the dark haze he counted fifty marble green gas masks littered across the floor. He glanced to the left of the cage and saw neat stacks of wooden crates nailed shut. On top of the crates were piles of papers and hardback books and some khaki shirts.

It was time to go, the sensible voice in his head screamed. Hastily making his way back through the murky corridor the stairs to normality suddenly appeared.

Joel returned to the stuffy room where Boyd sat on one of the beds reading FHM and Summers pumped dumbbells in another corner. He threw himself on the bed and stared at a ceiling tile, hanging by a thread. The world below felt unreal somehow. He then wondered if the great Alfred Lundy had had his own little hideaway among the dust, commotion bristling above.

11.

A sharp frost appeared on the patches of grass lining HQ Block. Running along the side of the block like a white picket fence. Winter in full bloom.

Every morning when Joel was outside, smoking a cigarette, he would touch the grass with his fingertips. The grass was as hard as granite. He would breathe in the sharp air every morning, as the cold snap which hung over Ziegborn showed no signs of abating.

The following weeks were spent in a loose routine as Joel slowly acclimatised to battalion life. Rear-party duties had to be filled such as guard duty, block cleaning and endless roll calls; by and large the new recruits were left to their own devices. Summers and Boyd sat on their bed's playing video games and reading lads' magazines. Joel sat on his bed, doodling on a notepad. The wet day on the destiny bus seemed an age ago.

"Oh, Lundy! Why did he do that? Why?" Boyd bellowed into the musty air, bashing a control pad in the process. Joel ignored the unanswerable.

All new recruits were addressed as their surname or number by their superiors, which would filter down amongst the lower ranks (or the '*cannon lemmings*' Ivan would call them). On numerous occasions Joel heard a Christian name he would use it, much to the disapproval of his superiors. Countless times he would find himself running around the parade square holding a rifle above his head – a punishment for this ghastliest of crimes.

Summers took hold of the control pad, a glazed fixation burning into his retinas. Summers was tall and gangly, around eighteen years of age with bright yellow spots dotted around his moon-shaped face. His character was an archetype of new recruits: submissive to superiors yet cocksure towards his level. 'The hyena' he was called in basic training, for Summers would constantly be testing the water amongst other recruits to exploit possible weaknesses. Unfortunately for him his deception was too transparent, often leading him into trouble.

Boyd stood a few inches less than Summers, his shoulders permanently locked together like a pair of rocks; a light brown complexion covered his face, accentuating his sea blue serpentine eyes and slim nose. Boyd's character was more capricious; amongst peers his motives were unclear yet transparent amongst the NCOs. Boyd would have no inhibitions running naked around camp if an NCO gave an inclination this would get him brownie points.

Joel, Summers and Boyd found themselves under the temporary command of Corporal Orpington of HQ Company. Orpington looked over thirty years; he had sustained a minor knee injury which had placed him into HQ Company as a store-man. He was a tubby man standing next to the fresh recruits, well past his prime. A detached look of a career escaping him drained his countenance.

The first few weeks on Gallipoli barracks passed by relatively calm, Joel kept himself to himself, passing the dead time by reading any literature he could get his hands on, doodling on his sketch pad and avoiding drinking activities in downtown Ziegborn. He knew he could not hold out too much longer without trying to save face. The weekly pilgrimages to Eddie's bar were becoming more frequent amongst the recruits, thus came the pressure to join the pilgrims for one night. He had no connection to Summers, Boyd, Orpington, anyone. Like a distant relative forcing small talk and getting sentimental, he was polite and shut his mouth, all the time wishing he was somewhere else, but unsure where.

One Thursday evening Summers and Boyd had taken early leave ready to hit Eddie's bar, downtown. Joel locked the door and stared blankly at the night sky from the small submarine window, from beside his bed was a notepad; he scribbled on the lined paper, drawing pictures of gargoyles wrapped around large buildings.

The night was here, no excuses. Macho pressure pushed down on his shoulders. Tonight, the young soldier would be baptised in a bath of blood and pale beer. Joel could count on one hand the amount of times he had sniffed the alcohol plant, each time ending the night in bed sheets of vomit with abject memory loss. Boyd and Summers arrived back from the NAAFI bar in playful mood.

Anderson, another of the fresh recruits from the West Country entered the room. "You ready or what, boys?" he strolled into the room, cocksure, a man on a mission. His Ben Sherman shirt ironed with perfect creases, loafers bulled to a crisp sheen, cheap aftershave stinging the cuts on his neck. Joel looked across at the impressionable boy. He could already see the metaphorical war paint.

"Woo, woo, let's do it!" Boyd yelled from behind a locker door.

"And remember we're squaddies now. No more recruit bullshit," said Summers.

"C'mon lad, all the lads are going down. Don't be jack lad," said Mackie, a recruit from Liverpool. "Orders from the corporal, no choice, lad," he continued.

Joel tried to hide behind his locker door.

"Ok, Eddies yeah?" Joel forced a reply out of his lips.

"Yeah, get down about nine; we wanna get there well before any Woofers turn up. See ya down there, lad!"

The four boys soon to be ritualised checked themselves in the mirror: splatting on handfuls of hair gel and turning up the collars on their shirts.

Joel grabbed a red chequered shirt and a pair of tatty jeans.

"Let's do it!" They moved out of the room like a drill formation into the corridor.

"Fucking Woofers, who they think they are!" Their circuits already programmed to take a beating for the team. Joel tried to picture the barracks across town identical in all aspects to Gallipoli barracks except the regimental colouring; housing the Worcestershire and Forest Regiment full of boys getting ready to scrap it out, all for a cap badge pinned to a beret. Joel looked around the locker door, he pitied them in a way, young men forced to conform or be ostracised. He joined them in the corridor like an outsider ready to join the flock.

Anderson, Boyd, Summers and Joel left the barracks and headed down the Ziegborn Main Straße. As they purposefully marched down the street Joel caught a glimpse of a clock-face in a petrol station window: nine minutes past nine.

They briskly walked down the street. Joel could feel his armpits warming up. As they marched past a food shop closing for the night Boyd and Summers began to play-fight in the middle of the pavement, "Get off, dickhead!" Summers bellowed.

"You're so gay, man!" Boyd replied. They both had an insatiable excitement in their juvenile eyes akin to bayonet training back in Chipping Burse. He felt warmth gently caressing his face and imagined a bubbling cauldron getting ever closer. The four soldiers, no longer recruits, hit the town centre and quickly located Eddie's with the yellow neon sign glistening in the nighttide.

Anderson was the first to enter the bar, Joel followed behind, his attention focused on an untreated pine bar that swerved around a concrete pillar smelling of sawdust. The walls were painted dark yellow with regimental photographs of differing battalions hanging off the plaster. High ceilings made the room feel airy despite the lack of floor space underneath. He looked from the ceiling down and noticed darker stains further down the wall. The beer, bile and blood spilt over the years.

The bar was lively. Oasis songs blurred out of a jukebox. Tobacco smoke filled the intimate atmosphere. Joel crammed his body between Anderson and Boyd and awaited Summers from the bar. Squaddies filled the bar area, varying from eighteen to thirty odd years of age. Joel took a quick look around; they all looked the same, shaved heads, Ben Sherman shirts, loafers, pink skin. He couldn't tell who was King's Hampshire, and who was not. With a casual indifference he rolled a cigarette.

"This the place then?" said Anderson.

Boyd nodded. "They'll turn up later on I reckon, that's what Orpington said."

Both Anderson and Boyd scanned the bar, taking in little details from every soul in the vicinity. The female of the species were lacking, Joel quickly poked his head around the pillar but could only see big stubbly heads shaped like ripe swedes. He felt even more tense and anxious, as if a safety blanket had been ripped from his shivering corpse.

"Who's that then?"

"What do you care, Lundy?" Boyd replied.

"I just wondered who you were…"

"Jeez Lundy, chill out man. Been spending too much time on that notepad of yours. Woofers man, Woofers!"

"Oh they come around here do they?" the words quietly fell from his mouth.

"They do indeedy," said Boyd. "And when they do…" he gesticulated with his right fist and stroked his knuckles.

The strong Bavarian beer poured down each gullet over the next two hours. With each sip Joel felt uneasy on his knees. Something was about to happen, he could feel it in the smoky testosterone filled air.

"What about those lot?" Anderson nodded in the direction of a group of squaddies loitering near the jukebox.

"Nah, I recognise the one with the 'tache, he's one of ours – signal platoon I think," Summers replied.

Anderson, Summers and Boyd carried on fooling around amongst themselves, every couple of minutes checking the competition in the bar. Joel stood with them hanging an elbow off the curved bar, the Hoegaarden blurring his focus.

The bar began to open up, a big expanse of smiling faces and glistening bottles. Every face in the vicinity began to look at him, more jovial and animated. A breezy sensation ran around his limbs. The three recruits turned soldiers continued their boisterous conversing, each trying to out-shout one another. He lost count of the amount of times he heard "bollocks!" or "wankdirch!" in a sentence. He gazed blurrily at the plethora of shiny beer bottles behind the bar and the overweight German man with a hooked nose serving the thirsty.

"You don't say much do ya, Lundy?" said Boyd.

Joel twitched, letting out a nervy smile.

"What's the time?" Anderson shouted.

"Eleven… quarter past," Summers replied.

Anderson waved his hand. "Let's head."

The squaddie's shuffled their feet away from the sticky mulch clinging to the wooden floorboards and into the fresh air. Joel lit a cigarette and followed the group into an underpass that ran under the town centre into an unloading area for the shops above.

"Oi! Oi", "aaaarrrrghhhh!" the war cries bounced around the concrete pillars and corrugated iron. He managed to focus on

Anderson's protruding earlobes as the march continued, into a dimly lit underpass smelling of ammonia and spilt diesel. He stumbled into some wooden crates labelled: **'GAP' 'DIESEL'** strewn on the floor.

The fuzzy feeling started to wear off. He felt the alcohol pushing his senses into an uncontrollable haze, the further they ventured down the creepy underpass. Anderson's earlobes stopped at a group of young men queuing outside a metal staircase. Joel shook his head and focused on a murky grey staircase, noticing a black door at the top. He felt like a lemming following the group up a cliff.

"This is it," Anderson said.

"How do you know?" Summers replied.

"Yeah I don't see a sign for Savoy's, Andy," Boyd protested.

"It has to be, look! I recognise that guy from HQ, and that guy there says he's in B Company," Anderson's index finger vaguely pointed in the direction of a group about to enter through the mysterious door.

Joel had heard the Savoy's name banded around the block, like a soldier's Mecca whereby kudos would be instantly granted to the pilgrim willing to make a noisy nuisance of themselves. And here he stood, waiting.

Each group in the queue was clearly

distinguishable from each other: There were the squaddies, the locals and a few teenagers who were in Ziegborn because they had no choice (commonly known as pad-brats). Joel was a pad brat, albeit not through choice. He scanned the queue of people through his watery vision.

The locals had unconventional haircuts varying in colours, shapes and textures. They had ear piercings, wore oversized puffer jackets and flared trousers. They stood in the queue, hands in pockets with a peep barely registering while the squaddies hollered and conducted play-fights, sounding like an excitable group of chimpanzees. The squaddie dress code was formulaic and conventional: loafer shoes, Sherman/YSL/Ralph Lauren shirts, Armani jeans. All with varying degrees of authenticity.

The pad-brats drifted in and out of the queue, scouting around the entrance, looking for the best way to get in and avoid detection from the door-men. Entrance into this sort of establishment was always difficult for a cocksure sixteen-year-old with fresh tonsils. Joel looked at the twitchy kids with their rogue cheeks and bronzed effervescent complexions and wondered how he had turned out so different. Teenage years spent in his room, scribbling on a drawing pad and drinking pineapple juice. It was like looking through a looking glass, visualising what he could have been doing two years ago, avoiding the same type of pad-brats he could now see standing in his blurred vision.

"Next!" the burly door-man shouted, fixing his pokey eyes at the next group in the queue. The door-man's enormous bulk towered over the small door frame like a storm cloud gathering over a small island.

"I said... NEXT!"

The door-man looked not far from seven feet tall, with shoulders the size of mountains. His neck fat hung over his shirt collar, adding more mass to his colossal monster's head. Tattoos winded up the side of his neck all the way to the base of his earlobe. Joel looked at the door-man's attire: pitch black from shirt collar to boot tip, almost blending straight into the door. An authoritarian disdain gripped the door-man's face as he grimaced and snarled at each punter walking towards him. *"I have the power; don't you forget that! Now kneel before me!"* Joel could see it in his primeval eyes.

Summers was the first to get the door-man's animalistic stare; upper lip curled, nose flaring, eyebrows scrunched together. Joel looked at the big imposing figure; all he could see was a gorilla in the Congo, King Kong, Gorillas in the Mist.

The door-man finished frisking Summers. "Next!" His tone was high, chirpy. Joel couldn't make out if he was ex-forces or just a random Brit washed ashore in

Ziegborn town. His enormous hands felt
around Joel's pockets, down his trouser
leg and patted his behind. "Yeah next!"
he shouted.

"Don't be getting above your station
boys, alright. I ain't kidding!" the
door-man sternly spoke.

Anderson and Boyd hollered in a stairway
that led upstairs into the nightclub.
"Woooo! This is it boys! This is it!
Woofers watch out, ha!" Joel followed
behind, stumbling against the banister
and stepping on fine segments of broken
glass. The bass drone ping ponged around
the walls of the downstairs foyer. He
felt a falling sensation in the pit of
his stomach, the drone rumbled then shot
in bursts from wall to wall. As they
approached the top of the stairs a
plastic moose head greeted them on a
wall. The head appeared like a bad joke,
with a light-hearted look carved onto its
cartoonish features. The other recruits
marched into the club, fists clenched,
salivating from the lip, ready to be the
man for a night. Joel was the last one
to enter through a shady brown door into
the nightclub.

Aftershave clung to the air, an enticing
aroma in the most unromantic of settings.
The inside of the club was small, no
bigger than sixty metres squared with a
u-shaped bar and a rectangular dance
floor squeezed inside. The interior
decorated like a 1970's kitsch
discotheque: glitter-balls from the
ceiling, flashing beams projecting onto

the empty dance floor and robes draped around the empty wall space. The DJ stood inconspicuously in a corner of the dance floor, pumping out a mixture of Euro-pop and UK chart hits as a wave of low-end frequencies crackled and hummed to a distorted melody. "Blue da ba deed a ba di" blurted out of a pair of tinny speakers hidden underneath the DJ booth.

Men, both civilian and non-civilian loitered. Scanning the opposition like a group of shifty pimps in packs around the periphery of the dance floor. In between the packs of men small groups of German girls stood silently sipping Jägermeister cocktails and casually blowing smoke around the room. Joel followed Boyd and Summers to the bar and ordered four steins of Hoegaarden. The barmaid looked at him with an alluring beam and flicked her blonde locks behind her ear. Joel took stock of her breasts, tightly packed into a low-cut top. Quickly he diverted his stare towards a fruit machine in the corner, picked up the hefty glasses and tried to locate the others amongst the ever- widening crowd. Summers slender frame appeared in the mist near another fruit machine. He carefully nurtured the steins through the crowd.

Boyd took a big thirst-quenching gulp of the beer, as if he was stranded on the Sahara. "Think I can see some of them over there," he shouted into Anderson's ear and took another slurp. Joel stood at eye level with Anderson, watching the excitement flush through his translucent skin. "Ready?"

"Ready!"

"Ha ha," they laughed in unison.

The evening progressed quickly. Joel rocked back and forth, feeling prickles on his back like someone was about to smash his head from behind. He edged towards one of the walls and let Anderson and Boyd continue their animated conversation over the high pitch squeal bouncing out of the speakers.

Summers came back from the bar holding four steins of beer and four glasses of pale looking shorts. 'Cha-ching!' The short glasses clinked together. Joel tasted bitter lemon-infused alcohol; a fireball racing into his fragile stomach. Summers, Boyd and Anderson grimaced, then set upon the steins. Joel attempted to watch them; his vision now a dreary fuzz of darkened colours and steam. It was like looking out of a car window on a blustery day. The club started to spin on its axis and he thought about the foundations in the Germanic soil creaking and groaning with the weight above. He looked towards the dance floor through a smoke screen of rainbow colours and tall bodies.

The German girls were starting to get noticed by the groups loitering around the dance floor periphery. The girls moved their stiff limbs, waving to and fro with the generic Euro-pop beat. Every few seconds they glanced for attention from the lustful packs. Joel looked at the girls with their tightly packed ponytails and baggy clothes with demeanours stoic and devoid of emotion. He almost felt sorry for them, flirting with the opposite sex waiting for the cage doors to open.

More bodies poured into the club from downstairs, each body taking up more of the crowded floor. He felt nudges on his elbows. The temperature rose, sweat began to drip from the ceiling, the air became thinner, the irritating melody increased in volume. As the music became louder he felt the pressure cooker begin to tremble inside the club; voices became harsher, drinks spilled over the floor, the stench of heated body odour clung to the hairs in his nostrils. He leant against a high table and tried to roll a cigarette but his fingers were numb and the tobacco spilt over the table as the darkened room whooshed like a turbo charged merry-go-round. He felt his bladder pushing against the walls of his stomach but couldn't muster the energy to find the toilets. The room continued to spin: round and round, round and round.

Suddenly a game of human dominoes took place at the foot of the bar; he caught a glimpse of it from the corner of his left eye. As he turned his head a girl with peroxide blonde hair went running towards the exit. Bodies started to fall over the bar. Fists flew in from every angle. All he could see were knuckles and glasses smashing amongst the strobe lights. The squaddies who had been set upon started to punch back; causing the dominoes to push in the opposite direction. He gawped at the incident; every punch, every crack, every head-butt slowed down to walking pace.

From the corner of his eye he saw Summers and Anderson rushing towards the melee like a pack of excited dogs. The DJ lifted the needle off the record, lulling the ambience to sickening thuds and screaming profanities. Right by his nose Joel saw a squaddie pummel another's face with wild hay-makers while others stood around with mouths wide open, gawping devilish. Details suddenly crystallised: the buttons on the squaddie's shirts, the lettering on a beer bottle, rings on fingers flashing in the darkness.

In came the door-man, bursting onto the scene with the tail of his coat dwarfing bodies underneath. His bald head shone under the spotlights, making his flesh look bronzed. He pushed bodies out of the way and glided into the ruckus like an inconspicuous assassin. In he went, targeting the main perpetrators, grabbing one in a stress position while kicking another with his size ten boot. Bodies fell on the bar, their hands making screeching noises on the polished wood. Others fell to the floor in a rain of kicks and stomps. "Gorillas! Dirty gorillas!" a shout came from the back of the nightclub. Joel stared into the whites of the door-man's eyes; wild, excitable, insatiable, the black of his clothing and the size of his fists resembling the angry primate. This was the door-man's orgasm, a wild instinct to hurt another. The door-man signalled to his cohort and hauled a squaddie's limp frame through the club.

The fight heightened Joel's senses, kicking away the intoxicated lethargy floating around his body. He looked on at the ongoing chaos carefully avoiding eye contact with the fighters. He counted eight, twelve, all swinging their arms and jerking their heads. Bodies shot into the ring from awkward angles, helping one then taking a hit from another. Summers and Anderson looked on from the periphery, confused as to who was Kings and who was not. Joel stumbled into the table he had been leaning on and rushed through the entrance.

The melee rippled out; beer bottles, sweaty bodies, spittle, the shriek of frightened girls, a tsunami of waste spilling out of the club. He pushed past the girls and rushed down the stairs, his pupils pierced, body core shivering. Only the cool of the mid-morning breeze calmed him down, gently blowing against his face.

He marched away from the club into the dark underpass. As he turned a corner towards the main shopping precinct, he passed a passion-fuelled embrace next to a skip at the back of a loading bay. A couple kissing each other's necks like bloodthirsty vampires. The side profile of the male had a resemblance to Pilman, a private with an ankle injury.

"What's Daaave gonna say?" the woman slurred.

"Sssshhh…" Pilman continued kissing her left cheek.

"He's back in a few days."

"Mine or yours?"

"But what about…"

"Sssshhh…"

The man caressed the woman's chunky left thigh, thrusting his groin into the other thigh. She reciprocated by grabbing Pilman's buttocks and kissing him on the lips.

Joel continued out of the underpass, thinking of Summers, Boyd and Anderson stuck in Savoy's; lighting a damp cigarette, he walked back onto the main Straße and sat on the steps of a disused government office, drawing faces in the dusty marble with the tips of his jittery fingers.

"Coward. Gutless scardy cat coward!"

12.

Joel peered out of the little nautical window at rainclouds forming: dense, ash coloured clouds that hovered over Ziegborn town. The clouds were the same colour from the Westhamton clouds that had blighted the spring of '96. A dense blanket of darkness that took an age to move on, so it seemed at the time.

It was early the following Sunday morning and he couldn't sleep. Summers and Boyd shuffled in their beds with brass bands leaping out of their dry mouths and acidic sweat staining their bed sheets. From his vantage point he couldn't tell if either had sustained injuries from the Savoy's rumble.

His head felt heavy on his shoulders and a sharp pain pinged across his forehead. Licking the roof of his mouth he tasted dried-up beer. He hadn't felt this bad since doing bourbon shots with Julie Jay last year. He mused… The last conversation with his mother, talking about a fine art course she wanted to enrol on. The one Julie Jay had told her about. It dawned on him. He'd forgotten to say goodbye to Julie Jay. *"Oh Jules."*

Joel had befriended Julie Jay in year ten at secondary school. Julie was a wannabe environmentalist with ambitions to save the rainforests; she just hadn't figured it out quite yet.

Her dark red Rapunzel hair would often

catch the eye of the boys at St Benedict's High. But she was above the wolf whistles and the crass remarks. Rich ocean blue eyes, mysterious and tangibly inviting would stop him in the corridor, asking for some tobacco. He would oblige and a smile would often leap from her mouth, stopping him dead in his tracks. The kind of smile that was hard to ignore.

Joel and Julie had spent time together in the post GCSE summer. The *'break-free'* summer. They would discuss George Orwell and their favourite Rolling Stones songs, the state of the environment, New Labour. Career, future, destiny an alien topic.

Joel admired her unconventional outlook compared to the other girls at St Benedict's – airy, happy-go-lucky, vivacious. The other girls would hang around in packs, making snide remarks every time her red mane glided through the canteen, commenting on her unkempt, gypsy appearance as if a wolf had been dragged in from the wilds.

"Joel Lundy is a bender, Lundy is a bender!" A red shade would spread across Joel's face when the girls teased him. He never knew how to react. All the while sitting there and waiting for a higher being to slap the immature brats across the face. Julie was above all the bitchy politics; she didn't care about school hierarchies or in-crowds. She was just herself.

"You really need to get some scissors on that hair of yours, Joel," she said, touching his scalp with her smooth fingers.

He embarrassingly stared at woodchips on the playground floor. "Sound like my dad now."

"You're too bashful for that place. Can't see you in the army."

The lack of real enemies and her benevolent nature meant Julie was never short of friends; Joel being an extension of her big social network. The network would involve many echelons of kids from the socially awkward geeks to the uber-confident networkers who were always useful for the odd bit of weed or magic mushrooms. He remembered a scorching hot July day with senses heightened and minds expanded; the dull grey of the Westhamton skyline replaced by glorious sunshine. They sat on a park bench, enthralled by the brightened blue of the sky and the faded moon with her head on his shoulder, beaming at him.

Sunday rolled on. He walked down to the YMCA on the main straße and ordered a big breakfast; sausages, fried eggs, tomatoes, black pudding and a round of fried bread. The grease helped his hangover, easing the pain in his forehead. Julie's image kept appearing in front of him as he strolled back along the main straße towards the barracks.

"Be strong!" she kept whispering. "Be strong, Joel."

13.

Boots clattered along the old floorboards, creaking and groaning as the squaddies packed up their belongings into army issued holdalls. Joel threw all his possessions into a grey bag: a Discman, CD storage book, Golden Virginia tobacco packets, a rusty Swiss army knife, two drawing pads, a pencil case, multi-coloured toiletry bag, one pair of stonewash jeans, one pair of brown cords, a black denim jacket, a couple of T-shirts, a shabby chequered shirt, a woollen jumper, a pair of trainers and some letters that needed posting. He then grabbed a Bergen backpack containing all his army issued kit and dashed to the washrooms.

The newly issued boots stomped along the tiled floor, giving off a squelching noise. He went over to a mirror and took off his beret. Creases were appearing in the corner of his eyes from the nights spent staring at the ceiling. He gawped at the rabbit in the headlights, "Another day, just another day!" he whispered. Recurring memories had been rumbling around his head all week: the spilt Coke incident on his first day at St Benedict's school, running out of the canteen before Ollie, the biggest brute in the year had a chance to find the perpetrator. And then meeting the recruiting sergeant in London with his square head, eyes like a brown bear and inviting hand gestures. *The sergeant knew how to sell the career, give him that!*

The wintry air gnawed at the tips of Joel's fingers as Boyd, Summers and he exited HQ Block. They walked along the wide road that circled Gallipoli barracks and past D Company's block. He had passed D Block many times on route to the NAAFI to pick up pineapple juice or tobacco over the weeks. Eerily silent and devoid of any being it had been, but today the large rectangular windows sitting in the rendered night blue walls he caught a glimpse of olive coloured reflections pressing against the frosted glass. The green abstract reflections appeared like poltergeist, flittering away from the light in differing shapes and forms. They left the road and approached the steps to A Company HQ. As the three soldiers trudged up the concrete steps Joel looked at Summers' angst-ridden face looking like he was beginning a long walk to the gallows.

'Rat-a-tat rat-a-tat!' A rhythmic stomping noise, like a tap-dancer performing, suddenly caught their attention. The three of them turned around to where the noise was bouncing off the buildings. 'Rat-a-tat!' It was the battalion provost sergeant surveying the morning.

The sergeant's stomp sang a merry song to the battalion, resurrecting the gallant troops ready for another day. The tip of his cap and the bulls of his boots glistened like a diamond in the rough as the trio shielded their eyes. "On your way grunts, on your way!" he barked at Summers.

They headed down the busy corridor of A Company in staggered formation, Joel clinging to the back of the trio. He always felt safer at the back. Corporals breezed past with sharpshooter badges sewn onto their jumpers with an air of authority over their dog o'war faces. Summers braced suddenly when an officer floated past; all three locked their arms into their sides and saluted the second lieutenant. The salute was limp and lacked motion like a pack of cards bent out of shape. They continued along the corridor gingerly, eyes locked on the grey linoleum floor, shoulders hunched, hoping someone would recognise them.

"Oi! You lot!" Boyd was the first to react, turning his head towards a poky office they had just passed.

"In 'ere!" a gruff East London accent bellowed into the corridor. Boyd turned towards the office and instantaneously saluted at the desk. Joel and Summers quickly followed Boyd around the corner. The waiting was over, time for the soldiers to meet the new king.

Joel turned around a shiny gloss doorframe and hung around the door entrance. The door was painted in regimental colours with a '3 PLATOON - A COY' template hiding within the rich blue gloss. Joel looked at the bold black lettering with the dark background: *a failed colour scheme*! he thought. His attention quickly darted towards the black skin of Sergeant Thompson slouching on the side of a desk, chewing a biro pen.

"New lot I assume?" the sergeant asked, his foggy eyes scanning each recruit from the feet up. "Well speak up then!" his big lips barely moved. Joel quickly realised what Orpington was talking about: a casual yet menacing stare with a body frame muscular in all the right places from years spent in the regiment's boxing team.

"Yes, Sergeant!" Boyd replied.

"Well, well," the sergeant replied. "You two forget how to salute an officer now?" His words were quick and sharp, almost too quick to decipher. Joel and Summers quickly stretched out the palms of their right hands, locked their fingers together and shot their hands into the ear. The sergeant went from left to right casually waiting for the first recruit to make eye contact. Joel fixed his stare onto a plant pot on the window-sill, feeling the blacks of the sergeant's pupils fixed, ready to pounce. The sergeant placed the biro pen on the desk and crossed his arms in a bored, nonplussed gesture. A silence descended.

"Gentlemen, welccccccooooome!" the lieutenant sat behind the shadow of the sergeant, stringing out vowels that accentuated the toff in his accent.

"At ease!" With the distraction Joel took

a quick glance at the smirk plastered on the sergeant's face. The lieutenant looked small compared to the sergeant, a medium frame of less bulk more akin to a middle-distance runner. His visage friendlier, un-menacing. A square rock stuck out from his smooth chin.

"This is your Platoon Sergeant Thompson and I am Lieutenant Briars. As you are aware gentlemen we have been on exercise in Poland." He flicked away his blonde fringe from his scrupulous, glistened eyes.

"So. You have had plenty of time to recuperate gentleman. We are expecting good things from all three of you." He arose from a swivel chair and joined Sergeant Thompson at the edge of the desk, puffing out his chest in a vain attempt to add inches to the height disadvantage next to the sergeant. His resemblance uncanny to Lieutenant Cuthbert Smythe at Chipping Burse.

"Sergeant Thompson will get you kitted out from the company stores, for now goodbye, gentlemeeeen!" Joel glanced at the lieutenant. His casual use of 'gentlemen' was confusing as he stood there all blue eyed and enthusiastic and he couldn't help but feel the term was a euphemism for 'runt' or 'shithead'. The lieutenant left the room, with him the room went silent again.

The sergeant stood up. "Don't let us down, you lot! All I've gotta say!" he mumbled in a low tone. Picking the biro off the desk he eyeballed them one by one, this time inching his puffy lips right up to their noses before walking out of the room, whistling a merry tone.

The next few weeks were an especially edgy time for Joel, even worse than the first few weeks at Chipping Burse. In training boys were turning into soldiers from the same baseline, in battalion a complicated system of respect and kudos was in place and he was firmly at the bottom of the ocean. He kept his head firmly down in the coming weeks.

"Get up! Get up!" the duty corporal barked into the room one morning. It was mid-March and the mornings were beginning to lighten up. A ray of light beamed into Joel's bed-space, welcoming him into another coarse revile.

The bed-space in A Company was marginally bigger than the space he had occupied in HQ Block. The rooms had higher ceilings and newer fittings; long curtains made from blue velvet, dark blue carpets that smelt of grass rather than mildew and tall lockers with shiny silver locks. He gazed up at a small hole appearing in the roof of his allocated locker. It didn't feel right, all the newness, he preferred the old crummy block.

He had been awake for the past hour, thinking about cold rainy mornings staring out of a dirty kitchen window in Londonderry, waiting for the garrison kids to move off the kerb. So much time spent in that cramped house: taps leaking stagnant water under the kitchen sink, central heating kaput during the winter, rats scurrying around the rubbish disposal unit outside.

"Fuck me it's six already!" Summers groaned. Joel was housed in a room with Summers, Boyd and a mixed-race kid called Agyina. The newbie room (or the 'New In Germany *NIG* room).

The seniors of 3 Platoon strutted in like peacocks on a mating call, giving them the cold sneer and poking fun at the *NIG's*. Joel's section commander Corporal Bronson had introduced himself the previous evening. Bronson was known as 'Charlie' amongst his cohorts, in reference to the infamous prisoner. He stood over six feet tall with protruding ears like giant coins. Bronson walked with a slight limp on his left side. Rumours floated through the corridors that he had been shot in Belfast.

"The newbie, eh?" Bronson sniggered, his hooked nose peering south like an ugly witch. He was joined by Corporal Pinkton, a gregarious, ginger haired fellow with a slight beer gut. Pinkton always felt the need to shout quotes from Sharpe's rifles whenever he felt he was not being heard. "Who is Captain Richard Sharpe? Who is he? Who is he?" he would bellow at the top of his voice.

Hunt wandered into their room later in the evening. A private of average build with shovel-like hands and beady brown eyes sunken into his eye sockets. Hunt refrained from eye contact, even the newbies. His disposition was somewhat nervy, like a spy was watching the very hairs on the back of his head. "Hmm…" he mumbled incoherently, "Hmm…" and disappeared from sight. Other privates from the platoon drifted into the room, eager to check out the new freak show. A curious glint was in their eyes as they recounted war stories from the great plains of Poland many times over:

"Remember that last section attack, Winny? I was up on the ridge laying it down thick and you bayoneted the wrong kraut, wankdirch!"

"Fuck off, I'd already done six of them. No stopping me, mate!"

"Skip-lickers wouldn't have a chance against us eh?"

"Hell no!"

"3 Platoon. We proud!"

Simone ventured into the room later in the evening, with dark Mediterranean looks and a cheeky twinkle in his eye. His demeanour assured without being boastful, cocksure without the need to play the cock.

The stories came fast, each squaddie drifting into the room with another gallant tale; the distance covered, the kit humped, the amount of sandbag dummies cut to shreds. Joel smiled politely at each story, obeying the unwritten protocol: smile at everyone, speak when spat at. Summers and Boyd nodded their heads to every story like a couple of loyal pups. The only words appearing from their lips "Wow", "No!", "Really", "Sounds good!" Joel sat on his bed and let Summers and Boyd continue with their trite platitudes while the rest of the platoon hovered, sending out warning shots to the impressionable young men.

This went on for days, weeks. Joel kept up the niceties, all the while retreating into his sketchpad, creating new characters in a complex narrative with no idea of the ending.

14.

"Alright, Lundy."

Pratt brushed past Joel who was sweeping the linoleum floor of the corridor with a coarse brush. He looked up at Pratt, somewhat surprised. Five weeks he had been with the platoon now and was only beginning to get recognised.

"What's 'aaappening?" Pratt's tone seemed less abrasive than a few weeks ago. A calm softening to his Devonian accent.

Private Pratt was another tied to the army machine. His father was a retired colour sergeant from the King's Hampshire and his grandfather a sapper who had gained his commission and retired at major rank. "Out tonight then?" Pratt asked.

"Oh, I didn't know there was anything going on tonight," Joel replied.

Pratt turned to face Joel, his hazel eyes enticing like a serpent, his fine strawberry blonde hair glistening in the fading light. "Well there is, mate. Savoy's. Reckon it's all gonna kick off!"

"Oh… ok." Sweat pores quickly dampened under his armpits. "See you… see you there then."

"Good lad, Lundy. Don't forget your balls!" Pratt sauntered through the corridor like a gloating promoter who had just organised the big fight. Sweeping up the last ball of dust off a skirting board, all of a sudden Joel felt a pushing in his bowels. He ran to the toilets, clenching his buttocks.

The day rolled on, repetition upon repetition. Joel stared solemnly at the piles of dirty equipment stacked up around him. Piles grew and grew as A Company ruffled their soft hands with Scotch-brite and soap: Pans with charcoal-burned stains, Giant Norwegian flasks stained orange from fermenting tea, mud-caked ponchos, tin containers caked in lime-scale. Three-week field exercises meant three weeks filthy kit to clean.

As 3 Platoon marched back from HQ Stores, Joel looked around the barracks while a calm breeze blew around his feet: The sky a bright blue, an ocean of serene clarity. He thought back to the fist pumping rhetoric at Chipping Burse: *"Wait till you get to battalion. You'll be on your feet all day waiting for the orders. You'll need to impress the guys above because when those orders come down you better be ready!"* All he had witnessed so far were mundane drills, ticking boxes on sheets and endless cleaning assignments. Only yesterday he was in the NAAFI watching the news on the BFBS channel: **'Historic peace deal signed in Bosnia Herzegovina'** The images flicked across the screen of slaughtered bodies and gunfire ricocheting from villages in the Yugoslav hills followed by Bosnian leaders and NATO generals signing peace deals on blue marble tables.

Rumours had floated around the barracks for a number of weeks about the next possible deployment every time a breaking news story flashed across the enormous TV screen in the NAAFI bar:

'Serbian Police kill terrorist gangs in Kosovo'

'Oued Bouaicha massacre in Algeria: 52 people killed'

'Pakistan tests medium-range missiles capable of hitting India'

'Iraq disarmament crisis: Iraqi President Saddam Hussein negotiates a deal with UN Secretary General Kofi Annan, allowing weapons inspectors to return to Baghdad, preventing military action by the United States and Britain'

Many of the King's Hampshire Regiment had served in Bosnia Herzegovina. A six-month tour holed up in large makeshift tents or disused police stations, chewing the same piece of mint gum, cleaning the same gun barrel, patrolling the same village. Waiting, waiting… That was the impression listening to the senior privates and the NCOs chewing the fat in the NAAFI. A touch paper was waiting to be lit by an unknown force: *When? How? If?* Riddles with no specific answer in peacetime. The term 'grunt' crystallised his current predicament of an army in peacetime: endless routine, waiting, boredom holed up in the great machine.

The platoon marched off the road to retire for the evening and Joel felt exhausted. He lay on his bed and curled up. Tonight, he just wanted to sit in the subterranean wilderness under HQ Block. Away from it all.

Nine o'clock that evening Pratt came barging into Joel's room kicking at his feet. "Ten at Savoy's don't be late!" Pratt marched back out of the room, a caustic aftershave tone lingering. Joel sat up and looked at the blank wall straight ahead. An image appeared in the faded magnolia paint: a thick muscular head, receding hairline and moustache. The image uncannily looked like his father back home looking out of the kitchen window, contemplating.

"What's going on, Lundy, what's going on?" Summers barged into Joel's bed-space eating a portion of soggy-looking chips. Mayonnaise was smeared on his lower lip.

"Just Pratt wanting me to go down Savoy's tonight."

"Oh yeah?"

He was tired and irritable from the sudden wake-up call. "Yeah."

"What for? How come we didn't get an invite?" Summers protested.

He was feeling unusually spiky. "I don't know. Why don't you ask him?"

"You got a special arrangement yeah? In the back alleys behind Oi Oi's yeah? Hear this, Boydey?"

Joel shook his head. "Yeah I've got a special arrangement. I'm going to have bum sex with him is that what you mean?"

Summers took a step back, shocked by the comeback. "Bet you do! Bet you do! Ha!" Summers retreated to his bed-space, petulantly throwing a chip on the floor. Joel then hesitantly threw a shirt and pair of jeans on and hurried out of the block.

The big Swiss clock on the Ziegborn main straße ticked six minutes past ten. Joel upped the pace and briskly walked past the clock and into the underpass.

It felt like a big hand was pushing him into the unknown. A hand of a hulking great machine. He approached the stairway leading to the black door of Savoy's. His nerves were tingly, the hairs on the back of his neck wet and alert. He rolled a cigarette, took a long drag, nearly swallowing the filter tip.

The door-man frisked Joel down from shoulders to ankles and waved him through. As the door-man raised his clumpy hand Joel's feet suddenly went numb. He felt the confusion: brain saying one thing, heart another.

"Well?" the door-man gesticulated towards the door. He felt the battle going on above; conflicting arguments each trying to out-shout another. *In?*

Out?… He pushed forward against his natural instincts and walked through the pitch-black entrance. As he stepped from the winding staircase and past the moose head he smelt the acrid testosterone dripping from the walls inside the nightclub. Once inside he was confronted by a mass of bodies, mostly squaddies, loitering in groups by the entrance, smoking cigarettes and downing steins. A boy crossed his path looking no older than sixteen, pupils alert and shaky, jaw bulging. Joel paused in the middle of the walkway and licked his dry bottom lip. He made out a few familiar faces from the King's Hampshire, the other faces seemed sinister and unfamiliar; a blur of a crowd illuminated by weak strobe lights. A door-man was stationed at each corner of the club like a post on a boxing ring, quietly analysing the situation about to develop.

The glitter-ball appeared dimmer, the music quieter. He felt the atmosphere rush through his body like a runaway express train, an intense explosive force about to be unleashed. His hands tingled uncontrollably as the voices in his head upped the ante. "*What are you doing, you idiot? Can't you see what's going to happen? Get out now!*"

"*Stand up, be strong! Show your mettle you wimp! You'll be a hero!*" The voices snapped around his ears until he couldn't even see straight. Suddenly he felt a tap on his right shoulder, it was Pratt, his light hair unrecognisable in the darkness.

Pratt looked taller in the darkness, like a mythical monster from a comic book. "What took you so long?" he shouted into Joel's ear.

"Oh, just took ages trying to get past the bouncer."

"Well you're here now."

"Yeah, here now." He followed Pratt away from the entrance into a corner next to a cigarette machine. Bodies blocked his route through; he twisted his hips around muscular buttocks and protruding shoulders caps, eager not to spill drinks hanging precariously from a thousand sweaty palms. The bodies seemed to merge into one big mass, extending all around the bar, sucking the oxygen from the cramped air. Pratt stopped by a group playing drinking games with tequila shots and signalled to the one leaning against the cigarette machine.

He recognised the squaddie from the cookhouse, of an average build with pumped biceps bulging from his tightly fitted polo shirt, on his right forearm a Chinese dragon tattoo. Always accompanied by a horde of hangers-on like military Mafia Don.

"This here's Lundy," Pratt said.

The Don's shaved cranium sparkled pink against the strobe lights, showing up a scar that ran from the top of his skull towards his right ear lobe. Joel couldn't help staring at the dark scar, wondering what story attached itself to the laceration.

The Don motioned his head, continuing to look beyond Pratt at the faces in the crowd. The rest of the group carried on chattering and gesturing amongst themselves, ignoring Joel. Joel stood on the outskirts of the group, biting his nails and lighting cigarettes.

"You getting the beers in then? Pratt asked Joel.

"What do you want?"

"Hoegaarden. Get one for Baz as well." Pratt gestured towards the Don. Joel carefully scooted around a tubby body blocking the gangway and ordered three steins of Hoegaarden at the bar. As he gazed through the glass at the pale frothy beer he contemplated the absurdity of the situation; in a bar, to be ignored, just to try and get brownie points. He was never one for mingling in big groups and chewing the fat over the tedious, the mundane, and the safe conversations. He waited for his change, watching the barmaid getting flustered with a big surge in orders. The squaddies shouted over the din trying to convey beer names in slow English, only for the barmaid to ask for the order to be repeated multiple times. Tonight the language barrier seemed worse than ever.

He weaved his way back to the cigarette machine, placing the heavy glasses on a plastic table. Baz took a swig of a stein, without even noticing him.

"Ta," Pratt shouted.

The wall of bodies spread out across his panorama; tall, short, stocky, waif; a sea of shoulders piled up to the ceiling. He pricked his ears near a speaker hanging from a wall; the music sounded clearer, less distorted. A cigarette butt left his fingers, dropping to the floor with divine grace. The tenseness around his chest began to unwind slightly. He headed for the toilets to clear his head.

Two sets of sheepish eyes peered out of the darkness; then disappeared into the haze. He walked a few steps on the sticky floor, then suddenly felt a shove in his back, hurtling his body forward. His shoulder collided with a glass, spilling beer over a squaddie with a gelled quiff. Joel looked at the damp patch covering the squaddie's Ben Sherman shirt and a fear of dread spiked his spinal cord. The squaddie glared at Joel with teeth glued together, like a wild cat about to jump its prey.

"What the fuck? What's up, eh?" the victim shouted at Joel. Joel noticed a WFR cap badge tattooed on his forearm. "I'm sorry… I was…" Joel mumbled. He felt the words stuck in his brain as a thud collided with his left ear. Dazed, he tried to plead innocence to the Woofer. Another blow hit the back of his head sending him into another squaddie slouched on the bar. Joel and the squaddie slumped to the floor, the DJ ripped the needle from the record;

signalling the start of the ruckus like the opening bell. The bar erupted.

Glasses fell around him like raindrops. He caught site of the Don rushing into the melee using uppercuts and hooks to floor two other Woofers. A boot caught Joel on his lower back as he lay helpless on the sticky floor. Pratt followed the Don, wildly swinging at anybody within ten metres of the Woofer group. As Pratt swung his fists the other members of their group hollered, trampling over Joel to get in on the action. A short Woofer with a thick moustache hit back at Pratt forcing him against the cigarette machine with a head-butt and a shot to the stomach. Two door-men suddenly arrived, grabbing them with bear hugs. One of the door-men picked up a scrawny looking squaddie and flung him against the bar. Then a squaddie threw a knee in the back of the door-man.

Smash! Smash! A glass connected with a skull, thickening the dense reverberations of the club. Joel managed to crawl out of the epicentre and ran to the stairwell. He puffed and groaned while his heart pumped a thousand beats and blood trickled around his ear. The din of violence rang through his eardrums, deafening high pitch tones crashing through his skull bone. All he could see were bloody faces, slumped corpses and broken glass, a bloody battle still raging between the door-men and the last squaddie left standing. Joel stumbled down the staircase and rushed out of the black door into the calm of the night.

A silent vortex replaced the sounds of violence as RMP cars arrived on the scene. The policemen dashed from their glistening Mercedes and ran into the club with handcuffs glowing a silver beam. On the kerbside groups of spectators eagerly peered into the black door. Shouts and screams still faded down the staircase and into the street, enticing the lookers on to cross the **DO NOT PASS** imaginary line. Amongst the crowd injured squaddies nursed their wounds, spitting out warm blood on the pavement and cursing their assailants. Looking around at the carnage Joel felt nauseous. He imagined being in the Somme trenches in the calm after a big battle, looking on helplessly as the wounded waited for death with a fearful silence rolling across the French countryside.

The piercing tones increased in volume. "Fuckers! I'll kill 'em! I'll kill 'em!" a squaddie protested on the ground. His left eye was swollen red. Joel quickly made an exit along a side road that headed north out of the underpass. As he trampled down the quiet road he caught sight of Anderson gawping at the club, transfixed by a ruckus he was not part of. Anderson's feet hesitantly twitched towards the black door like a junkie given the co-ordinates of a free stash. Joel wandered back onto the tarmac above, dazed and shell shocked. He meandered along the Ziegborn main straße to the barracks, swaying along the pavement like a madman.

"Had a good night then?" the guard facetiously smirked.

Joel nodded hesitantly. He ran past the guard room up the main road that snaked around the barracks and entered A Company's block. He felt the left side of his cranium; dried-up blood marked the skin of his hands, a rubicund colour staining the fresh pigmentation. He stumbled up the staircase like a wounded rebel fighter seeking a hideaway. The only solace he could think of was the toilet block. A yeasty smell wafted through the corridor as he barged through the swing door into the toilet block and went straight towards the mirrors. His head tingled as he looked into the reflection and saw a shy ghost; dilated pupils, pasty skin with spots appearing and a chin quivering uncontrollably. He felt the top of his head for the wound but couldn't make it out, all he felt was a mound pulsating from the side of his head. The bleeding had stopped, caked into his hair. The side of his jaw ached, he felt the inside of his mouth but couldn't find the strike spot.

He glared at the ghost. The lines around his head moved outwards bending around the cheeks. His cheekbones submerged, causing the fat to sag near his jawline. The colour in his eyes darkened to a tree bark tone. He crossed his brow in curious fascination: "Hello? Hello?" His top lip suddenly went dark with heavy stubble, spreading all the way to the corner of his lips like a rash, within seconds it had turned into a thick moustache. He took a step back and realised who the ghost was in the mirror. It was him. The strings in his chest tightened, closing his airway. A surge of adrenalin rushed along his right arm into his fist.

The cracks in the mirror had reached all the way to the beige tiles; the glass hole in the middle of the mirror, sending shrapnel over the sink. He looked down at his bloody knuckles and picked out the tiny crystals lodged into the thin layer of skin. "I can't do it, Dad. I can't fight back, I just can't!" he shrieked at the smashed mirror.

His inner animal felt the bars of the cage press even tighter against his ribs.

"There has to be a way out! Has to be!" he yelled.

15.

June was the month. Joel looked at the calendar on the wall, wondering where the months had disappeared to. Sparrows could be heard outside crying out the noisy morning song, the chirps drowning out the cacophony of slamming doors and shouts cascading through the corridor. Penfold, a short bespectacled lance corporal, grazed through the room. "Up let's get up!" His screechy voice echoed around the walls. He reminded Joel of a Pekingese dog.

The block was abuzz with rumours concerning Chambers and Brown from 2 Platoon. Joel quickly found his combats and beret, tied his boots and joined the rest of A Company outside, 3 platoons of 28. 3 Platoon were gathered nearest the block entrance ready for the sergeant major. Joel joined the furthest rank as the rhythmic thumps on the road picked up pace and a sergeant yelled "A COMPANY!"

Heels snapped into action, heads locked to zero degrees. The sergeant major appeared from the right, a shining beacon of military tidiness and discipline. He stomped towards the block with his bent posture; radiating a larger than life aura and respect into every eyeball on parade. Every soldier knew the sergeant major may not have been the officer commanding A Company, but the real power lay in his hands. A rock star and headmaster amalgamated into one.

The sergeant major took large strides toward the block, swinging a cane like an outer extension of his arm. He then stopped and felt his moustache which nestled underneath a broken nose. Joel had noticed that many of the senior NCOs had noses bent out of shape. He thought about fraternal rituals performed on a newly promoted sergeant in the sergeant's mess involving a smack on the nose. The sergeant major turned towards the company of men, his blue eyes scouring the ranks.

"Company!" the sergeant major began. "You may or may not know that two mindless twerps have failed to show up for muster parade since yesterday. The two guilty parties are Private Chambers and Private Brown. That is all you need to know for now, all I will say is God help them if they are found." The look on the sergeant major's exterior screamed murder.

"DISMISSED!" He turned off the road and marched back to A Company HQ.

"I never had Brownie down as AWOL." Joel eavesdropped on a conversation as the soldiers dispersed.

"What a muppet. He'll end up in the nick for this!"

"Bet it's over some bird."

"Course it is… y'know how quickly he falls. Probably already hitched!"

"One shag that's all it takes!"

"Dirty bastard!"

"How do they know it's over a girl?" Joel asked Simone as they walked past the company stores into the corridor.

"Lundy, that's the default answer to anyone going AWOL. Always think a bird has polluted their mind or something." Simone stroked his chin and looked at the ceiling. "Thrown them off course toward a voyage of uncertainty, shit don't you know anything?"

Simone always knew what was going on way before anyone else did. Some of the platoon had him down for espionage on behalf of the Italian government.

"First AWOL case I know about," Joel said.

"Won't be your last."

"What you think will happen to them, say if they get caught?"

"Don't know, Lundy man. Could be time up in Colchester, could be a court martial, could be block cleaning for a week, all depends on the judge. That's if they even get fucking caught."

Simone veered left toward his room seemingly unfazed by the morning's announcement. Joel looked down at the floor: the disinfected, polished linoleum that was home to a river of beer not so long ago.

The weeks of restless routine rolled on for 3 Platoon. A routine that would become an archetype of a soldier's life in peacetime: weapon-cleaning, weapon handling tests, drill, cleaning the company stores, block cleaning, drill… The monotony rolled over into another trite week. One overcast morning Joel looked out of his bedroom window. A neon sign was stuck to an office window on the outside: 'Montag! Guden-tag!'

Mondays involved fitness sessions followed by weapon-cleaning all afternoon; Joel didn't mind the fitness, his tarred lungs seemed to withhold the physical pain, much to his surprise. The fitness regimes would involve long distance running, gym work, marches carrying Bergen rucksacks, webbing strapped around their waists and rifles stuck to their palms. "A mere tab" the NCO's would call it. Much as he didn't mind the running or gym work, the marches (or tabs) he dreaded.

The weather was changing as spring started to give way to the muggy warmth of June. This change of season brought about new revised fitness regimes, devised by over-zealous physical training instructors looking to prove a point. June also meant Combat Fitness Tests: eight miles, twenty kilos, as fast as the platoon could get around. CFTs were relished by the PTIs; the perfect opportunity to create more punishing routines and help climb the greasy pole. *"Cometh the man cometh the hour"* rhetoric would ring around the block like a nasty smell.

The platoon was roused early on Tuesday in preparation for the annual CFT. Joel vaguely recollected the shouts of Penfold waking the room, but his body would not move. He smelt the sweat of the coming hours in the warm air. Beneath the bed cover his legs froze, his head nodded off to the side of the pillow and a cooling sensation of the untouched side brushed against his cheek. His eyes glued together as he entered through paradise's gates once again:

A cage could be seen in the distance toppled over onto one side. Small yellow birds flooded from the cage towards the gate he found himself stood by. A steady stream of bright yellow, whizzing around his shoulders, cheeping a joyous song, waiting for the large gates to open…

"Lundy what the fuck are you still doing in the sack? Get up now!" Penfold barked at Joel's lumpen body. The gates of paradise slammed shut and his eyes opened with a sudden flicker.

"Don't forget block inspection at seven!" Penfold sauntered out of the room. Joel quickly sat up in bed "Shit! Block inspection!" he yelped. Sweat suddenly beaded on his forehead. He looked at the digital clock next to his bed – 06:45 – remembering he had not cleaned the washrooms yet. He leapt out of bed forthwith, fumbling around in his locker for some DPM clothing and a pair of dirty old boots he had used in the field. Only to find the boots without laces. He panicked as a second layer of sweat appeared on his forehead. Setting about de-lacing his parade shoes, without a moment's hesitation he laced up his secondary boots and shook dried mud from the grey soles.

Summers was sweeping the corridor as he entered the washrooms. He grabbed a wet Scotch-brite and scrubbed grime from the porcelain sinks.

"What time is it?" he shouted in the vain hope somebody was next door. A lone voice echoed back at Joel: "Five to. Hurry up Lundy, the sarge will be 'ere soon."

"Nearly there." He wiped the corroded mirrors with a length of toilet-roll.

Sergeant Thompson barged into the bedroom at five past seven. The sergeant's charcoal skin accentuating the deranged look in the whites of his eyes. He threw a hefty looking Bergen on the carpet and glared at Boyd with an icy stare. The rucksack thudded on the carpet like a boulder off a cliff.

"You lot ready then?" The sergeant left the room before Boyd could muster a reply.

The block inspection passed by without any harsh words from the sergeant. He seemed a bit more sympathetic to the odd millimetre of dust today. Joel gathered his webbing and Bergen from the locker and ascended the stairs to the A Company armoury. The rest of the platoon lined the staircase ready to pick up their weapons.

"Walnut, you been playing tongue tennis with those Slovakian hookers again?" A roar of laughter cascaded down the staircase. Everyone stared at the dolefully eyed Walnut.

"What do you mean? I haven't been near a woman in days!" Walnut replied in the direction of Corporal Bronson.

Walnut was a veteran private with a sex problem. Most weekends he could be found frequenting the whorehouses of Ziegborn looking to quell his lustful hunger.

"What's that shit over the side of your mouth then Walnut eh?" Bronson poked his finger in the air.

Walnut touched around his lips seductively, feeling orange sauce lodged in the corner of his lips. He licked the tip of his finger. "Just beans, Charlie, few baked beans. Wish they were beans of another variety, mind!" the platoon giggled in a more muted tone.

"Still the brekkie hit the spot!" Walnut added.

The words stabbed into Joel's heart. He suddenly realised: *"Breakfast. Sustenance. Bollocks!"* The company were setting off in minutes. His mind raced back to last night's meal of Pot Noodles and chocolate biscuits and whether the protein would be enough for a CFT.

The Bedford truck parked outside the block awaited the platoon. Within ten minutes eighteen privates, four lance-corporals, four corporals, one sergeant, one lieutenant and twenty-eight SA80 rifles, sets of webbing, Bergens and helmets were loaded. Joel looked around the truck at the hardened countenances, masking a fear and trepidation deep within their make-up.

The Bedford grinded its way through Ziegborn, passing the German civilians and dogs and shops and factories like a leaf falling off a tree; only one direction, no turning back, gravity was pulling the leaf to the floor just like the Bedford was being pulled towards a track that would lead around a range in the German countryside. The Bedford stopped at a traffic light as Joel sat in the back of the truck like a ghost, gazing at cars passing either side of the giant wheels and ignoring steely eyeballs of the platoon ready for the big test. "*Cometh the man, cometh the man.*"

The truck took a left turn off the main straße onto the range road. The range road led for three miles before the Bedford swung onto a narrow gravel track. The engine became quieter and the wheels turned slower. The store-man hit the brakes with a jerking thud and the platoon alighted from the truck.

Joel was last off the tailgate. Sweat was already forming around his lips, the early morning conditions a taste of the day. His boots landed onto the delicate surface, placing deep marks into the light brown soil. He picked up his rifle and took a deep breath; the sun was starting to shine through the tall oaks and sycamores lining the track. The sky was a clear turquoise blue and sparrow's sung in the trees overhead. It felt like the trees were watching him, nobody else.

His helmet lay on the sand, Bronson barked at him to pick it up and get his chin strap tied. Joel could already see the salivating animal dying to get out of Bronson's body. He felt the metal clip join on the chinstrap, forming a solid tumour to his sweaty temple. A rumble roared in his stomach, untying the tight knots around his pancreas. *All over in a couple of hours,"* he thought. Walnut looked shaky, as did Peterson and Hunt standing next to him. The only men laughing and joking were the NCOs. The lower ranks awaited their sentence.

The rows of helmets made the fearsome war machine resemble a merry bunch of camouflaged button mushrooms as 3 Platoon lined up in rows of three with Lieutenant Briars heading the expedition into the German forest. The men took gulps of salty sweet water from their metal canisters like it was their last on planet Earth then followed in unison by a barrage of phlegm directed off the soft grounded path.

"Ok, we are the first platoon to set off!" the lieutenant bellowed, adjusting his rifle strap. "2 Platoon set off one minute behind us and we do not I repeat DO NOT want to be overtaken! Flaking will not be tolerated, because this platoon IS the best in A Company. The wankdirch platoon! The OC expects good things from 3 Platoon chaps." The chest pumping rhetoric echoed around the tree-lined path. Joel was always amused when the lieutenant tried to use squaddie colloquialisms like 'flaking' and 'wankdirch'. His prep school accent never convinced. Prince Charles trying to speak cockney, it just didn't work.

The platoon set off on a steady pace, stomping on the forest floor towards a lake in the near distance. Boots trampled against the broken twigs and dead acorns littering the forest floor like an industrial machine clearing the path. Bergens wobbled from left to right; rifles hung loose from every soldiers palm as the platoon tried to establish a rhythm early on. He could already hear Hunt panting to his left, lungs trying to pump carbon dioxide through a needle's eye. Joel's lungs pumped at a steady rate, keeping his pace close to Agyina in front whose long legs stumbled and staggered along the brown path, causing him to constantly adjust his pace. The lake approached on the right-hand side, the path becoming narrower, forcing the platoon to shrink down to banks of two. Joel started to struggle with the softer ground under his feet, each step gently pulling at his boots from underneath.

"Two miles!" Sergeant Thompson boomed from the back of the squad. This precipitated an increase in pace at the front. The jog turned into a sprint within seconds as the lieutenant over-zealously stretched the pace. The ranks began to break and the wolf packs came out from under the shade picking on the strugglers. First it was Corporal Pinkton and a shady accomplice: "Get up there, Hunt. You don't want to let me down!" Pinkton snarled. Hunt slowly managed to catch up with the next rank while Penfold and Bronson double teamed on Agyina who had fallen behind Joel.

Bronson ran in front of Joel, chasing Agyina down the narrow path and on toward the lake. "Please, please don't tell me you're struggling already, Agyina! Remember what we talked about last week, knob head? Well get the fuck up there NOW!" Bronson hissed. A look of mild glee in his viper eyes.

Fresh air from the lake filled Joel's heavy lungs as the pace dropped and the weary men broke into a march. He could feel cracks in the front of his legs. Raking pains all the way up his shins that got worse with every stride. Sergeant Thompson ran to the front of the pack. "Left, right, left, swing your gat!" The sergeant kept looking to the rear for 2 Platoon.

Panting filled the airwaves. Heartbeats raced through the platoon's veins. Pounding the Earth's core. Sweat stuck to Joel's forehead like treacle, an ever-flowing salty waterfall pouring down from his helmet into his eyes. He quickly glanced to the rear. The platoon's ranks were not in bad shape considering the exertion. He glanced at the path ahead past Sergeant Thompson's helmet. The brown soil was flowing out onto a white shiny surface that sparkled next to the water.

"Ok this is the surprise we forgot to mention, men!" the lieutenant shouted from the front. "Hold onto your guns; it gets harder from here!" The lieutenant paused for a catch his breath. Joel peered out of the side of his helmet at the officer; all the young officers never seemed to be out of breath. *Super fit and super bloody enthusiastic,*" he thought.

"No falling behind. The OC still expects. Remember!" the lieutenant continued as they marched on. A sharp pain continued to gnaw in his legs, scraping his shins along the gravel. The platoon's boots clattering in unison toward the incandescent river bank like a centipede headed for battle. Moisture filled the hot air, giving off scents of fresh clay and water lilies. The panting slowed and the ground became thick. Joel looked to his feet at the grains of silvery sand sucking his boots inwards.

Lifting his boots out from the sand became harder. His boots sunk with each step, exerting more pressure on the motor working at full kilter inside. The ranks broke again. First to fall back was Agyina followed by the short figure of Robinson. Each body a dead weight in the all-consuming quick-sand. The lieutenant continued to sprint ahead, gliding across the sand like a desert snake.

The centipede's legs gradually dropped off. "Get up there, Lundy. What do you think you're doing here?" Penfold shouted at Joel, poking him with his rifle butt. "Because I want to be here, sweat, sand, rock and roll," Joel mumbled under his panting breath. He tried to get past the wretched figure of Parks being pushed along the sandbank by Bronson. "Parky, c'mon stick with me!" he yelled.

His throat felt intensely dry as he swallowed the arid air. The shouts became more frequent.

"Get up here! Up here now!"

"You better not be flaking!"

"Think of the other members of the platoon!"

"2 Platoon are not going to beat us today!" The words sounded muddy and distant.

The sun blazed, baking white rays on the sand as the expedition continued apace, each NCO berating the weaker members of the platoon. They were hurting themselves, breathing hard, kicking through the muddy sand but had to show the platoon commander they were fine-tuning their leadership skills. This resulted in the unfit corporals conveniently positioning themselves next to platoon members they knew would be the first to drop back.

The lieutenant stopped under a row of oak trees out of the sun's pulsating glare.

"Get up here! Get up here now! You've got one minute to get a drink and sort yourselves out!" Sergeant Thompson shouted into the trees.

Joel panted like a lame old dog as he raced to a smaller oak tree, sat on a large boulder and fumbled around the back of his webbing for a water cannister. On his tongue all he tasted was sea salt and Golden Virginia. The sweat had dried out his face, blurring his vision. The water bottle lid popped off. The taste of cool, sweet water was like nothing else he had ever tasted, each gulp of the sugary water flowed from an Alpine retreat straight into his parched body; zesty orange aftertastes bubbled on his tongue. His lips insatiably craved the water bottle, wanting more.

"Take small sips. DO NOT drink too much or you'll end up with a stitch. Stitches mean we separate, which means 2 Platoon will pass us!" the lieutenant shouted.

Joel looked around. Some of the men already looked past it. The forlorn figures of Parks and Agyina had the look of death in their scared, beaten eyes. Agyina was a fit lad overcome by the sticky sand; Parks was just not built for physical endurance and Robinson had given up a long time ago. Joel levered his exhausted body off the rock. He took a few deep breaths and focused on the sandy path about to merge into a bank of mud ahead. He rubbed his eyes and wobbled on the rock…

Two white figures, like elves, appeared under a bush just ahead. They strolled a few steps onto the path then vaporised into the air. "Who the fuck is tha…" Joel asked Simone.

"What… what you on about, Lundy?" Simone replied.

"Did you not see that? Nothing, sure it was nothing."

Walnut raced past Joel like his pants were burning hot. "Whore house that way," said Simone, pointing in the opposite direction back up the sandy path. Nobody heard Simone except Joel, still taken back by the vision he had just seen.

The platoon marched on, up the muddy bank back into the full glare of the mighty sun. The legs of the great insect neatly back in place. Joel felt his whole body aching with each stride. His shins felt like they had been hit with an axe. His helmet weighed down on his temple like a cast iron weight and his lungs pumped and pumped, making his chest muscles feel tight and constricted. He felt so weak. Pains shot down his spine from the Bergen perched on his back… The elves appeared again, hanging from the willow trees lining the path.

The lieutenant picked up the pace. "On

the double… double!" shouted Sergeant Thompson. This time it was Boyd who fell behind. Pinkton nestled next to Boyd's tired frame.

"This isn't you, Boydey. No this is not you, pal!" Pinkton could be heard. His suggestion was a lot nicer in tone. Joel could feel the platoon racing further and further ahead. He tried to widen his stride and lift his listless arms. Summers shot past, then Bronson, Agyina, Mac McCullen and Penfold.

Joel swung his rifle looser and wilder, out of kilter with the platoon's broken time signature. "Lundy you're not flaking it are ya? Get up there!" The voice pinged around his eardrums. He felt a strong push from behind. The strong salt was back amongst his saliva, synthesising with a metallic aftertaste. His leg span became shorter, beats pounded out of his chest, exhalations flew out of his lungs. "Balls!" he shouted.

"Come on, Platoon, swing those arms. Open those legs!" cried the lieutenant.

A deluge of sweat poured into his eyes, clouding his already blurred vision. The elves multiplied in front of him, skipping along the path singing a merry folk song. Joel smiled. He kept moving. "Must keep moving," he murmured. The platoon raced ahead. His body creaked and groaned. Second gear burned out.

The big orange ball in the blue sky shone. The orange incandescence blinded him until a sheet of white eclipsed his line of sight and all he could taste was mud. His body lay on the forest floor, lifeless.

16.

The white elves faded away into the sunset. He was floating among the clouds, limbs numb.

In the near distance he could see a silver gate, with dots of people surrounding the gate. As he drew closer, he could see they were soldiers dressed in khaki uniform.

The soldiers stood to attention at the gate entrance, hundreds, thousands. Awaiting the cog in the machine that had escaped them. Suddenly the soldiers burst out into an ear rattling laugh and the piercing laughter turned the white world crimson. Blood dripping from space.

He awoke to find a nurse attending a drip in his arm. He was shaking profusely.

"There there, it's ok…" said the nurse.

He looked at the slight nurse with a neat brown bob. She had a kind face like his mother. The nurse casually adjusted the bed sheets.

He sat up in the bed, off the sticky patch of bed sheet. "What happened?"

"Heat exhaustion, you've been out for the past twelve hours," she replied in a Cornish accent.

Feeling a numbing sensation in his left arm he glanced over to see a drip attached to his arm, hanging precariously from his translucent flesh. He tried focusing straight ahead, at a red clock on the wall opposite but his vision was blurry. The colours indistinct.

"Hot. It's really hot." He squinted at the clock again. The room felt stuffy and looked like a child's drawing through a kaleidoscope.

"It's ten pm try and get some rest. You're not going anywhere just yet," said the nurse.

Remembering patches of the morning's events his brain slowly began to add pieces to the puzzle.

"Heat exhaustion? I remember it being hot. Just had no energy. My legs wouldn't move," he said.

The nurse looked him in the eye with a subtle grin. "Just try and get some rest, you're making a good recovery. It could have been a lot worse you, knowww." Her West Country speak was the warmest most soothing human chords he had heard in a long time.

He took a swig of water from a plastic cup, still tasting metallic on his taste-buds. The red clock came back into his line of sight.

"Was I hallucinating when I saw the elves this morning?" he asked the nurse.

"It's likely." She went to open a window. "When your body is too hot and dehydrated it starts to shut down and you'll become weak. Hallucinations are common. Elves eh? Normally the guys with heat exhaustion see stars, that's about it. Looks like you had it lucky!" The nurse beamed at him.

He looked up at the low, green ceiling, realising he had witnessed a rare moment of joy stuck in the machine. "White elves hopping along a trail in the woods. Now I know what Syd Barrett and Bowie were on about."

The nurse felt his forehead. "Did you eat breakfast this morning?" The question attacked his delicate vitality with a sudden jerk. He paused, trying to recollect the morning trek to the mess hall.

"Breakfast yeah err… I… toast… lots of it… with marmalade." He remembered within a flash: *"Damn Penfold and his lousy wake-up call!"*

The nurse left his room soon after. He wriggled about all night trying to get comfortable in the damp, sweaty sheets before the morning sun begun peeping through the velvet curtains.

The inevitable entrance of the powers that be charged towards his bed mid-morning, the rhythmic stomps awakening him from his awkward sleep.

A faint aniseed aroma wafted through the sanitised hospital corridors. Tiny cracks appeared in the green paintwork. The sound of cars hurtling down the autobahn could be heard miles away. He ran his tongue around his mouth: the dry metallic taste had left his taste-buds, replaced by a fruity tang.

The sergeant major turned the corner into the green room. He stood under the door frame; shoulders wide, legs exactly thirty centimetres apart. It was a Saturday morning, yet the sergeant major was still immaculately presented. Silver incandescence shined from his lapels. Razor-sharp trouser creases blended into the floor tile symmetry. He stood straight as a pole, beaming proud. Suddenly he snapped his neck towards Joel's bed. "Feeling better this morning, Private Lundy?" his charred blue eyes locked onto Joel.

Joel sat up in bed, squirming his tired body into an attention of sorts. Elf tomfoolery now felt very distant.

"I slept well, sir. Feel a bit better, sir," he spluttered.

"Good. That's good, Private Lundy!" The sergeant major strolled up and down the near side of the bed, hands clumped together at his rear. He stopped halfway along the bed, stroking his moustache. "Word has it, Private Lundy, this could have been avoided…" the look on his chiselled face was suggestive.

"I asked your platoon sergeant this afternoon about you, Private Lundy, and interestingly he told me your fitness levels were not bad. Not great, but not bad. I also happen to know that you,

Private Lundy, do not have medical conditions that could possibly have caused you to faint from exhaustion." The words rolled off his tongue with the professionalism of a prosecution lawyer.

His pulse raced. The voice in his head rattled: *"Just get on with it. Say it please, just say it!"*

The sergeant major moved towards the drip and stared straight at the green wall above the headboard. "So that brings me to the next question…" he ratcheted up the tone of his voice. "Why would a fit soldier that has no history of flaky behaviour when it comes to fitness and is also medically in good condition collapse like a sack of spuds, Private Lundy?"

He stood poised: fists clenched, lips swollen. Ice formed around the green ward. The sergeant major had turned into the archetypal wise guy detective ready to lift the lid.

Joel felt his insides twisting up.

"You didn't have breakfast did you, Private Lundy?" The sergeant major raised his fist. Joel felt like he was being chased by a pack of wild dogs and was now on the cliff's edge. Jump or be mauled to death. *"All this over a bacon sarnie!"* he sardonically thought before jumping.

"Yes sir, I did not have breakfast. I tried to I did… but there was so much to do in the morning. I was about to go to the mess but just as I was about to go I was called upon to do area clearing, sir. By the time we finished area cleaning the Bedford was ready to go. For that I am sorry, sir."

He looked the scraggy blue eyes dead on, knowing his half-hearted explanation would not be enough. The sergeant major lowered his fist, his icy glare veering off Joel's left ear. "Pathetic! Private Lundy. Pathetic!" he snarled. Creases formed on the sergeant major's forehead, pushing his broken nose into his eye sockets.

"What do you think would happen in the field if you didn't get some food down your neck?" His menacingly calm voice heated up again.

"I would be beee beee hungry, sir."

"Hungry? You'd be more than fucking hungry my friend. Your platoon members would pick up the slack for you being fucking careless. Dragging your limp body along as the enemy closed in. You, Private Lundy, would be a dead fucking weight!" Joel could literally see the steam bellowing out of his hairy nostrils.

The sergeant major prowled along the side of the bed again. "You will be charged, Private Lundy, for gross negligence," the sergeant major informed his underlay, the venom subsiding from his lips.

Joel looked at a magpie perched on a

telephone wire through the window. A strange serenity gripped his chest. He felt like a convicted criminal finally knowing his sentence. "But sir… I did try to get to get to the mess… No one wants to miss those oak smoked bacon sandwiches!"

"Don't get funny with me, Private Lundy!" He stopped by the window, peering at the magpie. "You will find out your fate when you are back at barracks from Lieutenant Briars. Failure to look after yourself both before and after a CFT is a very serious crime in the King's Regiment. Just remember that!" he poked his index finger on his brow.

The rage subsided. He stopped next to the drip, straightened up his back, parted his legs and pushed back his shoulders; a finely tuned stance from a young age. The steely blues took one last look into the black of Joel's pupils and stomped out of the room, making a peculiar grunting noise as he vacated.

Joel laid back. The pillow felt moist, dewy. He moved his ankles around to get the blood flowing; strength was slowly beginning to return. Paradoxically a depression gnawed at his insides. The charge he was indifferent about, he knew it was coming, but going back to the machine he dreaded. The magpie flew from the telephone wire, leaving him to count the seconds on the red clock alone, in silence, waiting to fit back into the machine. The bars grew tighter and tighter.

The minibus dropped Joel off outside Gallipoli barracks the following day. His aching feet gingerly moved toward the front gate as the guard yawned like an overfed tomcat. The walking wounded had returned. The guard peered at the bruises on Joel's arms where the drips had punctured. "Alright?" said the guard. Joel nodded.

The block seemed dormant, unusually quiet. He slithered past the stores and climbed the steps into 3 Platoon's corridors. The corridors smelt like an East End brewery. He opened the door to the corridor. Broken beer bottles were scattered on the floor: Heineken, Stella Artois, Leffe. Hundreds of glass pieces swimming in a light brown river. He navigated carefully around the sharp glass pieces, noticing soggy chips and half eaten Bratwursts in the mix. The wretched smell nearly made him retch on the spot. As he turned the handle into his room Walnut appeared from the room opposite with both hands down his tracksuit bottoms, looking frisky. "Eh it's the return of the casualty! So, you remember much of what happened, Lundy boy?" He slapped Joel on the shoulder.

"Not really. Just a dry mouth then I'm in a hospital bed," Joel replied.

Walnut laughed. "You know this doesn't look good for the platoon, Lundy boy. A grunt fainting on a CFT. The sarge was proper pissed off!"

Joel turned his back on Walnut pushed

down hard on the handle and hurried inside. All was quiet in the room, not a body in sight. The bed springs squeaked loudly as he flopped onto his bed.

Peering out of the window he took stock of the last few days. The charges that were incoming didn't even register. He started playing with his nails, removing the omnipresent dirt that had turned the tips black. "Wonder if Dad ever got charged for not eating breakfast? Probably not. He was too keen to fall for that one."

He felt like his body had hit a brick wall head on. His body shattered into trillions of pieces. A wind of sadness sunk into his chest, a melancholia gripping his soul tight. He was so, so, sick of feeling this way. Everything felt helpless.

He tried to think of positives in the current predicament: food, shelter, a career, a chance to see the world. He didn't feel lucky. The army felt like a curse, a wicked curse that had gripped the Lundy family for generations. The prerogative of the generals became clearer by the second:

Institutionalising the brave men who had fought for what they believed to be a just cause… polluting the young men's psyche with militarized dogma… telling them they were better for nothing else except cannon fodder. The whole dirty ethos was laid on the kitchen table of Reigate Terrace. Kitchener and that poster had a lot to answer for.

But he didn't want to feel bitter. He was bored of the melancholy and the apathy. He searched for a ray of light out of the window; a guiding light, an epiphany, anything. His numb skeleton rolled towards a wall and stared at the magnolia paint as a teardrop dropped down his cheek and into his mouth. He felt so alone. Alone amongst a group of men he could not empathise with, no matter how hard he tried.

He turned onto his other side, arm still aching, legs numbed.

"Were you here Dad, were you? Talk to me, you old bastard!" he mumbled at the locker opposite. The brief conversation with Simone in the corridor whirled around his head. *"ANOTHER WAY! ANOTHER WAY!"*

"I'M NOT YOU, DAD! I'M NOT!"

17.

Joel was summoned to the lieutenant's office on the Monday morning ready for the charges. Sergeant Thompson and Corporal Bronson stood behind the lieutenant's neck, breathing their dehydrated liquor fumes into his ears.

Joel marched into the lieutenant's office and limply saluted the officer. The lieutenant told Joel in no uncertain terms that he had let the Platoon down and brought great shame on the King's Hampshire Regiment. Sergeant Thompson and Corporal Bronson stood behind, rubbernecking every scathing criticism that left the lieutenant's lips, dropping in cowardly anecdotes any opportunity they could. Joel stood there listening to the barrage while sinking further into a lazy apathy. Words drifted past his ears into the corridor. He daydreamed about his father being in this position twenty years ago. Would he be thinking exactly the same thing? Every word leaving the lieutenant's straight lips seemed to mould into one dirge.

"Blah… Blah… Platoon… Blah… Let down… Blah blah… The regiment…"

Joel refocused on a tiny birthmark on the lieutenant's right cheek. He was told he would be charged by the OC of A Company and be put in the barrack prison for one to two weeks. The words failed to sink into his brain, feeling abstract.

He just didn't care anymore.

"Get out of here, Lundy!" Sergeant Thompson barked.

A breeze brushed past his cheeks as he dragged the soles of his boots against the tarmac to the block. A sudden urge to be alone took hold. He avoided the corridor and turned into the toilet block. The polished taps gleamed, fending off the grey clouds hovering over his cranium. He felt the clouds hovering over his head sucking his youthful zest. Draining him of hope.

A smell of hopelessness hung in the sterile, bleached air. He sat back on the porcelain seat inhaling the fresh bleach smell, wishing the smell would knock him unconscious, away from this coerced society. Anywhere…anywhere…

The cage doors were firmly slammed shut in Ziegborn. Like they slammed shut in Londonderry, Gutersloh, Cyprus; An impenetrable prison hovering over his soul, pushing it back into the abyss and oppressing every aspect of this existence. He imagined what it would be like to reach through the cage bars and touch the other side with his fingertips. To feel freedom, proper freedom.

Out of the cage.

18.

A dirty window radiated a burned orange sheen around the cellar room where Joel sat, rocking back and forth on a rocking chair. His focus a network of intricately made cobwebs made from the finest silk which peered over the side of a mesh wire fence. Joel looked at the rows of dead flies tangled in the cobwebs, waiting to be eaten by a spider in the corner of the web.

Silvery vapours clung to the passageway that separated the cage from the subterranean entrance, hanging in the dank air like spirits summoned. His foot hit the cold floor, crushing mouse droppings that littered the cemented floor like seeds in a chicken coup. The stench of the cellar room was vinegary, like rotting fruit – but somehow warm and pleasant.

A murmur from above; Joel looked to the low, withered ceiling; stomps, shouts, bass-lines from stereos. The harmonics of life sounded muffled and convoluted. "Are they looking for me? Do they know I am here?" A grandfather clock ticked in the corner. He peered at the clock-face: one hand over VI, another halfway between VII and VIII. It was like staring back in time; before wristwatches and the digital revolution. He picked out dirt from under his fingernails then bit the calcium until his fingertips were red raw.

The harmonics of the building suddenly fell silent. Looking past the mesh he stared at hundreds of gas masks scattered on rows of wooden shelving. The masks stared straight back at him, taunting him. It felt like he was in a complex maze from Alice in Wonderland. "What to do?" he contemplated. "What to do? Which path…" His father dressed in full parade regalia had haunted his dreams for many nights, marching up and down the parade square into his conscience. "I've let the old man down. Let him down…"

He leapt up off the rocking chair toward the sealed off cage, pacing up and down the mesh barrier like a ravenous mutt. The building creaked with the muffled sound of footsteps two floors above once more. He thought about his mother: Poor old Belinda tied to the army machine. He wanted to pick up the NAAFI payphone and talk to his dear mum. This army machine was not for him, he couldn't be another cog. The played-out conversation hit his heart with a heavy spear.

"I tried, Mum, honest I tried…"

"I know you did, love."

"I love you, Mum." No reply.

He paced up and down the cold floor, kicking up dust-balls; the masks gawping at the agitated figure through the wire mesh. He could see emotion on their dusty faces, an almost arrogant, sardonic grin. As he turned away from the window a chink in the mesh became noticeable. He walked up to the small hole and began kicking it with his trainer, making the hole bigger. He kept kicking, the force increasing with each kick of his worn trainer. The masks looked on, chuckling amongst themselves. He upped the ante and kicked with both feet, the hole growing bigger.

"Fuckers!" he mumbled pounding the fence with all his worth until his hand fitted through the gap. The sharp wire caught his wrist as he reached for a mask on the bottom shelf. Blood drops began to make splotches on the grey floor, penetrating the dust defence. His fingers stretched until he could feel his middle finger about to spasm and hooked a mask. Slowly he retracted his grazed arm and pulled the mask through the hole. He blew on it. Thick dust flew off the rubber seal. "What's your story?" he said.

Cradling the mask in his shaking hand a past was visible: a mask that had seen and felt world wars, cold wars, banana wars. "How many depended on you, I wonder?" The glass eyepieces had no reflection; it was like staring into a black hole. Beneath the glass protectors sat the air canister housing, his fingers felt around the brown rubber seal. It was a rough grainy texture matured through time. He thought about the soldiers who had worn this mask – a mask of preservation – and the ones who were not so lucky. "Poor bastards," he said.

Cradling the rubber mask, he sat on the floor and focused on the lifeless glass eyes that had given up hope a long time ago. His memory travelled back to the gas chamber at Chipping Burse:

"Gas! Gas! Gas!" Three words of panic, ten seconds to get the rubber seal around his neck. Completely blind, his fingers would be shaking, palpitations trebling. Then the stinging sensation like a swarm of bees creeping through his eyelids and the sickly smell of strawberries rotting in a field. The relief! Oh the relief! Once the rubber seals slapped the back of his skull and he took his first breath through the tasty oxygen. The oxygen tasted stale but heavenly.

He suddenly realised that he was feeling empathy toward this lifeless thing cradled in his hands, which only moments ago facetiously laughed at him behind the mesh. He dropped the mask on the floor, the thud echoing around the dungeon.

"Why did you make the decision, old man?" He looked to the ceiling. "You could have been somebody, a free man, except you chose this! This life! Polluting us all with that dogma."

An irk rose. He bit his nails and kicked cobwebs on the floor. "Mum didn't want this life. I know she didn't. She wanted to go to art college for Christ's sake! Ha! And she ends up marrying you," he chuckled; a snorting fit, quickly morphing into a roaring laugh.

The laugh rumbled around the dungeon, bouncing from wall to wall. His cheeks turned devilled red and his paces grew quicker. The dust flew around the room, kicking up a wild wind. Amongst the dust cloud the mask lay on one side as if it had taken a bullet. He picked it up and peered closer into the dark vortex of glass. He stared and concentrated, looking for some sign of life. The mask stood still in the sands of time, a crystal ball awaiting instruction from above. Suddenly an image appeared: his father, sitting in an armchair. He shrieked, flinging the mask into the corner. The shriek bounced across every crumbling wall before hitting his left ear drum with a thump.

Every muscle in his body tightened. His eyes focused on the mask in a predatory glare. The rubber relic had become the prey. Without a moment's hesitation he sprinted toward the corner. "Argh! Is this what you meant, huh?" he screamed.

"Rage? Aggression? Kill that fucking enemy!!! Arrrrrrggghhhh!" the rabid dog was released in his pneuma, flicking the switch between love and hate.

His trainer came crashing down on the mask with an almighty stomp. A kick from his left flung the relic toward the cage. Red filled the whites of his eyes. He stamped on the mask until an eyepiece popped out and smashed on the floor. He then pounded with his fists at the rubber, then at the wire mesh. Dried-up flies fell to the floor; he kicked and punched, kicked and punched at the wire mesh.

"You bastards! Bastards!" He repeated "Bastards!" until he was exasperated and slumping on the cold concrete. A cathartic groan yelped out of his lungs.

Sweat dripped from his forehead, blood dripped from his knuckles. Panting, he looked up at the window. The sun was beginning to set, casting tiny rays around the subterranean museum turning burned orange to silver grey. He grabbed the rocking chair and stood on the base of the chair underneath the window and touched the murky window. The rays warmed his palm sending serene, halcyon waves through his veins. It felt like angels of hope were knocking on the window and an inner demon was not far away.

He trudged back up the stairs breathing heavily like a pugilist on the twelfth round and floated around the barrack perimeter to A Company's block. Summers and Boyd's tones echoed around the corridor, boyish laughter admiring Walnut's latest B-movie purchase. He walked straight pass them into his room. A flicker of a bulb caught his attention about to go in the high ceiling; varying in pulses, about to die. He was drawn to it like a moth. It flickered and flashed calling out for help. The next time the switch was turned off would be his last.

His body slumped on the bed, numb, no longer angry. Turning on the lamp next to his bed he fumbled around for a drawing hidden on the shelf. 'Carpe Diem' was written on the front of the drawing in a large, italic font. He sat up in bed feeling a cold numbness gripping his spine, and reached out for a pencil case hidden underneath a pile of books on the shelf. He placed a book to one side and grabbed the case with a renewed gusto. The lead touched the paper in a light symphony. He began to draw kestrels and buzzards. Always hovering over the same stretch of the M1, scouring the small grassy patches and wheat fields for juicy rodents. The image was clear: visits to Nana's house with his mother in the clapped-out Fiesta, while his father was away on tour. The graceful birds a picture of patience and elegance, floating in the sky, free, as the world rushed by at seventy miles an hour beneath them. On another page he sketched bird characters. There was Bronski the Bulgarian budgie and Trevor the unkempt parakeet rocking back and forth on a cage swing. Both had baggage under their eyes with faded feather colours, beaks as blunt as a paper clip and demeanours reeking of middle-aged men whose youth had regrettably passed by.

He placed the pencil and sketch pad to the side of the bed and rolled a cigarette. Smoke filled the cosy space as he exhaled. He continued on with the drawings: Bengal tigers in cages, lions prowling the Serengeti. A calm excitement manifested in his face, a mild glee, an insatiable need to put lead to paper. He hadn't felt this way in a while.

He carried on with the drawings right through the night. It was three in the morning before he stopped to look at the sketches. Eight sheets of A4 paper had been filled, with anything from monks chanting on a mountain top to teddy boys strutting down an alley in the East End of London. All walking towards some kind of utopia left behind on planet Earth, a nirvana, no-holds barred, frivolous, dirty nirvana. Lying back on the bed he surveyed his work. Then it dawned on him that Penfold's revile was three hours away.

Off the bed he sprung, energised and sprightly. The subterranean hole downstairs felt a trillion miles away. Taking a last drag of the cigarette he saw the dried blood stained on his knuckles. The rouge splotches glared on his translucent skin like measles.

"Idiot! Don't waste it beating up on old gas masks and wire fences you fool!" a voice appeared. With a quick step he rushed through the corridor into the calm evening, listening intently while the barracks slept.

Birds chirped in the overhanging elm trees of the perimeter road. The odd rev of an engine. A siren echoed in the distance, fading into the Ziegborn main straße. All was quiet, peaceful in the war machine. He tiptoed around the high steel fence, as if the fence posts were watching the tiny cog below. He then took a deep breath. The air smelt clean and crisp. Exhaling slowly through his nose he could feel the poison from inside, blowing into the wind.

"Out on the hunt for a bird?" a voice called from the sergeant's mess. Joel turned around at the private in combats, rifle in hand, about six feet with a gangly, wire frame similar to his own. Joel shook his head, a vacant look in his eyes.

"So what you doing out here at this time? It's gotta be a bird. You don't look that pissed," the private chuckled, taking off his beret and rustling his fine hair with his fingernails. His fringe flopped halfway down his forehead. Yellow spots covered the tip of his chin, waiting to explode into the night sky. Joel took a deep breath and looked straight into the private's doleful, marble-coloured eyes.

"You know what? I'm just walking, walking that's it. No ulterior motive, no women, I'm not drunk I… I can't explain it. I'm… I'm just here… Here in Ziegborn… walking and now talking to you, friend. How are you? Life good?" The private took a step back hesitantly. His eyebrows arched at Joel, somewhat bewildered. Hippie bullshit lingo equalled an incorrect order.

"I'm alright, mate. You sure you're alright?" The private was out of his comfort zone, looking at the strange specimen of a soldier dressed in combat trousers, a cotton shirt and scruffy trainers.

Joel fumbled around in his pockets. "You want one?" he asked. The private put his SA80 on the ground.

"Yeah, sure."

Joel inhaled the tobacco fumes, causing his lungs to tickle. The guard dolefully gazed at the tarmac around Joel's feet. "Can I ask you something? You know, squad to squad, man to man." Joel fidgeted with his nails.

"What's up, man?"

"What's it all about? This military life? Why are we here?"

The private smirked. "Jeez, who are you, my dad?" he took the cigarette from Joel.

"It's just I'm, well… trying to figure it all out. Can't say it's all it's cracked up to be."

The private clenched his lips together. "It's not so bad is it?" the private cradled the cigarette in the corner of his mouth and took a short drag. "We get to be proper men don't we? Travel the world, shag birds and get paid for it."

"Do we?"

"C'mon man, this ain't so bad from where I'm standing."

Joel sighed. "I must be in a different world then."

"Then there's the kudos you get back home. Proper kudos, know what I mean man!"

"Yeah I guess." Reluctant acceptance shadowed Joel's face. It was the same, same old story. "But don't you ever get the urge to get outta here and try something else? I don't know what. Just leave, experience something else? Know what I mean?"

The shutters came down on the private's eyes as if Joel was speaking another language. "Like what?"

"Another… Another way… of life."

"I love it, man!" He waved his cigarette like a conductor's wand. "Beats being back in Brum working some shitty job or being on the dole."

Joel looked down at the SA80.

"This is what it's all about being young n'all. Maybe going to war. Gets me blood going. How can you not like this man?" The private had the animalistic look in his youthful gaze he was now accustomed to. "How long you done anyway?"

"Six months depot, five here," Joel replied.

The private gawped. "Well I think you're nuts!" He toked on the cigarette, blowing a smoke hoop into the air. "But you could leave this and be back on Civvy Street in a couple of years."

"Two years, how could I forget. Been living this my whole life and will continue to when I get out."

The private picked up the rifle and tapped him on the shoulder. "Anyway, stalker of the night, I've gotta do the rounds. I'll see you around. And remember don't be a wuss. It'll be wankdirch soon! Think about all the good stuff we'll be doing soon. Heard it could be going off in Kosovo soon. Imagine!" The private slung the rifle under his arm, moulded his beret back on his scalp and wandered back towards the guard room.

"One other thing – what time do you close the gates?" Joel asked.

"It's gone man. Think they changed it to midnight."

"Because of?"

"Y'know B Company kicking off last week, the arrests. Weekends I think the gates stay open with a guard."

"See you around then."

"Laters! And get to bed, man!"

Joel watched the private swinging his gangly legs in a purposeful stomp. A stick insect on the march. He imagined the young private back in Birmingham, hanging around the local boozer on Friday nights, quarrelling with his mum during the week. AN ACADEMIC FAILURE according to the school system. A boy, nothing less, with limited paths to follow in life. Had he seen the same poster on a bus one day directing him on this path? Now he rolled and rolled and rolled inside the cage.

He rubbed his eyes and looked to the heavens. "Over two years!" he sighed.

The regimental emblem appeared, painted

on the signal stores of B Company. A sudden jerk thrust his body forthright. The emblem peered at him through the thick, gloss paint. Realisation manifested its shy head as he looked up at the stars faintly glimmering in the sky and contemplated his predicament: years of following his father, and his father, and his father. And for what?

The stars watched on as Joel took the long route along the fence perimeter. He stared dumfounded at the ground, paths that led into patches of neatly trimmed grass. Daisies and buttercups were clumped together on the patches. The flowers appeared different to the ones over the fence, with larger leaves and a duller sheen and appeared to be growing closer together, on top of one another.

He passed the REME workshops where faint red flashes caught the corner of his eye in the darkness. The flashes appeared to be coming from a perimeter section that seemed to flow into a black hole. He moved towards the flashes.

A section of the fence was hanging loose from a support wire and had been sectioned off with red tape and traffic cones. He moved closer, looking from side to side for guards in the vicinity; the steel barricade was hanging on its last limb, causing a dip on the barbed wire surrounding the top section. He poked the loosened support wire, then took out a tobacco packet and left the fence section. *Where were the guards?* he wondered.

The parade square lit up under the phosphorescent rays of the mysterious moon. His figure all magnified and burning bright. The man sat up high on the dark blue waves watching the insignificant dot muddling around trying to find his senses on planet Earth. He trembled. Tomorrow he will be in front of the OC leading to jail time, eating filthy mop water for breakfast while the regimental police got their kicks. "Think. Be calm." His pupils beamed at the stars.

"This is your destiny!" Each time a different speaker would take the microphone to yell the prophecy: his father. Vague images of Grandad. Sergeant Thompson. Corporal James. The caged birds. The careers advisor from the secondary school in Westhamton.

His body was moving on a conveyor belt of contrived dogma and rhetoric: round, round, round. He sighed and finished the cigarette, hands quivering and nails jagged like the teeth of a saw. Shifting his weight onto the left leg he headed for A Company's block.

Boyd's snoring filled the room as he entered on tip toe. He poked his head around Summers' bed-space. Summers was lying on his side directly facing Joel, with half an eye open.

Out of the locker came the grubby rucksack he was going to use for R&R in September. He dusted it off and gathered some clothing. As he lifted the rucksack up a ticket dropped on the carpet. He picked it up:

ARMY ISSUE 28/03/98 London Waterloo – Westhamton one way £21.13

In went a scratched Discman, wash bag, leftover tobacco and drawing pads. He opened another locker softly and grabbed a black denim jacket (the same denim jacket that had been entertaining moths for the past year) and swung it round his shoulders. He then grabbed a black woolly hat and caught a glimpse of his reflection in the window "This morning I'm James Dean!" he pondered, and swaggered out of the room.

The gap in the fence had arrows pointing to the new world; a clear path to the Promised Land. Up he climbed onto the fence section, carefully avoiding the barbed wire jutting outwards. All he needed was a stripy set of slacks with a ball and chain. He threw the rucksack on the pavement and slipped through the gap, cutting his hand on the wire. The pain did not register. Starlings had begun their morning call, beckoning him from the other side.

The outside flashed before his eyes, appearing iridescent and fantastic in colour. He glanced up at Venus, who had been the one watching him the whole time, ablaze in all its splendour in the blue waves of morning. Julie was right, Venus was beautiful.

19.

The lights of Ziegborn glowed in the dawn; dulled red sex shop signs, fading yellow petrol stations, dim orange glowing from the tall street lights. All glimmering into a cauldron of hope and optimism. Sweat dried on Joel's forehead as the soldier turned escapee darted along the Ziegborn main straße, dashing between phone booths and bus shelters while looking over his shoulder. He looked down at his hands, which had become an extension of his paranoid being, with fingers shivering in the glorious summer morning.

He stopped at a phone booth by a parade of shops, panting heavily and adjusted his hat to cover his eyebrows. In the handset he could see his enlarged reflection: A droopy bottom lip and shifty, paranoid eyes stared back. If he looked closer he could see salty stains around his eyebrows.

The Ziegborn train station was just short of two miles. He had to get to the station quick, before the alarm was raised on the barracks. The evasion felt exhilarating then wildly perilous. He glanced at the digital clock in the phone machine: 06:09. Twenty minutes he had been on the run; already the doubts were kicking in. His father's deep voice flanked his left ear lobe questioning his son's destiny: "Disappointed. Sad. Let down. SON." A cacophony of tones reached his right ear lobe: jet planes and tanks rolling through the fields, intertwined with chit chat amongst the ranks of soldiers. The voices became muddled into a messy synthesis of war mongering and that word again: Destiny.

Slamming the booth door, he raced down the main straße, past a taxi rank, the YMCA, buildings upon buildings monitoring the escapee. He headed down the underpass that burrowed under the town centre. The early sun rays bounced off the shop windowpanes, rebounding failed hope and broken dreams flush into his haunted countenance. Vampire instincts took hold. He focused on the train station amongst the concrete battleground. His pace quickened through the shopping centre, past the old Gothic cathedral housed in the middle of the shopping precinct. The bells were about to chime. Ziegborn was awakening.

He took deep breaths, trying to control his breathing. The old launderette appeared on his left, where he had spent Saturday afternoon's staring at dirty khaki clothes spinning round and round in a fuzzy, catatonic haze. He then passed the Turkish kebab shops where greasy meat aromas filled the air every evening; German beer-houses, squaddie bars, ice cream parlours all dotted the route, before his legs motored underground past Savoy's. Ammonia fumes floated through the dark underpass as the door-men closed the black door for the last time that morning.

The ground level approached; groups of Polish builders drank coffee on park benches as he passed the big department store on the edge of the shopping precinct. Shifty eyes followed Joel along the walkway: women going to work in the factories, street cleaners collecting the morning waste and podgy bus drivers waiting to start a shift.

Ziegborn had become an alien world and he felt like the canary in the coal mine again. He slowed down to a fast walk, shuffling out of the town centre and onto a tree-lined back-road, towards the bahnhoff sign. He then sprinted through the corrugated iron entrance, scanning the train timetables. Every face in the crowd turned on him, exacerbating the manic paranoia gripping his senses tight. Each eyeball seemed to be tracking each footstep into the station, hawk eyes blindly staring at the suspicious-looking figure with a woolly hat and rucksack. He glanced back at the timetable.

Numbers mixed with German words and glistening lights flashed in front of him. White fizzy stars buzzed like fireflies in the night. He remembered the sensation well from the CFT; popping stars, the whirling rush, then the descent into the black.

Pounding thumps pulsed inside his head. He sat on a bench encrusted with pigeon defecation, took a deep breath and tried to retain focus on the timetable puzzle.

Gutersloh, Hannover, Bielefeld… all place names with no resonance. The large clock at the ticket office read thirty-two minutes past six. Night was now day. "C'mon make a decision, make it make it!!" rampaged through his rationale. Trying desperately to sweep the procrastinating demons from his brain he picked the one place he had heard of: Hannover.

"Ein Ticket nach Hannover," he said to the ticket seller.

The ticket seller, a bespectacled man with wavy, silver hair looked Joel up and down "So oder Rückkehr?"

"One way… One way," Joel replied.

"Entschuldigen?"

His heart pulsated with an intense rapidity "Oh. Ein Weg bitte."

Joel looked at the ticket seller's eyes, hidden under thick glass. "He knows something. He knows."

The ticket seller handed the ticket through a gap in the glass barrier.

"Danke," Joel said.

He sat on the same bench, this time avoiding the dried-up faeces. The great Hannover express was due in fifteen minutes. Out of the corner of his eye he noticed two men getting off the train from Bielefeld on the opposite platform. One of the men was completely bald, with bronzed skin. Gold earrings in both ears sparkled against the carriage window. His slightly taller companion was wearing a tight t-shirt, showing off his muscular, tattooed torso. The man was moustached with a buzz cut like a marine and beady iron eyes. He scanned the platform from left to right then grabbed his companion by the hand and began stroking his arm.

Joel looked at the taller man. A lightning bolt struck. It was Bronson.

A survival instinct took hold. He dashed for cover behind a newspaper kiosk, keeping a close eye on the two men. The slighter built man grabbed Bronson by the buttocks and pulled him into a homo-erotic embrace and their lips met in a sloppy kiss, right there on the Ziegborn station platform. Their bodies then unlocked, each going a separate way.

Joel crawled out from the kiosk, somewhat bemused. His pulse slowed and he felt his cheeks warming up. A smile forced itself from his sweat drenched, anaemic face. He then sniggered like a child at what he had just seen: Corporal Bronson, the archetypal tough guy, living a lurid second life.

The Hannover express entered the platform, ready to whisk the young renegade off to his new nirvana. The morning sunshine warmed the side of his face. Nerves began to loosen off and a new kind of trepidation entered into his soul.

Two images stuck in his head. His mother

washing spuds in the sink and his father polishing his boots in the garden. He entered one of the train carriages and sat down away from the prying eyes. His eyes hung like potato bags from their sockets, getting heavier by the second. Resting his head against a pane of crystal clear glass he looked at the empty platform at the sandy brown concrete floor, a board advertising car parts painted a sharp red… and drifted off to sleep.

20.

Black clouds, like a shade of tyres burning, hovered. The clouds appeared rapidly, dwarfing the sky as far as the eye could see. The pupils dashed for shelter, under the bike sheds, as the first drops of rain pinged off the goalposts on the football field.

"Oi! Lundy! What you listening to?" It was Joe Nelson, the B Company sergeant major's son.

"Jimi Hendrix," Joel replied.

Blackbrook Secondary School, the school of pad-brats attached to the Bulford garrison. There were children of all cap badges: Adjutant General Corps, Army Air Corps, RMP, Tank Regiments and the King's Hampshire Regiment. Joel huddled into a corner of the bike sheds amongst the other kids, gazing at the thunderstorm blanketing the football field. A netball court in desperate need of a paintjob divided the field and the tennis courts.

Joe Nelson, according to the other pupils, was an extension of his father: all-seeing, all-conquering, of medium height for his age but with a habit of getting on his heels at every opportunity to enhance his stature. Joel Nelson's scalp shone like a bowling ball against the glow of shiny metal bike grates. He was top of the pyramid in the school year, hardest of the lot, without really being challenged.

"Jimi Hendrix? Music for dads you mean! What you listening to that for? Lundy is an old man, old man ha ha!" Nelson shrilled to the pitch of a drunken cabaret singer. Joel turned off his Walkman and stared at the deluge pouring down on the playground. Out of the corner of his eye he noticed a figure moving close.

"Reckon the rain can stop us going to class?" It was Ivan Vickers. A short kid whose dad was a REME engineer attached to a tank battalion. Ivan sported a long auburn ponytail which covered his protruding ears, instantly making him a tad unconventional alongside the other pad-brats.

"These classes, I mean what's the point eh?" said Ivan.

"Wish I could answer. Jimi just distracted me for a second," Joel replied.

"Hendrix eh? Don't listen to Joe Nelson. He's just acting like his dad would like him to."

"A real shining star eh?"

"He could either end up a company sergeant major or a career store-man with a drink problem."

Joel brushed his mop of a fringe to one side, sniggering. Ivan always had a way of seeing people for who they were, even at the tender age of fifteen.

"What you boys sniggering about?" Adrian

Farmer approached Joel and Ivan.

"Nothing, we were just talking about Mr Hodgkinson," Joel replied pensively. Adrian Farmer was Nelson's right-hand man, his father a colour sergeant in C Company. Rumour had it both fathers were war buddies from Northern Ireland.

"Girls, girls… giggling like little girls you know that?" Farmer edged up to Joel's chin. Joel backed away in a shy retreat. They both felt a hostile atmosphere brewing and headed into the rain.

"That Farmer has a chip on his shoulder the size of China," Ivan protested.

"Doesn't matter, he's probably just trying to impress Nelson," Joel replied.

"Know what I heard?"

"What?"

Ivan let out a shy smile. "A rumour that the King Nelson had a dangerous liaison with Mrs Farmer." His jester eyes suggestively looked down at the paving, like he had taken down the president.

"You're kidding! Who told you that?"

"Got my contacts, Joel, have my contacts. Let's be honest not much gets kept secret in here does it?" He stroked his ponytail.

"Bloody hell!" The two boys walked into a classroom, out of the rain.

History lessons occupied Thursday

mornings with the bumbling Mr Hodgkinson in the newly built F block. F block had been built the previous year to cope with the swelling number of military offspring coming through the doors. Each classroom resembled a malfunctioning jungle with its dark green painted walls and plastic pot plants dotted around the room.

"Which bright spark had the idea to pacify unruly children with calming plants?" Ivan theorised. The graffiti signatures were starting to show through the green shield of paint on the walls. The very antithesis of the original concept.

"So class, who can tell me the role the Middle East has played in world politics since the end of the Second World War?" Mr Hodgkinson speculated. The silver-haired teacher with a peculiarly pointed beard looked somewhat younger than his dour appearance. Hopelessly passive and prone to erratic outbursts, unruly children would constantly walk over Mr Hodgkinson.

"That's Iraq, right?" Joe Nelson answered.

"That's correct, Joe. Formally Mesopotamia, Iraq is in the Middle East," replied Mr Hodgkinson. "Care to add any more?"

Joel sat back in his marble green chair in the front of the class, awaiting the spectacle.

"My dad told me they've got this scumbag tyrant who invaded another country a few years ago so he went out there and they kicked him back to Iraq," Nelson slouched in his chair at the back of the classroom.

Mr Hodgkinson stroked his beard, curiously peering at Joe Nelson at the back of the class. "Kuwait was invaded by Iraq. Following this a coalition of international forces including the UK were sent in to overthrow him."

"But why did we have to kick this guy out? Why couldn't these Kiwit's do it themselves?" a girl asked from the back of the class.

"Well that raises an interesting question: Iraq had broken international law but an argument could be made that other countries around the world did not receive the kind of assistance KUWAIT did, Joanne."

"What the hell does that mean, sir?" Nelson said.

Mr Hodgkinson peered into the general direction of Nelson, twiddling a pencil in his right hand. "All I am saying, class, is have an open mind. Other interests could have played a major part in the removal of Saddam Hussein."

"What kind of interests?" Nelson interjected.

"Well what I will say, Joe, is that Kuwait has very large oil reserves that western countries would have wanted to protect, that is all I will say."

Mr Hodgkinson's statement flummoxed Joel. His father had served in the Gulf, as had many of the kids in class. The reason for war was plain and simple: Saddam Hussein was a bad egg who had invaded an innocent country and killed innocent people; this bad egg had to be stopped. A storm began to brew in the jungle classroom.

"So, sir. You saying what the government said was a pack of lies?" chirped in Suzanne Hart, removing her thick glasses.

Mr Hodgkinson paced to the back of the class both hands clenched in a ball on his chest. "That's not entirely true. Governments did mention oil fields in Kuwait but quite clearly they had a big concern for Saudi Arabian oil fields. Class, my point is: why were poorer countries, for example in Africa, not given such grand protection as Kuwait? Could that not be classed as favouritism?"

A wave of groans echoed around the classroom. Mr Hodgkinson sat down.

"Well sir, my dad was sent out there cos that's his job. He didn't ask any poncey questions, he was doing what he was told for the good of the country," Nelson replied.

"Yeah, sir!" A cacophony of approvals rung around the class. Mr Hodgkinson attempted to swing the debate to colonialism in Africa, only to be met with restless noise and babble. Joel looked around the class of preposterous blankets, carpeting their eyes and mouths. They had all heard it before from Mr Hodgkinson, the non-believer. His father, Alfred would have been sat in a similar classroom twenty years ago. "Don't listen to the fool! He knows nothing!"

Joel and Ivan left the classroom at 3.30 with the scent of frustration and anger in the air. Hundreds of kids sauntered out of the school gates. Ivan noticed Nelson, Farmer and little Rakito hanging around the bus square on the other side of the road, kicking a plastic ball around and smoking cigarettes.

Ivan looked across the road. "Think we've caught their attention."

"What do you mean?" Joel replied. His face whitened.

"They're eyeballing us that's what I mean. Shit! Start looking around for Christ's sake."

Joel bent down, pretending to re-tie his shoelaces. His eyes followed the line of the pavement: left onto the road, past a yellow single-decker bus and onto a grass bank where the three loitered with intent. Farmer stood by the kerb shoulders pinned back, chest puffed out like a frigate bird. His nose jutted out like a pointed blade, shadowing a pair of curled lips. His six-foot frame surveying the bodies walking along the wide pavement dictatorially.

Joel got to his feet, his chest twisting into knots. "Let's get going. Hopefully they'll get distracted or something," he said. They hurried down a back street away from the crowds towards a disused petrol station.

"Don't worry yourself, Joel. Neanderthals with nothing to do. Daddy's probably forced it into them. Be tough at school! Be tough!" Ivan gruffed his vocal chords to sound like a sergeant major.

"Easier said than done."

Ivan grinned. "Well they don't worry me, Lundy boy, just keep your head down."

They passed a dilapidated garage where the smell of petrol still lingered. "You're not honestly scared of little Rakito are you?"

Joel shrugged his shoulders.

"He just so happens to have got in with the in-crowd," said Ivan.

"No not really. Just want to avoid the other two."

Ivan kicked a stone into the road, his expression doleful and dreamy. "That Rakito is something else. His dad is probably a made-up major. You know one of those lifers that go beyond the twenty-two, get some made-up commission then hang around the barracks like an old relic because the CO doesn't know what to do with him. Bit like Prince Philip."

Joel smiled at Ivan. "Why do you say that?"

"Can just tell Rakito has an old daddy. The way he lords it about regimental history."

"It's that Nelson who worries me the most. Got a lot to live up to being a sergeant major's son. And he doesn't like me for some reason."

"Just keep out of their way; they'll have bigger fish to fry."

Joel and Ivan wandered down a cul-de-sac, keeping a tentative eye on their surroundings; Joel rubbed his forehead, peering at a puddle in the quiet road. He stopped in the middle of the road, biting his nails. "I reckon Nelson's dad knows my dad. In fact I don't reckon, I know. There's beef he's got with him, but I don't know what, and here we are. Collateral damage. Collateral bloody damage." His solemn countenance looked up at Ivan.

They carried on into the cul-de-sac, through a graffiti-covered alleyway reeking of fresh cat faeces. Ivan leapt over a freshly laid stool, his fairy grin still ever-present. He turned round to Joel. "C'mon man you're reading into it too much, there's no conspiracy. Chill."

"Oi!" A shout suddenly rung around the

grey walls of the alleyway.

Joel and Ivan turned towards the screech. Out of the corner of his eye Joel saw two shadowy figures appearing from behind. "Oi! Lundy!"

It was Nelson. Mouth ajar, shoulders hunched. He had placed his body by the entrance to the alleyway. Joel looked at his head shining. Two more figures approached them from behind, blocking their exit. Joel and Ivan turned around with a fear of dread tearing in their chests. It was Farmer and Rakito. Joel and Ivan backed off to a brown fence connecting the walls to the edge of the alleyway. Farmer and Rakito strolled up to them.

In a blind panic Joel looked at the two figures: Two Ronnie's, Mice n' Men he thought. *Let it be over quick. Please.* Ivan stood still next to the fence, still somewhat unperturbed as his fingers nervously made loops out of his ponytail. The two boys stood, hugging the fence. Farmer fronted up to Joel's nose, breathing stale tobacco over his forehead. A fire burned in his eyes.

"Didn't like you laughing at me earlier, Lundy." Farmer's nose pointed down into Joel's fringe.

"Wasn't… Wasn't laughing at you Adrian, honest," Joel stammered.

"Is that so? Are you lying to me? What you reckon Rak?"

Joel looked at Rakito's oriental features poking through his white skin wondering what part of the world his father had dipped his wick into the sultry beauty of an Asian queen. Singapore seemed likely.

"He's lying. I saw him talking with this joker Vickers. Know what I saw, Ade," Rakito replied. Farmer stared at the two scared boys, the fire still burning through his retinas. He glanced towards Nelson's direction. Nelson was casually leaning on a concrete pillar chewing a blade of grass. He winked at Farmer.

Crack! The hit arrived like a flash, numbing Joel's right cheek. Popping stars appeared in both arcs of his sight. Joel cowered, holding his face in an instinctive defensive pose. Ivan clenched his lips like he was sucking a lemon. Joel's neck drooped down at the paving slabs, avoiding the deathly glare of Adrian Farmer. Rakito chuckled like an excitable hyena.

"You'll be next if you're not careful you hippy freak!" Farmer pointed his chubby figure into Ivan's chest. The towering figure of Adrian Farmer sauntered towards Nelson with Rakito following impish. Joel stared at the grey slabs on the floor, fearful of eye contact with the bully's gaze. Adrian lit up a cigarette as the gang of three disappeared.

"They're gone now." Ivan kicked at the brown fence. "I'm sorry."

Joel stared and stared at the cracks in the weathered paving slabs in a deep trance. Patterns of wings were forming in the dust and dirt, very faintly. A small cut began to bleed on his cheek. "Sorry for what?"

"I should have said something. You didn't deserve that. Christ you didn't even do anything to annoy them. Bastards!"

Joel crouched down, shocked but relieved the altercation was over; until tomorrow or next week or next month anyway. He continued to stare into the black cracks of the slabs.

21.

"Bitte steigen sie ihren sitzplatz!" the conductor boomed down the carriage corridor, then carried on talking to a cleaner sweeping the floors. Joel arose from his slumber and looked out of the train window, admiring the Gothic architecture holding up the grand Hannover station. He reached for the rucksack glowing in olive green, which was overhanging the carriage rail.

As he disembarked from the carriage a man walked purposefully across him, heading for the edge of the platform. The man's posture when he sauntered across the platform was just like that of Adrian Farmer, shoulders wide, arms locked to his side with a sneer on his lip. The strider turned and stared at Joel for a brief second.

The platform was busy with commuter activity. Every commuter looked like a character from his previous life; a pretty redhead with multiple body piercings to a stocky labourer reeking of sweat. Every face in the crowd blurred into one. "Why would Julie be in Hannover? And why is Dad here? Has he left Mum?"

British squaddies were the easiest to spot in any crowd; from the clothing to the tattoos, demeanours, facial expressions. He rubbed his cheeks with both hands then sat on the clean tiled floor next to a small cafe. Freshly ground coffee and newly baked pastry smells perfumed the air. He took a big, exaggerated sniff. There was something refreshingly beautiful about the aromas wafting from the little kitchen. He bought a large cappuccino and a flaky dark pastry and walked towards the station entrance. The frothy coffee tasted good, so much better than the insipid powder coffee dished out at the barracks.

Coffee stirred thoughts of his mother; ever the connoisseur. He remembered the arguments his parents used to have about coffee.

"We're not paying over four quid for bloody coffee. Coffee is coffee, Belinda!" his father would protest every time she bought Arabic filter coffee from Tesco's finest range.

"I can't drink that other poor excuse for coffee, Alfie. I like to TASTE coffee not just drink it because I want to stay awake," she would constantly moan.

"Well I'm telling you we can't afford it ok?" his father would reply.

Money; It was always about money. Killed the romance before it was allowed to flower.

He looked from side to side, noticing a sign outside the station:

Hannover mit Perpignan, Frankreich & Bristol, Großbritannien Partnerstadt.

He felt uneasy again. Imagining spies from Bristol eating cakes and reading broadsheet papers, ready to pounce on the newly arrived convict.

A humidity filled the air. Grey clouds were forming over the Hannover skyline, eating up the sea blue sky. He left the grand station, took a last bite of the sweet pastry and reached for a tobacco packet dug into his jacket pocket. A memorial of Ernst August passed his left, a murky blue statue pointing into the sky.

He didn't know where to go or what to do. Over busy autobahns and tram lines he followed the Zentrum signs; his forlorn figure cut a lost boy, now on the run with nowhere to go.

A cool breeze closed the pores on his forehead. His pulse turned from reckless thudding to rhythmic flows, gradually clearing the pent-up tension that had run through his veins all morning. His instinct was telling him to lie low, not act suspicious and avoid unnecessary contact, instincts that had been battered over the year. He walked on through the city centre. Street pigeons pecked away at mouldy crumbs left on the street floor, the bells of a church rang loud, much louder than Ziegborn. Aeroplanes hung in the sky like arrows defying gravity. Bodies barged past. It felt like a proper city.

He sat on a bench around the State Opera House, soothing the achy soles of his feet while smoking a cigarette. Dribs and drabs wandered past; the homeless, dog owners, Turkish migrants and the occasional office worker talking on a mobile phone. A fresh dew smell hung in the air like the beginning of a rainstorm.

He wandered through the old town, taking a room in a simple guest house near the red-light district. With a reluctant shake of his wrist he handed over ten Deutschemarks to a petit lady with platted peroxide blonde hair who was sat behind a desk full of flyers promoting dance music events. The woman guided him into a room on the first floor next to a disused washroom. The poky room felt like a shoe cupboard, with walls made from a paper-thin plaster. A smell of vegetables cooking hugged the thin walls. Across the faded cream plasterboard messages were scribbled in English:

The king is dead, long live the king!

BAADER MEINHOFF

Kurt Cobain forever in our hearts x

He teleported back in time: the far-left wing organisation from the 1960s fighting for their so-called just cause… the angst-ridden idol of grunge holed up in a room with a gun to his head… the king, whoever that could be…

The coils on the bed squeaked as he laid down in the comfort of shelter, away from the double agents scouring the Hannover streets. The squeak became more rapid. Squeak! Squeak! He looked around the bed. He lied still, trying to find the noise. His bed was completely still. The noise felt like someone was banging the bed posts from underneath. He looked underneath the old mattress at spider webs and strands of hair.

Squeak! Squeak! It became louder and more frequent; a human harmonic now added. He listened carefully around the tiny room.

Squeak! Uhhh! Squeak! Uhh!

The groan synchronised with the high pitch noise. He remembered walking past Simone's room at 4 am one morning, the same groaning and squeaking, like a panting woman running up a hill trying to escape the big monster on the low budget movie set.

He then moved to the corner of the room where the skirting board curved around a small alcove. The panting became louder. He lit a cigarette. With the exhalation he put his fingertips into his ear lobes, wondering when the lucky couple would come crashing through the thin wall.

The din continued. Uhh! Squeak! Uhh! He paced up and down the laminate floor then sat on the squeaky mattress. An awakening had begun; an awakening of rusty sensual feelings. Urges and feelings he had not felt for months.

The groans continued to penetrate the stale-smelling fingers covering his ears. His penis slowly moved around in his loose boxer shorts, wriggling. It slowly erected and came alive. He felt his prostate gland warming. "Awaken! Come alive! Where have you been?"

It felt unnatural, grubby. Yet the groans punched and kicked his genitals into an animalistic, lustful submission. He fought the erotic lust welling up with images of the old WRVS woman at Gallipoli barracks, sitting in her armchair stroking her cat.

Squeak! Uhh! Squeak! The zenith was reached with a loud bang on the wall. The sexual thrusts stopping just as he was about to hit the wall in frustration.

He looked down at the bulge in his blue denims deflating back into the depths. The awakening had commenced. He threw on his jacket and smiled at the blonde woman behind the desk, venturing into the underbelly of the sinful city.

"Wo finder ich die bibliothek?" A tall, tanned man with creases on his brow asked him on the street. The man was wearing an expensive-looking leather jacket and snakeskin boots. He shrugged at the man. "Nein." The man looked puzzled.

The afternoon sun arrived, warming the city air. He looked around the thin claustrophobic street: Motorbikes jostled for position with bicycles and mopeds on the tightly squeezed curb-side. Mercedes taxis flew past, one taxi barely missing an old woman running for the bus. Lorry horns reverberated around the city, a constant drone to the natural acoustics of the metropolis.

He bit his fingernail and walked along the pavement, coolly peering at the laptop computers and televisions displayed in the shop windows. There were widescreen television screens, portable DVD players, CD stereo towers and state of the art camcorders. The silver objects burned brilliant through the windows, beckoning the consumers: "Ditch your old fangled technology. Join the elite set. Don't be left behind!" VHS players, tape recorders, bulky televisions were on the way out.

He approached a T-junction where bright pink lights dazzled from the other side of the road. Hungry lights, flashing lights, beacons that flashed to the rhythm of his animalistic pulse. He waited for a green light to appear and walked across the busy intersection, a curious sensation gripping tight. A naughty, intrepid adventure felt like it was about to be embarked upon.

Men of all sizes and ages passed him on the road, hurriedly heading for the great pink castles in the sky. Oriental women headed in the opposite direction looking not much older than twenty, talking amongst themselves in Vietnamese or Thai. He approached the other side of the road and rolled a cigarette, glancing at the neon signs that had lured him to the seedy, spell-binding part of Hannover:

Madchen…

Sex show…

Viele videos…

He took a puff on the cigarette.

Pigeons hung around the dips in the road drinking stagnant water. Aromas of honey wafted from the shops ahead. He ventured off the main street and down a back street where the natural light narrowed into a thin passage above townhouses, four stories high. Out of the thin doors of the townhouses where the dazzling pink signs hung joss sticks fanned thin smoke circles into the alleyway. He carried on down the darkened street, inhaling and taking in the view.

African men passed with fake gold jewellery hanging from their pockets. An old woman crossed the street, lugging two heavy shopping bags. She stopped by the entrance of a beer house, took out a bottle from her coat pocket and took a sip. Lanky German men hung around the doorways watching the world go past, stroking their mullet hairstyles and moustaches shaped like elongated handlebars. Little spots of red flickered amongst the skinny buildings like butterflies circling a fresh flower; Joel passed a large door where two young women and a bespectacled man were playing cards, drinking absinthe.

"You! Ja! You!" a bald man with baggy combat trousers and a skin- tight t-shirt called from across the alley.

"Vant to zee two women. Gud show, come!"

his low pitch rumbled around the narrow street. Joel scuttled down the alleyway toward a large set of rectangular windows. Either side of the windows frames oriental decorations of flowers flowed. Pinks and reds glowed out of the windows, lighting up the dark street.

The street took a sharp turn past a shop specialising in rubber fetish wear, into a kaleidoscope of sparkling colours buzzing around the viewing windows. An industrial, synthetic rubber smell hung in the enclosed space. He glanced at the tinkling glass, having no idea what was behind the windows. All the teasing Walnut used to get, all the kudos Boyd wished he would get, the secret, seedy world he knew nothing about.

A slender Caucasian girl with jet-black hair, dressed in stockings, with leather boots up to her kneecaps sat on a stool behind the first window he approached. Her perfectly groomed hair hung out to one side, covering one side of a high forehead. Lipstick, a shade of blackened red adorned her fat lips with mascara accentuating her attractive Baltic features. The girl's index finger beckoned him through the window like a sorceress waving a magic wand. He stared at the specimen through the looking glass on the other side; the girl stared back with contrived lust. She resembled a blank canvass: "Just at work is all I'm doing. Getting paid to support my family back in Latvia!" He imagined the justifications.

He immediately felt a sad guilt. "Why? Why? Why do they have to sit there like a piece of meat?" It felt so unjust. In the window next door a Chinese girl excitedly jumped up and down like a hyperactive Jack Russell dog. "Ello! Ello!" she bellowed through the dazzling lights, frantically trying to grab his attention.

She wore a lacy garment that barely covered her petit frame and stilettos that clunked against the polished wooden flooring; drowning out the Euro-pop coming from another street. Through the narrow door slats he could smell perfume scented like garden herbs. "Ello mister!" she stuck her tongue out and rubbed her small breasts.

Between the two prostitutes a burly man with a wispy moustache patrolled the walkway, huffing and grunting. Joel could recognise the aggressive posture, the steely gaze and the clunk of steel toe caps. The man crossed his palms and gave him a stern look. He turned and had a look down the windy, narrow street; sex shops began sprouting up, daisies on a spring meadow.

He smelt the sinful lust in the air leading to the dirty nirvana; Intriguing peep shows, shops selling mint-flavoured dildos, looking glasses selling a woman's soul. Dirty, it felt so dirty. He continued down the street, his shabby trainers lightly touching the filth on the pavement. The tarmac turned into a cobbled street, leading to a disused car park. He continued through the car park until a beer house appeared, nestled between a main road and the far end of the parking lot. He counted eight, ten, twelve steps before descending into the establishment.

The atmosphere was lively for a Wednesday afternoon in the drinking house; men in suits mingled with student girls around a large, square-shaped bar. The walls were decorated with scarves, placards and posters of German football teams. The memorabilia broke up the insipid, cream walls with jets of red and bright blue.

"Eine stein Leffe," he said to a waitress before slumping down on a wooden chair.

The legs of the chair stuck to the floor, glued. He fiddled with a beer-mat and bit off skin from his thumbnail. The nectar beer arrived. He took a small sip, the alcohol nicely taking the edge off. Ziegborn felt like a safe distance for now.

Looking around the beer house nobody espionage-quality stood out. He took another glug of the beer. The beer was warm on top but cold inside, a perfect temperature for the unsettled August day. Another thirsty glug of the beer, his mind raced back to the girls being paraded in the brothel windows; having sex with hairy, fat men and answering to pimps while being caged up like wild animals. At the back of his conscience away from the sorrow, regret and lamentation for the prostitutes a small fire was burning. Burning in the distance like a star in another galaxy. It kept nagging at the strings tied to his conscience. Feelings, urges… "What's it like?"

The squeaking and the rumbling in the shabby guest house would not leave him. "Is it painful? Embarrassing? Does it take a long time to climax? I'd never make noises like those animals."

The afternoon sun soon disappeared, and evening was born. The lone AWOL soldier wobbled on the wooden chair. All around him people were making lots of noise. A techno mix blurted from the sound system, groups of young locals spoke at the top of their voice; all trying to out-shout one another. He just stared into the golden bubbles floating around the heavy glass. His intoxication blurred the indentations of the glass, making the glass seem like an abstract painting. His father's face appeared on the side of the stein glass, looking weather-beaten and tired. He gazed at the sad old man with his neat moustache and balding head.

"Old man… what did I get myself into?" The volume of the chatter around him quietened. "Bet you had thoughts of leaving didn't you? Sitting in your bunk one night while the harem passed by. Maybe you didn't… Maybe you just wanted to keep Grandad happy… Too late now, old man, too late… I did all this for you. For you!"

With all the laughter and the music, his

mood hung on a precipice; desperate for a new direction away from the cliff. He couldn't go back, he just couldn't. But deep down could not think of a way forward. A group of slender women entered the bar through a side door, dressed in office suits and high heels. He smelt their sweet perfume from across the bar. It smelt of lavender. The fragrant smell reminded him of the brothels up the road; enticing, alluring, enchanting.

The brothels of Ziegborn these were not, so it went. Simone had already given him the lowdown. Payday every month always meant big business for the seedy whorehouses dotted around the periphery of Ziegborn. Rumour had it their takings for the first squaddie payday would be double their takings for the third and fourth weeks of the month. Security was always tightened around boom week; erection malfunctioning drunken squaddies could be the most volatile of creatures, even to the over-zealous door-men patrolling the steamy corridors.

He remembered the same old botched story floating around the block the same time of the month. "Eight hundred marks I blew! That's me skint for the rest of the month! Can't even remember half of it I was so hammered!" The youthful naivety brought a certain kind of kudos to the ranks. It was like an auction of intoxicated stupidity.

The taste of the beer stuck to his lips, sickly sweet. He stretched his legs and wandered towards the toilet. The room froze while he groped for his balance, the ceiling shrank, and the table grew.

A jet of translucent liquid sprayed into the urinal. "Damn fly."

"Move. Why don't you move?" The painted insect stubbornly kept its ground. He focused on the fly until the spray stopped.

Zipping his jeans, he stared morbidly into a mirror. The stress of the chase had caused tiny white spots to form on his chin. He rubbed the raw skin; it felt rough like the freshest of sandpaper. Lack of sleep had opened blood shoots in the white of his eyes, the red lines plaguing the once beautiful brown shades. He turned the tap and splashed cold water onto his face. "I AM CONVICTED," he said.

The group of office workers had doubled in size when he returned. Young professional-looking women with short hair and fake gold earrings mingled with middle-aged men sporting peculiar facial hair and wearing baggy suits. He looked on suspiciously from one end of the bar to the other, the bar still moving from side to side, blurred and murky.

Hazy cigarette smoke clung to the freshly painted ceiling. The group laughed and joked. A younger man with fair, Nordic features hung his tall frame over the counter and turned up the stereo. "Ja sunshine, we having fun!" it coughed out. The drone of the sludgy kick drum repeated and repeated in one long monotonous cycle.

"Fun, having fun!" the lyrics went on. Joel caught the eye of a slight blonde girl, perched at the edge of the group dressed in a cheap-looking blouse suit. His blurry vision caught hers in an abstract embrace. She smiled at him, revealing a silver stud nailed through her tongue. The silver caught his eye, calling out from across the bar. The same senses that felt dirty; clumsy fumbling in the block, illicit liaisons in Savoy's, back-alley lust while the rats played hide and seek.

The group grew rowdier by the minute. "Ja ja sunshine!" they sang, spilling orange drink over the sticky floor. He stared at the group, akin to an outsider desperately wanting to join the cult. The blonde girl turned her back and joined in with the sing-a-long, the silver flash disappearing into the crowd. Taking one last sip of the sweet beer he slammed down the stein glass on the table.

Hannover was coming to life. As Ziegborn was when he left, in a more ordered way. He began the ascent up the lime-stained steps to street-level, floating from one side of the railings to the other, having no sense of the other punters trying to push past. The air was fresh outside. He buttoned up his jacket and spat yellow phlegm to the ground. Young groups in bright coloured jackets and red jeans loitered around the bar entrance, shouting German colloquialisms at each other. He turned around to the group, balancing on one leg. The words sounded jumbled up, like a game of German scrabble hooked on vodka.

The mood was jovial and lacked aggression; boys mixing with girls, girls mixing with boys. A platonic utopia. Sex didn't seem to play a part. He tried to lock his gaze onto one of the girls sitting on a bench. She looked around sixteen with a tom-boy crop.

"Hi! Sorry guden-tag! How are you? You… you want a cigarette? I love this place I really do. You come to this place often? I'm… I'm on holiday. Yeah on holiday. Taking a break from things. Want to escape with me?" The words tumbled out of his brain catatonic.

Swaying from side to side he loitered on the periphery of the crowd, his drab blue and black clothing melting onto the dark streets away from the vibrant rainbow in front. As he was about to approach the girl a man shouted from the other side of the street. The group headed south away from the red-light district towards a large bistro bar, leaving him rocking back and forth against a bin.

He staggered down the bustling street. Hannover felt like a dark dream: Fading colours, blurred lines, his vision watery. He stared down the cobbled street at the bright pinks, sparkling blues and florescent yellows weaving an enticing design of webs lighting up the warm evening. The city resembled a large fish tank without the fake coral, bright pebbles or exotic fish. Like an excitable moth he walked toward the colourful web, veering off the cobbled street. A dog barked out of an apartment window, the yelp caused his body to stumble off the kerb onto his ankle. He slurred a curse while continuing to limp down the narrowing street.

The seedy back street had blossomed. He smelt the dirty enticing air; the incense strong.

Men of all ages passed him on the street, bald men, young men, black men, white men, groups of men, solitary men, queer-looking men, men looking like Rambo, men resembling plane-spotters. All on a mission to get somewhere quick. He looked around at the invasion of the Y chromosomes filling the street, wondering where the female of the species had fled to. He panicked for a split second, imagining every female on planet Earth had been abducted: leaving the rotten planet with one disgusting macho gender, fighting it out amongst themselves for alpha male supremacy. Grimacing, he bit his nails. This wasn't the block now. He turned a corner, pink light radiating from window panes onto the alleyway.

His head swayed, heavy and cumbersome as the alcoholic slumber tried to register a location. The pink lights grew in intensity. It beamed into the back of his skull, warm and sensual. He turned around. It was an angel. The prostitute in leather stood before him; her lips looking redder, juicier. Black locks lustrous and slick. She stood, hand on hip, posture domineering of Joan of Arc quality.

He walked up to the window to get a closer look. A different door-man watched him, with slick back blonde hair tied up in a small ponytail. The door-man gave him a quick once over then stepped away from the doorway. The prostitute beckoned him through the glass with her deep brown eyes like a daughter of Lucifer enticing a recruit through the gates of hell. He picked out of his pocket some Rizla papers and quickly rolled a cigarette. On closer inspection he saw a small dimple on her chin, an imperfect bump that made her bottom lip stick out and long fingernails painted mauve. Her body was beautiful, curved in all the right places. His hazy memory thought of Elvira princess of darkness, seductively sitting on a large boulder.

A group of middle-aged men speaking in Arabic slithered up to the window next to Joel. The men were dressed in Armani suits and Oakley sunglasses with expensive aftershave pouring over the big glass panes. The door-man gestured to the men and broke into a wry smile; the men reciprocated and gestured to each other, then mumbled in broken English to the door-man. The door-man's shoulders loosened. Joel stared blankly at the youngest of the bunch, his own courage growing in intensity.

The younger man, with thick black hair, produced Deutschmark notes from his trouser freely. "Money, see we got money!" The man said to the door-man, then pointed at a young girl with piggy tails. The door-man gazed excitedly at the fresh banknotes, grunting at the group. He showed them the way, his big hairy hand slanted towards the small door like a statesman showing authority on a world visit. The group uniformly took off their sunglasses and entered through a red gloss door.

"Ello mister! 'Ello mister!" rang into the street. The last of the group turned around and smirked at the door-man. Thanking him for granting royalty for the next hour: grapes fed on the vine, oxygen scented like roses, flesh as smooth as silk. Joel loitered by the entrance, rolling the cigarette. The Elvira stood still at the window; hand on hip, mouth ajar. Bits of tobacco spilled on the pavement as he tried to adjust his blurred vision.

He lit the cigarette and took a short drag, singeing his top lip. The black-haired princess looked around the street, eager for custom. The red door closed. His heart thumped out of his chest. He felt the blood flowing around his testicles. An urge began to rear its ugly head again. He bit his nails one by one until they were rubicund. The Elvira stared at him, licking her puffy lips. The door-man took a sideways step away from the red door, clearing the path to sin. Bashing against his ribs, Joel felt his heart beating uncontrollably.

The red neon sign ceased flashing, stuck on red. As if the devil himself had re-wired the electrics and given him the dirty subliminal instruction. Joel took a deep breath and focused on the enchanting, alluring red door and placed a quivering foot onto the plank as the sea of unadulterated desire floated calmly underneath.

The Elvira winked.

22.

The door-man held his right hand aloft like a captain leading troops onto the battlefield "Komm hier her zurück!" he screamed "Komm hier!" Chalky white spittle clung to his lips, rage sprung out of his hollow belly. A slimmer accomplice with straggly grey hair and a tanned complexion joined him as they raced along the dark street lit up by pink butterflies weaving in and out of fidelity. Joel approached the intersection and looked behind; they both were clearly visible fifty metres away, with blue bomber jackets and tanned foreheads, both panting like old dogs in the sun.

"Hey! You! Hey!" The words forced from their tightened airways.

The intersection traffic whizzed past with no let up. Joel raced to a crossing to the right of the busy road and looked behind as tourists bumbled along the pavement, making welcome obstacles for his nemesis. The door-men pushed and barged their way through the crowd. Joel waited for the green light, stomping his trainers on the tarmac like he was running on the spot, his judgement still clouded from the alcohol. "C'mon! C'mon!" he shouted at the red light hung high in the heavens.

He glanced at the red light, wandering why so many bodies were at this crossing at 3 in the morning. This, he thought, was a crossroad of severe magnitude. "This is it! Life boiling down to a zebra crossing!" The traffic suddenly muted and all he could hear was his racing heartbeat and teeth grinding. The door-men pushed past a group of French tourists, sending an elderly man to his knees. With no remorse they stumbled toward the intersection crossing with the ponytailed door-man leading the way.

Joel awaited, feet frozen to the ground as the door-men closed in rapidly. Both sides of the busy intersection barrier were closed to pedestrians, with traffic cones blocking off the gaps in the barrier. The only exit on the crossing was a narrow path on the opposite side of the intersection. He tried to move left, then right but was stuck in the crowd waiting to cross the road. To his rear were poky shops a muddy grey shade, with mysterious dark eyes poking out from under Arabic newspapers. A calm fear pulled at his heart strings. The ponytail was twenty, fifteen metres away. He knew what he had to do. A sudden act of pugnacious bravery stiffened up all his muscles. He shoulder-barged a small, dishevelled man out of the way and freed his body from the crowd. With a sudden burst of fist pumping adrenalin he ran head on at the door-man.

The ponytail flapped and a grainy image of a sandbag suddenly appeared before him. The door-man's rabid gaze fixed on Joel. Just before the door-man had time to scoop a hairy hand onto Joel's shoulder he forced the heel of his scuffed trainer into the door-man's genitals. The other door-man waved his fist and upped his pace towards the crowd. The wounded door-man felt his groin area, short of breath. "Arrrgh!" he growled like a wounded lion "Arrrgh!" His accomplice was now ten metres behind with grey hair waving in the wind.

Without a second to think a primeval instinct kicked in and with a swing of his right fist Joel punched at the incoming enemy. The wind swept past his right ear. He looked at the door-man straight into his hazy green eyes, while all around him paused. The right hook missed the door-man and swung wildly into the late night traffic. The door-man backed off, completely unprepared for the sudden attack and the confident look in his face disappeared, replaced by shock.

He saw the opportunity and ran across the busy intersection, the beeps of cars, vans and HGV Lorries barely registering. He zigzagged across the tarmac:

"Pepper pot! Pepper pot!" Basic training kicked in. "Never run in a straight line. Make it as difficult as possible for the enemy. Remember you are the target. Weave! Pepper pot! Pepper pot!" The other side of the intersection was fifteen, ten, five metres away.

His lungs pumped nicotine carbon dioxide out of his nostrils with his heart beating at a thousand beats per second.

He reached the other side of the intersection and looked around. The door-men were hopping on the other side of the section, raging with vexation. Their fists raised into the air like a pair of comic villains, thwarted by the dashing hero at the end of an epic chase.

A wry smile left Joel's mouth. "Suckers!" he punched the air with wild excitement. He jumped up and down, purveying the hapless bouncers on the other side of the road.

"Suckers! Suckers! Ha ha!" he repeated over and over triumphantly. His cheeks glossed and his eyes shone glazed caramel. The catharsis that had lain dormant for so long sprung out of his body, kicking up a stale dust. "Ha ha!" he laughed. Two men in grubby clothes looked on at the excitable young man with bewilderment.

"I got you this time! I won! I won!" An air vent from a Polish restaurant blew his cheek with a warm, comforting, exuberant ray. Winning, this is what it felt like; winning against the odds with the enemy punch drunk in the corner. He kicked a can into the street in jubilation then made a quick dash around the back of a department store away from the intersection. The alcohol was starting to wear off, leaving a sickly taste at the back of his throat. A sweetened sickly taste, but it felt good, sticking it to the two burly door-men.

A clock inside the store ticked at 3:14

am. He looked through the winding streets, devoid of life away from the pink and red and blue lights on the other side of the intersection. He waited for the two grizzly door-men to appear through a window or to arise through the tarmac like poltergeists. Waiting, waiting. No sign.

Like a spy on a covert mission he darted in between parked cars and rubbish bins, shielding his face from sheepish eyes and the seedy characters that lived in the early hours. Each face appeared in the night, even more distorted and sinister with a look of knowing in their eyes. "AWOL soldier! Violent aggressor!"

He ran at full speed through the streets, wobbling and sliding from side to side until he reached the guest house and took a deep breath. The triumphant euphoria was starting to wear off and the air smelt of meat slowly cooking in an oven. Taking out a fresh packet of Golden Virginia he rolled a cigarette outside the entrance and took a long hard drag of the porky cigarette. The whole day and night felt surreal and otherworldly. As if his mind had departed, leaving his body to fend for itself on the mean streets of filthy, rotten Hannover. A funny thing, adrenalin, he thought. One minute you can take on the world and for a split second you are not afraid to die, next you are back to your usual insecure fearful self and are afraid to die. He became convinced the RMP's were about to come running around the corner; batons and handcuffs in hand; ready to bust his meagre existence. Now it was the whore house incident.

"What they don't know," he mused. "Was never going to sleep with the poor girl! How was I supposed to know she would go mental and scream strange Russian words at me?" Convoluted theories about army life, whorehouses and Hoegaarden began to untangle. An innocent crime he had apparently committed. His heartbeat slowed down, the sweat on his forehead dried up. With a click of his wrists his hands gained their normal composure.

As he climbed the dimly lit stairwell to his room a moment of clarity manifested. "All of it. Everything, what was it for? What am I worried about eh? This is my life. I've done nothing wrong, have I?" The clarity was masking something, something bigger; a hole about to open up his heart. A painful stitch manifested in his abdomen as he stumbled to his room sensing a tragedy.

Early the next morning he packed his rucksack, changed into a pair of baggy cord trousers and a plaid shirt and vacated the guest house. The blonde woman behind the desk smiled and gave him a suggestive look as he walked out of the entrance. "Gud night?" she said.

He ignored the woman and peered around the corner of the guest house expecting an ambush of sorts. A woman and child crossed the road. He glanced either side of the street and marched away towards the train station. The red-light district appeared in the near distance with the ubiquitous red and pink lights of Hannover fading in the bright morning sunshine. And with the fading lights the lust and the dirtiness appeared to ebb into the sewers for another day.

The strange feeling still gnawed away at his insides. He tried to think about a future away from the army: a beach in Thailand, a ski resort in Austria, a bohemian lifestyle in an American commune… It didn't work. All that was left was an urge, a need to get back to his parents in Westhamton. He slung the rucksack on a park bench and lit a cigarette, watching the tobacco smoke hang in the air as if a were spirit judging him. The voices bickered in his head:

"This is it, this is it! Take it. Time to banish this monkey off your back. Go! Go! Move on. Start your life, Joel. Start your life."

"You can be anything you want to be: an illustrator for a graphic novel, a singer in a band, an ambassador for world peace, choice is yours! You are wasted where you are. What family loyalty do you have? What did they do for you except make you become an insecure wreck?"

"How can you say all this? Do you have no loyalty to your parents? At least to your mum anyway, forget about him. They have raised you. Go see them, you imbecile. They don't even know you are AWOL for Christ's sake! They must be worried sick. What kind of son are you? And how do you know they are actually ok?"

The strings pulled tighter and tighter, squeezing the walls in his chest. He knew he had to go home at some point. An empty Coke can blew in the wind and he kicked it with frustration. Home was not home, it never had been, but something did not feel right. He looked at graffiti sprawled on the bench, all German words he could not understand. They were like an analogy of his life: words, drawings, symbols, all meaning different things, pointing in different directions, none the right answer.

The morning rush of commuters filled through the grand old straße: men in suits, school kids chasing pigeons, train station workers drinking cups of coffee and smoking cigarettes. The world was passing him by. He felt like the most invisible insignificant speck travelling through a micro space of time.

A middle-aged woman passed by. The woman was petit with a tightly pulled ponytail. A black leather jacket covered her shoulders all scratched and ruffled. A toddler trailed behind the woman pushing a toy cart. "Beep! beep!" the toddler yelled. The woman turned around and mumbled German kiddie phrases to the boy. Joel turned his head, only to hear the groan of the city. She picked the toddler up, stroked his straw like hair away from his blue eyes and proceeded to kiss the boy's pink forehead.

He remembered back in Bulford when primary school was about to start, butterflies in the stomach, a new scary world full of scary kids. His mum would hold him tight to her chest and stroke his hair.

The muscles in his chest froze. "It's ok, Joel, I'll be here when you get back. If any of those kids give you gip you tell me ok? Mummy loves you very much," she had said. He had not spoken to his mother in weeks; she had no idea the strife he was in. The cigarette butt fell to the floor. He stamped it out and moved off the bench.

The bahnhoff entrance came within sight, a big concrete arch with metal grates either side. This now felt like the crossroads he had ventured onto, crossroads leading to different emotions, destinies, mortality, immortality, heaven, hell, dying in Westhamton or in some barracks, a life in nirvana.

He sat on the edge of a raised flower bed just outside the station entrance next to a collection of pansies, wallflowers and geraniums and took a drawing pad from the rucksack. He sketched a bigger budgie to the one he had drawn back in Ziegborn, swinging to and fro in a rusty cage; apathetic, solemn. A ray of sunlight pierces through the metal bars lighting up a small quarter of the dark cage. The budgie looks ahead, into a black hole that has enchanted and vexed the bird its entire life; an enchantment the only focus in its sad life. Where would the black hole take the bird? He didn't look like he had the energy to find out. Years of entrapment had masked any zest for life he may have once had.

He sketched the rest of the drab, faded feathers, and the chipped beak then put the pad down. The tightness in his chest was getting worse. He knew deep down who was pulling at his heart strings. It wasn't the fate of the budgie, or the RMPs, or the door-men running around Hannover, it wasn't even the man who had forced this life upon him. It was love and affection, unconditional.

He slung the rucksack over his shoulder and felt the petals of a golden pansy in the flower bed. With the touch of the soft petals he attempted to clear all the clutter from his overburdened mind.

The bahnhoff sign appeared in the corner of his eye telling him which direction to move to: away, away, away from this madness.

23.

The cage hung over Joel like a gigantic shadow. Around his feet the earth was clumpy and boggy. He looked up at the rusty bars all around him; dark, cold pylons. Beyond the bars lay a sea of black stretching as far as he could see.

In the huge, all-encompassing cage were two privates from the Green Howards Regiment that he had befriended in Ziegborn. They were laughing and joking without a care that they were caged in like zoo animals.

"Lundy!" they shouted in unison. "What do you call a bunch of squads shitting their pants on the ranges?"

Joel shrugged his shoulders.

"King's Hampshire shitbags that's what. Ha ha ha!" The Green Howards rolled around in laughter as the tones of wicked, sinister laughter escaped through the cage bars into the abyss beyond.

Joel sat in the corner and smoked on a cigarette as the tobacco smoke rose out of the cage in small puffy circles. The earth had clumped together around his boots. Suddenly out of the corner of his eye a figure was running through the abyss towards the cage. He squinted but could barely see the figure in the darkness; all he could make out were a tatty pair of jogging bottoms and bare feet. The figure's running posture upright, solid. It continued out of the dark "Joel! Joel!" he heard.

Joel recognised the coarse southern English accent, it was him. The outline of his nearly bald head cut a strange image in the dark. The runner powered towards the cage. "What's the old man doing?' he thought, quivering in the dark. The Green Howards' giggling continued unabated. Alfred got within ten metres of the bars and tried to catch his breath. "Joel, it's me, it's Dad!"

"Yeah I can see that," he solemnly replied. "What are you doing here?"

Alfred wiped his brow and placed his hand in front of his mouth. His bulky frame had sunk into his shoulders. He looked nervous. The darkness camouflaged his blotchy face. "Been looking for you for a long time, Joel." sorrow poured out of Alfred's once steely eyes.

"This cage. What is this?" he asked his father.

Alfred tried to catch his breath. "Don't be scared, son, it's a cage. A cage that has surrounded you, me, your mum, your granddad all our lives." He spoke with a concise manner. "Don't be scared son! Don't!"

The rusty bars wobbled in the darkness as Joel felt the coarse metal with his fingertips.

"I don't understand what you are saying,

Dad. What do you mean? Is this a cage you put me in? How do I get out?"

Alfred walked around in a circle, shaking his head and muttering under his breath. He had the look of a madman about to confess a sinister crime. Suddenly a big groan echoed around the cage. Joel turned towards the heavy noise as a red flash appeared in the distance. The flash roared out of the black abyss and rolled like deadly lava towards the giant cage. He froze to the spot and stared at his father. "What do I do, Dad?"

"Don't worry, son. Don't worry. You'll be out of here soon I promise." His response was calm yet slightly panicked. He looked at his son and felt helpless. The groan of the red flash grew louder, picking up pace as it rushed out of the dark wilderness toward the cage. The groan became deafening, drowning out the screeches of the Green Howards and the squelching of boots on the mucky soil. Joel picked up a black stone lying on the ground. It had the texture of a burned sponge.

"What's going on, Dad, what do I do?" he shouted. The red liquid began hissing and foaming as it snaked its way downhill towards the cage. "Whhhhat do I do?"

Alfred quivered. A tear formed in his right duct; he quickly wiped it away. "It's going to set you free, son! Like a bird yeah?" His shouts became muted in the pounding noise. A sulphuric smell filled the thin air. Joel looked at the red sludge coming towards the cage; he tried to lift his boots from the sticky soil but felt exhausted and devoid of energy.

Hallucinations leapt in front of his strained vision: Monsters with no limbs, turtles the size of whales, strawberries shaped like cucumbers. All incomplete characters carved from another world. He slumped to the floor. The Green Howards lay in the corner unconscious.

"How did I… I get here? How?" he stuttered. His breath became shallow. White shades appeared all over his wafer-thin face. "Is this it…? This it?"

In an act of final lucidity before fate took hold he looked over at his father, tearful and distraught, and took a final deep breath of the fine oxygen. "Mum, where's Mum?" he screamed at his father. "WHERE IS MUM?!"

Alfred Lundy

24.

"Name?" asked a woman with thick, dark-rimmed glasses that appeared to be sucking her eyes into the back of her head.

"Name?" She was sitting behind a pale wooden desk, staring intently at a monitor screen.

A stocky man handed over a small paper booklet. "Lundy, Alfred Lundy," he replied.

The room was abuzz with activity: mothers shouting after their troublesome offspring, drunken vagabonds arguing by the doorway, security guards calling down walky-talkies. A strange concoction of body odour and fried food clung to the stuffy air.

"Been looking for work?" the woman asked, avoiding eye contact with the stocky man.

Alfred sat in a perfect vertical position with his legs exactly twenty centimetres apart at the knees. He looked down at his thick forearms where tattoos were poking out from under a crisp white shirt.

He moved his hand through his thinning dark hair. "Been looking around the agencies and the shopping centre and been asking around. Nothing has come up yet. Hopefully something soon." He fiddled with his neatly groomed moustache.

The clerk scribbled down notes on a slip of paper. She was big. Her hair was big. Breasts were big. Her hands encompassed the whole desk. "Go over to the job applications department, ask for Mr Dewsbury. What was it you specialised in again?"

A sudden disbelief hit Alfred's countenance. "Well… my speciality is not really in Civvy Street, you know what I mean?" her big brown eyes finally acknowledged his; squaring up to him with an agitated disregard.

"That is no concern of mine if you have served time in prison, Mr Lundy."

"Prison? No… No… I've never been in prison! I served the country. Was in the army for twenty-two years." He felt like he was back at school, being told off by the headmaster.

She sighed heavily, her doleful eyes nonchalantly looking around the stuffy office. "Well I apologise for that, Mr Lundy, however, you need to tell me what kind of work you are looking to go into. You know, an OCCUPATION."

"Just been doing the odd bit of security work since I got out, y'know. Retail, car parks, factories, that kinda thing." He strung out the answer in a dreary motion. "Few days here and there."

"And is that the field you want to carry on working in, Mr Lundy?"

"Well I guess. Need to earn some money. I'll take work if it's there."

"Go over to the vacancies section and ask for Mr Dewsbury. Give him this slip." She handed over a ragged looking Post-it Note with a code written in black ink.

Alfred looked across the room. Piles of people were shifting through the doors ready to snap up jobs and claim benefits. His eye caught a grey-haired man sitting in the row behind the signing-in desks. He had seen him two weeks before. The all too familiar look: tarnished ink on the arms, rubbery skin sagging at the jowls, a pot belly growing. 'Retired squaddie' written all over his grizzly face. The clerk handed back the signing-in book.

"Well thanks anyway." He left the desk.

Here he was again – the notice board of hope. White cards clung to the flimsy boards precariously, like golden tickets about to fly off into the wind. Many times he had visited the VACANCIES notice board, hoping he could gain a new direction to his life. Some days he imagined a gate keeper arising above the board with a winning lottery ticket or a flight ticket to the Bahamas.

Security officer. Negotiable hourly rate. Flexible benefits. Quote D34

Warehouse operative. £5.03 per hour.

Overtime opportunities. Fork lift licence essential. Quote B57

A card with red ink caught his attention on the bottom rack:

Lothario needed. Mega bucks per hour. Previous experience needed. Large dicks only apply. Quote S5X xx.

He sniggered at the card, reached out for a ticket slip and slumped into a chair.

"Exactly the kind of prank Smudge would have dreamed up," he reminisced. "Wonder what he's up to nowadays? Old Smudge, the joker in the pack, with his curly ginger hair and chipped front tooth. Why he thought putting itching powder in Brick Allen's pants was a good idea I'll never know." His lips curved upwards into the flaky skin masking his rugged, red cheeks.

51, Alfred's number flashed on an LED screen. Half of the number 1 failed to light up, the number resembling a squiggle on a chalk board. He strolled over to a desk with mountains of folders piled up to a polystyrene tiled ceiling; passing glum faces, disenchanted dreams, an imaginary wall between public and service.

"Name?" the man asked behind the counter, his attention transfixed with a bunch of forms lying on the cluttered desk. Alfred glanced at the faded ink on his name badge, all he could ascertain:

"Lundy. Alfred Lundy." He handed over the Post-it Note and glanced at Mr Dewsbury's face. His upper lip was stained orange and his eyes were so close together they were sitting on the ridge of his nose. The advisor looked down at a pile of forms away from Alfred's curious gaze. "So, you're interested in the security job over at Augustus Toys then?" Bits of snot dropped onto the desk as he wiped his nose with a damp tissue.

"Well yeah that's what she said. Come over here if I was interested. Is that right or not?" Alfred stuttered.

Mr Dewsbury looked up, revealing his piggy pupils. "Alright Jack, calm down was a simple question. You interested in this job or what?"

"Alfred actually," he replied, trying to claw back some respectability from the facetious advisor. "Well yeah of course I'm interested, what's the pay like?"

"£6.10 per hour."

"Any benefits?"

Mr Dewsbury smirked, knowing he had the upper hand. For now, he was the all-seeing card dealer, the great fixer, king for five minutes. "Benefits, well, let's see…" He tapped away at a keyboard. "Overtime available, progression opportunities, product discounts."

"What's that then. Product discounts?"

He smirked again. "I've got the upper hand just you remember that old man. Better be nice to me," transparent across his grey, dumpy face.

"Well I'm guessing discounts on toys, that kind of stuff."

"Oh, no discounts on food, travel that kinda thing?"

The advisor shrugged his shoulders. "Doesn't look like it. You could ask when you get there but I wouldn't count on much else except your wages."

"Ok then." Alfred stared into a paper clip poking out of a bunch of application forms. He stared transfixed, unable to veer the beam away from the clip. "1976," he said.

Mr Dewsbury's brows scrunched into his nose. "1976? Think you may be in the wrong decade!" he triumphantly declared.

Alfred awoke from his hypnosis. "Oh, sorry I just remembered the year I came into a centre like this to sign… anyway doesn't matter."

An awkward puzzlement filled Mr Dewsbury's face. "So Mr Lundy do you want to apply for this job or not?"

Alfred looked around the long-extended desk, men and women of varying ages with that helpless look in their eye, all hunting for work, wages, scraps, scared to do anything but look for work, support their families then collect a dire state pension. Competition was fierce in the jobs jungle.

"Sure, I'm interested. Just tell me what I need to do."

25.

A fan rattled furiously, sending dust particles around the tangerine interior of the old Cavalier. Grrrrrr! it chugged away, muting out the tones of Tom Jones on the stereo. Alfred thumped the steering wheel in frustration. "Bloody thing!" he tried to fix the fan by turning the lever off and on.

He looked at his reflection in the rear-view mirror: a neat brown moustache covered his upper lip descending into the corners of his mouth. The brown caterpillar was starting to get grey hairs. He put his foot on the accelerator to mute out the din.

A glistening sheen lit up the newly laid tarmac as the Cavalier left Westhamton town centre, towards Patchley town on the A346. Shiny new car bonnets nestled up to the worn blue Cavalier. Alfred caught a glimpse of the commuter rush whizzing past: suited men shouting into mobile phones, mothers screaming at quarrelsome children, courier vans dangerously lane-hopping to make the 9 AM drop-off.

"Rush. Everyone always in a bloody rush," he said under his breath.

Large retail parks straddled the sides of the A346, dwarfing the once tranquil setting with all the familiar names: IKEA, Tesco, MFI, Wickes, Burger King. Housed in red brick warehouses stretching for miles. He pulled into a gigantic car park and parked next to a burger van.

Turning the ignition off he stared at a grass bank, some ten metres from the kerb. Immigrants hopped off the bank towards the vehicles, selling wilted flowers and pirated CDs. He wound down the driver's window, smelling hints of sulphur in air. Around a hidden corner was the happy bear of Augustus Toys, all beaming and joyous, enticing children from all over Southern England.

He slammed the door shut and glanced around the car park. Children of all ages pouring into the big bear's mouth, dragging parents and siblings along for the ride. One little boy looked familiar: jet-black hair overhanging, purplish cheeks, a quiet submission in his innocent stare. He walked behind the young boy and his father into the store, feeling a pang in his heart.

A young girl sat behind a desk in the foyer. "Is Mr Wallace around?" Alfred asked.

"Wallace?" the girl's bottom lip jutted out. "Oh, Derek!"

"I think so yes. I'm here for the vacancy." Alfred tightened up a red tie that hung still from his collar and brushed down his sleeves. The girl picked up a receiver and dialled a 3-digit number. "I'll send him round." She shouted down the receiver.

The girl picked up a nail-file. "Round

the back."

"Which way?" Alfred asked.

A pink bubble expanded out of her jagged mouth, hanging like an unwelcome tumour. Her perky little blue eyes peered over the pink balloon and the bubble popped suddenly. Alfred twitched. The pop sounded familiar, an eerie déjà-vu. He looked down the desk and focused on a mouse mat the girl's hand rested on: elephants, tigers and bears of illuminating colours, unnaturally gleeful. His brain was unresponsive, the pop had triggered something. He couldn't figure out what.

"Right out of the exit then follow the building round the back," the girl responded.

Alfred's gaze uneasily gripped the mouse mat. "Why do the animals look devilish? What? How? Which?" His eyes clung to the mat.

He walked through the exit and nodded at a silver-haired security guard. Paranoia began to rear its ugly, disgusting head. In his panicked state a quantification of the response time varied; five, ten, fifteen seconds? Poor, so poor.

Alfred felt the whole store gawping at him from the inside, the worthless specimen who had struggled to produce an answer. Tills stopped beeping, bratty kids stopped crying, muzak stopped on the third beat. He reached inside his trouser pocket and pulled out a paper tissue, wiping his brow and both sides of his bullish neck.

"No fear. That's right no fear! They didn't serve their country, did they?" He made his way around the red brick store fronts, watching the judges from within the huge glass and turned a corner.

He approached the staff entrance, still confused by the inability to place the right response to the girl's answer. The Augustus sign appeared, shrunken and filthy compared to the front of the store. He opened a double-glazed door and rushed inside where a boy with gelled blonde hair sat behind the desk of the staff entrance. "I have an appointment with Mr Wallace," Alfred said to the boy. The boy picked up a handset and played with the gold stud in his left earlobe.

"Take a seat. He'll be down in a bit," said the boy. Alfred sat down on a red sofa facing the desk. Teenagers dressed in red polo shirts travelled in and out of the heavy glass door; armed with shrieks and mobile phones.

"That other guy what a muppet!" a gangly boy with acne covering his chin shouted into his handset. The boy at reception cordially acknowledged the spotty boy's derogatory remark. Alfred stared nervously at a blank space under the stairway: Pop! Pop! The cracking noise was stuck to his memory like a barnacle.

A dishevelled-looking man with dusty brown skin suddenly appeared. "Mr Lundy, is it?" The man's dark brown hair was wiry like a border terrier. A baggy polo shirt hung off his sunken chest, covering pointed nipples beginning to sag.

"Yes," Alfred replied, hazily focusing on the black hole under the staircase. A cardboard cut-out of an Augustus bear looked straight at him, reminding him of the all-seeing I.

Early 1982, he suddenly remembered. Exercises on Salisbury plain; looking for that safe place where the enemy wouldn't find him: rolling grasslands, big holes in the ground that looked like badger sets, Scimitar tanks shooting past, the Falklands not far away. A carefree attitude he had then; even with a twisted full screw taking it out on him because he didn't go to Vietnam with the Yanks. Exercises in the field always felt like a game of hide 'n' seek, but on a bigger playground with weapons and hairy assed attitude. Games of hide 'n' seek were rare in Alfred's childhood. Working and grinding were not.

"Mr Lundy?"

Alfred shot into the air like an adrenaline shot had smashed through his heart.

"Sorry, I was… I was miles away. Mr Wallace?" Alfred stammered.

Mr Wallace nodded. His jowls were so far down his cheeks they were nearly falling off his jawline. "Follow me." His voice was cracked and solemn sounding.

Mr Wallace led Alfred through dusty corridors with Perspex window doors sectioning each part of the corridors. The droopy shoulders and sludgy pace of the security manager infuriated Alfred. He begrudgingly held pace with Mr Wallace's clunky steps. "No wonder he looks like he's carrying a shell on his back. Shoulders! Way too slumped and his neck! Floppy like a ragdoll."

Alfred followed Mr Wallace, navigating around the steel cages in the corridors; no more than five metres away from his backside. Alfred had an eye for distances, drilled into him from numerous tours of Ulster. When the slumped shoulders of the security manager gained a few yards, so did Alfred. When Mr Wallace slowed down to eye up a young skirt Alfred slowed down abruptly. Space was the key, the right space. Not too little, not too much.

They entered a small office in the corner of the warehouse which smelt of mouldy oranges. A water cooler welcomed their entrance. "*Augustus suck my balls*" had been scrawled on the tank, the ink fading but still visible.

He looked around: the office appeared tighter than the cubby hole he had spotted under the stairs. Page 3 girls and cut-outs from FHM adorned the narrow walls, which sloped sharply downwards at the back of the office. A stereo sat in the corner, playing easy listening from a local radio station. It was cosy, if a tad cramped. Alfred looked down at piles of cigarette butts on the linoleum floor which had burned little holes in the material. "Take a seat, take a seat," Mr Wallace said.

Alfred brushed bread crumbs from a wooden stool and sat on it while Mr Wallace sifted through some forms on his desk, "So, what was it again. Alan?"

"Alfred, Alfred Lundy."

"That's it. Sorry, this says Alan. Anyway, you're interested in the security position then?" The wiry haired manager fiddled with some forms on his desk like he had lost an important document. Alfred noticed fingers small and bulky, resembling chipolata sausages.

"Yes," Alfred replied.

Mr Wallace continued to rifle through the forms, eyes locked downwards away from Alfred. "So, what's your experience in security then?"

"Well, done the odd bit of security work in car parks, shops since…" he paused to clear his throat, "just got out. Forces. Did a fair stint." A beam flashed across Alfred's puffy lips, lifting his moustache and blocking his nostrils.

Mr Wallace twitched before exhaling a deep sigh. "How long would that be then?" he scribbled on a notepad.

"Twenty-two. The full twenty-two. Years that is."

Mr Wallace scratched his thick head of

bristled hair and stared blankly at his notepad. The stereo moved onto a Steve Winwood song. Alfred waited for reciprocation, maybe even an acknowledgement. Mr Wallace looked around the office at the big breasts and dangly peroxide hair hanging off the walls, then opened a box of Embassy No. 1's. "So why security?"

"Well… thought this line of work I could slip into quite easily y'know? Did plenty of security work on tour, patrols, policing, and crowd dispersion. Even saw some riots in Londonderry."

The sagging jowls of Mr Wallace elevated into a facetious grin. "Listen Alfred. Seen many ex-squaddies wanting to do security work here, all the same. I had to get rid of an ex-marine only last week. Couldn't control that temper of his, you see what I'm saying?"

"Oh… but… hang on."

"Didn't want to, gave me no choice."

"But I've got references back at home. Honest!" Alfred pleaded.

A maelstrom of confrontation began to nibble away at the security manager. Sweat patches appeared under his arms, he tapped his fingers on the desk to a broken off-kilter beat, his own scattered pulse. "Not sure that's going to be any good," he replied. "Don't think I want to take the risk after last week."

Alfred stared straight into the murky

whites of Mr Wallace's eyes; he sensed a disillusioned middle-aged man trying his best to get on with the job, despite low self-esteem and a lonely existence outside of work. He kind of felt sorry for him.

"But didn't the job centre get in touch?"

Mr Wallace pulled his fingers away from the desk "A man got in touch, but he was very vague, didn't say where you were from and just gave me a time you were coming in. Was just a quick chat."

"Well did you not discuss it with him? My background and all that?"

"Like I said he was quite brief."

Alfred looked around the grubby office. Dead flies were piled up in a dusty corner awaiting decomposition.

"So, you can't consider me because I'm ex-forces?"

Mr Wallace tapped at the desk. "If you'd have come a few weeks ago I'd have given you a go but…" He lit a cigarette. "Tell you what if something new comes up I'll call you. You haven't started smashing glasses or shouting at me I'll give you that." Alfred reluctantly shrugged his shoulders at the compromise.

"Anyway, have to go now I'm afraid. I'll be in touch and sorry if it's been a waste of your time." He held out his hand. Alfred's bulky fingers gripped the soft tissue of Mr Wallace's palm; it felt wrinkly and weak, like the skin of an old apple.

They arose and headed back along the dusty corridors, Alfred making sure he was the right distance from the droopy figure in front.

26.

A lone sparrow perched on a washing line, singing a merry song to the Westhamton awakening. Alfred watched the little bird from the kitchen window while polishing a pair of leather shoes. The sparrow flew off, quickly fading from the picture. Alfred was sure it was the same sparrow that had been visiting the garden for weeks, entertaining him while he waited for work.

The past weeks were tense times, full of boredom, daytime TV and arguments. He placed his shoes on a piece of newspaper and drank his tea.

"What time do you need to get off?" A husky, feminine voice shouted down the stairs. It was Belinda. He finished the last mouthful of sweet tea and checked himself in the reflection of a kitchen cupboard window.

"Now," he said, brushing past a bunch of white envelopes stacked on the edge of the worktop. One of the envelopes fell to the floor. He picked it up:

EAST HAMPSHIRE DISTRICT COUNCIL — IMPORTANT

He'd been ignoring the deluge of bills building up week on week: council, water authority, power supplier, TV license, insurance companies. "Damn things LEAVE ME ALONE!"

"What?" Belinda shouted.

"Nothing, nothing…"

"Well make sure you're not late. Considering they weren't going to give you that job in the first place," she shouted back. The voice was a muffled conflation. He checked his tie and placed a badge onto his grey blazer:

Security/Augustus Toys/12789/A. Lundy

"Right Bel, I'm off!" he shouted up the stairs. A cacophony of footsteps moved from the bedroom down the stairs and Belinda suddenly appeared, wearing a black polo shirt and skinny blue jeans which clung to her petit figure. She moved to a kitchen drawer and took out a box of Benson & Hedges. "Be good then." She lit a cigarette and exhaled away from her husband.

Alfred glanced at his wife's mousy brown hair which shone a chocolate shade through the kitchen window. He wanted a good luck hug from her but couldn't pluck up the courage to ask. She turned her back and looked out of the window at the clouds gathering.

She took a deep drag on the cigarette and exhaled onto the window pane. The smoke formed a grey circle on the window. She stared out of the dirty glass, her sideways expression blasé and jaded. "I'll see you later then."

"See you later," he said and left the house.

The ignition grinded, chugging the old Cavalier into life. He brushed down the sleeves on his jacket and steered the Cavalier out of Reigate Terrace. The fan groaned and creaked.

He slammed his fist on the horn. "Idiot!" he screamed from inside his cocoon. He looked at his complexion in the rear-view mirror; it was milky, just like it was last week, last month. He remembered the golden complexion that had sizzled his skin in Cyprus; six months in the scorching Mediterranean heat. It was all downhill from there. He had a quick glance at his brow to check for sweat beads.

The A346 was clear. He stepped on the accelerator and followed signs to Patchley town. Within fifteen minutes he had arrived at the sprawling retail park where Augustus Toys sat. He pulled into the car park and applied the handbrake. The Cavalier's interior smelt odd, like sweaty trepidation. The same hints of anxiety that only certain situations could produce. He glanced at the clock: 08:50. The maths pinged in his head: four minutes to check his appearance, one minute to walk over to the spotty boy on reception. Five minutes early, always five minutes, no less. The drill ingrained from an early age. Looking in the wing mirror he fiddled with his moustache.

It was a fresh morning, a cooling breeze rushed along his cheek. Vauxhall Corsa's, Renault Meganes and Ford

Focuses were starting to fill the car spaces steadily. To his right ssshhing noises came from the burger van as the vendor pulled butane canisters from a car boot. Street sweepers hazily passed through, sweeping leaves and crisp packets into clunky dust-pans. "Our block inspection would have done that area twice as quickly!" he mumbled to himself.

Pigeons were perched on lampposts at the shop front avenue, watching the first shift of workers. Each face arrived looking tired, hungover, disconsolate. People of all ages, races and religions swung their dishevelled bodies out of cars, motorbikes and buses ready to step on to the conveyor belt of employment.

The workers all wore polo shirts: green for the ASDA workers, orange for the Halfords workers, grey for the bedding store on the corner, dark blue for the garden centre on the opposite corner. It was like going to a football match with more than two teams playing, each worker assigned a colour, an allegiance. Alfred looked around the retail park, gingerly taking a few steps on the pavement surrounding the car park to the gawping shop fronts.

He then turned the corner of Halfords and directly faced the joyous Augustus bear. The steel shutters were locked down. He slowly paced around the back of the store, passing the shutters of an automobile repair garage where petrol fumes were about to flood into the open.

The glass door opened with a hefty push, an overcompensating habit Alfred had gotten into, which would often cause the door hinges to creak. The reception was un-manned. He turned his head towards a corridor where muffled voices shouted from the warehouse, then sat down on the spongy sofa.

His hands trembled. He tried to place one hand on the other and took a couple of deep breaths. That used to work well in Northern Ireland on night patrol around the provinces. The corner of the cubby hole under the stairs appeared in his vision. Nobody had bothered turning the stairway lights on.

A boy with brown spiky hair suddenly raced through the glass door with the subtlety of a rhinoceros on a charge. He was chewing gum and eating a bag of crisps at the same time.

Spinning a wheeled chair around the boy spat the gum into a bin and began typing on a keyboard. He sat patiently awaiting an acknowledgement. The boy carried on typing and chewing the crisps. He heard scurrying noises of fingers tapping.

Trying to gage the teenager's attention he coughed, the boy's hair invisible from his vantage point. He cleared his throat again.

A group of excitable girls in Augustus uniforms passed through the reception. "You make me wanna… ooh time for relationships… relationships…" The girl's screechy laughter bounced off the

243

reception walls and into the dusty corridors beyond. He turned his wrist and glanced at his watch: 09:19. A creaking noise groaned from his kneecaps as he got to his feet and fastened his tie once more. He timidly looked from left to right. "Excuse me," he said to the spiky haired boy.

The boy continued typing, unaware of any presence. A black lead grew out of his ears, leading to a silver Discman vibrating on the desk.

"Excuse me!" he repeated. The boy fiddled with the volume control of the Discman, still failing to notice Alfred.

His blood began to boil. With a thump Alfred slammed his large fist on the desk.

"Deaf, dumb or stupid?" He glared at the teenager. The boy's bottom lip sunk, his chin extended, pulling the rest of his adolescent face into a big sulk. He took out one of the earphones. "Yeah?"

"I'm here to see Mr Wallace."

"Wallace? Don't know a Wallace."

Alfred felt his blood vessels contracting harder, faster. "Mr Wallace. Security manager."

The boy's eyes shifted. "You mean the half-cast fella with the hunch?"

"Well he does look like that but…" Alfred hastily replied.

"See if I can find him."

Alfred scowled at the spotty boy with spikes in his greasy hair, sitting right under his nose. "Fella with a hunch? I would have been knocked out if I'd referred to an old timer like that!"

The boy kicked the chair from under his desk and swung through the doors into the grey corridors. "Baaa baaa bee deee dah dah," he hummed into the corridor. Within a minute the boy leapt back through the doors. Mr Wallace followed the boy, all heavy footed and sunken into the grey tiled floor. The boy skipped around the old man like a fresh spring lamb.

Alfred glanced at the security manager, his new boss. Mr Wallace's natural complexion was looking even more lacklustre today, his lips red and crispy and eyes sunken even further into the dark rings circulating around his eyeballs. He greeted Alfred with a limp handshake.

"Mr Wallace. Hello."

"Hello, Alfred. Sorry, I was sorting out paperwork, lost track of time." His breath smelt of fried sausages.

"That's ok, no problem," Alfred replied.

"We'll go to the office and do an induction, I guess." The sunken eyelids caught the attention of a miniskirt drifting up the stairwell and immediately lifted, scanning the pink leg flesh up the stairs away from Alfred's attentive look.

"Yeah we'll go to the office, follow me," Mr Wallace let out a loud chesty cough and dragged his feet into the corridors. Alfred took another look at the cubby hole. "Just in case," he thought. "Just in case."

He followed the sunken posture of Mr Wallace once again, through the dust that clung to the white skirting boards and cobwebs that hung from the corners of the ceiling. The security manager walked ahead. Alfred's mind drifted: "Seven metres I reckon. We'll make it ten just to make sure. No more, never know who's going to come careering out of these doors." He took a quick glance over his shoulder; two boys were giggling near the shop-floor entrance. He felt a heightened sense of things, like something was not right.

They turned a corner and carried along the unkempt corridor, a mysterious silence took hold of the well-trodden space. A light bulb flickered, attracting a small fly. A subtle tapping noise came from the steel cages that covered half of the gangway. He kept his distance. Still feeling something not quite right. The last time he felt this was in the Gulf:

…petrified, rooted to the spot. Waiting, waiting, waiting for the order to move. Iraqi chemical weapons primed. Or at least that was what he was told. Every nook, every cranny of the small Kuwaiti town death could arrive; a shot, an explosion, a God-awful pain in the throat. A barrage of screams then white light. Mortality's question always hanging in the hot dried-up air…

He shook his head. Gloopy sweat puddles were forming on his brow. He wiped his brow and dusted down his neatly pressed blazer jacket. A couple of hair strands flew onto the floor. The two men were on the final stretch; he could see the water cooler poking out of the small office ahead. Just before they reached the office a bright light suddenly shone from a packing room to the left of the corridor as workers barked muffled orders inside. Alfred peered inside the flap door. Shadows floated around the room.

Crrrraaaaccck! It came full pelt out of the packing room, down Alfred's oesophagus and into his diaphragm like a missile. He took a few steps away from the flap doors; silence, crystalized silence. His head felt light. Pulse rippled. Confusion reigned in the silence.

He remembered the girl on the shop floor popping the bubble gum. "You mong!" Shrieks bounced around the walls of the packing room.

"Wasn't me. He bloody pushed me!"

"Well I'm not clearing it up."

Mr Wallace wandered up to him. "You ok, Alfred?"

The whites of Alfred's eyes shone piercing bright. He reached into his jacket pocket, to cover his shaking left hand. "I'm… I'm fine."

"Just kids messing about. Looks like a few crates went over. Least we don't have to clear it up."

Alfred took a further look into the packing room, the shadows had disappeared. He saw broken plastic crates and scattered toy soldiers all over the tiled floor. Crimson red blotches appeared on his slate cobby cheeks.

"Grenade… GRENADE!" He halted the words leaving his lips.

Mr Wallace looked at Alfred, his expression nonplussed. Alfred resumed ten metre spacing and followed Mr Wallace into the dingy office where breasts covered the walls and rotten fruit perfumed the stale air. They gathered around Mr Wallace's cluttered desk and discussed the role of security officer for Augustus Toys.

Alfred desperately tried to concentrate on the Augustus Security Policy apathetically flowing out of Mr Wallace's mouth. But his mind was elsewhere: explosions in Northern Ireland, the Falkland adventure, the Kuwaiti desert, Belinda shouting at him for leaving the toilet-seat up.

And his teenage son.

27.

"Hey kids wanna come on a ride… A magical adventure? Well it starts here kids… Augustus. The adventure of a lifetime all under one roof! Waaaahheeeyy!" The elf's voice looped over once again, sending the incoming children into frenzied excitement.

Sunshine blazed through the store as Alfred tightened his silk tie for the tenth time that morning and wiped his forehead. It was a warm August morning, the type of morning where the humid air stuck to his shoulders with a vice-like grip. His bulldog stance stood at the entrance of the store, monitoring the comings and goings with a posture supremely steadfast and hands clenched like they were squeezing imaginary oranges.

For three weeks now he had been working the entrance of Augustus Toys; four days on, four days off, on ten-hour shifts. Day by day he watched the shoppers like a hawk, using a technique called 'distant suspicion'. The technique involved a concentration to look at one spot while surveying each suspect from the corner of his eyes. Pow! Gotcha! Just when they thought he was looking elsewhere.

In the first week he scanned the entrance using imaginary x-ray specs: "Potential… Definite candidate… Shifty as hell… He'll nick something I know it," his monologue would instruct.

Mr Wallace had given each security officer a set of guidelines to adhere to: "Check people if you can, don't go overboard. Still want the customers coming into the store. Be sure they've stolen before confronting. If you are not sure ring me, but only in exceptional circumstances and preferably not when the races are about to start."

Alfred gazed at a fixed point, this time a traffic cone at the car park entrance, grimacing and hunching his shoulders. As much as he tried to look the part of a menacing gorilla the distraction of a small boy getting a piggy back from his older sister brought out a smile from the old soldier. He focused again. A grey squirrel jumped down from an overhanging elm tree and wandered past the cone onto a patch of grass. "Otterburn. Always had an abundance of grey squirrels there…" he reminisced. "Hordes of squaddies, tanks and weaponry treading unapologetically over their habitat. Never seemed to bother the poor blighters!"

Alfred grinned at his musings. Stag duties when the sun was peeking through the clouds at dawn always seemed to bring out the most hyperactive ones, trampling over leaves and swinging from branches. "Hey mate, I've got to watch these arcs stop distracting me! Any moment the enemy could turn up. When they do remember the procedure: If you are unsure signal a 'halt! Who goes there?' Inform the stag commander immediately. Send a warning shot. No response. Open fire. And don't ever sleep on stag duty! Not only are you endangering yourself you are endangering the platoon." (Another well practiced drill.)

He kept focus on his arcs, approximately forty-five and three hundred and fifteen degrees off the cone. "Teenagers, vagabonds, grandmas, toddlers, take no prisoners. Any one of them could be shoplifters! We can't let our colleagues of Augustus down. No!" It reminded him of all the insatiable excitement he was supposed to feel walking through the gates of Catterick barracks many years ago… "Young. No fear. The adventure begins here!"

"Charlie, come here please. Stop that! And come here now!" a mother shouted through the swing doors, interrupting Alfred's reminiscence. A pink tracksuit covered her voluptuous frame and big gold earrings shone from her lobes.

"Stop doing that!" A little boy darted in and out of the cardboard promotion stands next to where Alfred stood.

"Vrrroooomm…vrooommm," the boy gurgled, Alfred looked down at the boy. He looked about two years old, with shaggy dark locks slithering down his forehead.

"Vrrrooomm!" The boy held up a toy car into the air, imagining it to be a spaceship flying through the galaxy. Alfred couldn't help his line of sight being drawn away from the static position, towards the little intruder scurrying around the store entrance. The boy wove around the cardboard hoardings advertising computer games and Barbie dolls, his little legs carrying his sturdy body around with an amazing grace. The boy suddenly stopped in his tracks and glanced up at Alfred's badge shining off the store lights. Alfred looked down. A twinkle leapt off the boy's innocent countenance. Alfred wiped his brow; he knew all too well whom the young toddler reminded him of…

Sixteen years ago, running around the cramped living room floor with scraggy hair and skin fresh with infantile zest and that twinkle that would puncture Alfred's heart every now and then. He didn't mind the box of a living room, the mildew spreading around the window-frames or the peeling wallpaper. All he wanted to do was run. Run on his new legs, embrace limbs that were now in working order. "That twinkle! Oh, that twinkle!" he smiled.

"What the fuck are you doing, Lundy?" Alfred's focus quickly rebooted back. "Every shopper a suspect! Remember that!"

The mum grabbed the boy by the scruff of his neck and proceeded towards the aisle selling action figures. Alfred looked around, embarrassed by the diversion he had been dragged into. He looked around the store as checkout staff passed products along the scanners with a detached look on their faces and mothers chatted in the outdoor toy section. A blind man led a Labrador across the entrance, the dog panting and huffing.

A cold sweat dried on Alfred's forehead. He shook his head. First the popping noises, now young kids distracting him away from his professional duty. Aghast, he swallowed the dry phlegm from the back of his throat. The gulp of emotion dropped into the suppression well buried deep in his stomach. It felt like the well was beginning to suck up all the goodness and niceties in life. He felt it tugging harder with each day, each day a battle with the unknown. He craved that warm feeling that warmed his stomach, when life felt positive and full of possibilities.

"Focus! Focus!"

The store shutters went down at seven o'clock and Alfred solemnly slid into the seat of the old Cavalier. He could see the bottle hiding under the passenger seat but chose to ignore it and drove into the town centre. The Cavalier circled the town centre in an ever-increasing circle, munching up hours of the evening until Alfred pulled into a space on Westhamton High Street.

"What is the tipping point of sanity? When does calm reason turn into uncontrollable rage…?" A professor calmly conveyed his theory to the talk show host.

Alfred turned up the volume on the radio. "Insanity normally requires a trigger to kick-start the so-called madness. A switch flipped which can change a rational sense into an uncontrollable sense, completely out of touch with our perception of reality. Lots of people can encounter this, and the trigger is not defined by a certain time in life, the trigger can happen anytime in a lifespan our theory suggests."

He looked out of the misty car window with the professor's words floating around the Cavalier's interior.

The usual gang of drunks had gathered outside the off-licence opposite the old church graveyard on the Westhamton High Street. The small group congregated in a slapdash circle red faced, emotionally attached to the can cradled in their raggedy hands. Alfred turned the steering wheel of the Cavalier into a backstreet, behind the Jolly Roger pub and turned a knob on the radio: "That's why I'm easy aaahhh. Easy like a Sunday morning yeaaahhh."

He glanced at the clock in the dashboard: 09:02PM. The backstreet was getting darker. His blurred reflection bounced off the windscreen with the aid of a solitary streetlamp positioned next to the car. Droopy chin, bloodshot eyes and thinning hair glared back at him in the reflection. He undid his starched collar and loosened off the grey tie that had been sucking the life from him all day. He sighed, trying to smile at the ghostly reflection in the window.

The muscles in his right cheek froze and

he felt a sharp coldness that decapitated his smile. A 'field accident' on exercise in Cyprus had made the simple act of smiling a difficult one. The small red scar shone in the mirror, arguing with him, telling him to not even bother. He put a finger on the red dot and tried once again to elevate his cheek bones, again a sullen expression looked back. He turned towards the Jolly Roger.

A black alley-cat jumped off a window ledge outside the entrance of the pub and paced along the paving slabs. The cat looked down the murky alley and sniffed the ground, then tiptoed away from the pub. He monitored the feline out of the side window and slumped down in the car seat, staring into the deserted street. Laughter rang out of the side of the Jolly Roger in spurts like a release valve on a steam engine. Belinda's voice rang in his ears from the argument they had the night before…

"You said you didn't mind me starting the art classes," she said.

"I don't mind. But why do you want to do them now though, love? Thought you were over all that?"

Belinda sighed and took a deep breath; the flippant response placed a scowl the size of Jupiter on her delicate features. "All along! All along I wanted to start drawing lessons but no, every time I found a class, we were moving… moving someplace else."

He wiped his brow and took a seat at the

kitchen table. "You never mentioned this before."

"I did, but you never listened, did you? You know that's what I wanted to do at college all those years ago."

"But… you were happy to sacrifice that, Bel, I remember your words. Why do you want to start it all up again? We're not getting any younger!"

"Oh, for Christ's sake, Alfie, I've been following you all over the world for what is it? Twenty-two, three years. Making friends, losing friends, hot weather, cold weather didn't mean anything you know that?"

Alfred looked around the kitchen for a distraction; a crack was beginning to surface in the plaster above the cooker. He followed the crack line where it would end up in a few months, imagining the plaster loosening until the wall had split. He imagined the house falling into a pit.

"You listening to me?"

"Course I am."

Belinda walked around the kitchen, keeping her gaze locked onto her husband. "I bumped into Jackie Samson from school the other day. She's on the dole. Then there's Mel Caruthers, working in some factory packing cereal boxes or something. Even heard rumours that Paula Donald is working a street corner in Bristol." A sigh left her nose. "I'm…

anyway doesn't matter. Doesn't matter."

"You were happy with this life, Bel. I know you were. Those were your words." He cleared his throat like a Shakespearian actor about to start the first verse. "'I am grateful, Alfie, you know that.' Those were your words so don't lie to me."

On the side of his forehead a vein glowed. Belinda hovered around the thin wooden table, brushing her fine brown locks away from her beaten, hazel pupils. A downcast expression etched on her face. Her mouth opened in a slow-motion fashion, as if the words that were about to fill the raggedy kitchen had been regurgitated many times.

"Alfie, we're done with the army now. Why can't you accept that?" She fiddled with the tip of her tightly formed pony tail. "Why can't you accept that, why?" The words replayed over and over in his consciousness like a record stuck on the same loop.

"I've accepted it, I have," the voice in his head protested.

The clear bottle poked its head out from underneath the leather passenger seat, gleaming in the darkness star-like. The labelling had started to peel off. He grabbed the bottle and took a swig, maybe the whisky was his friend after all.

The alcohol shot down his neck, charring the lining of his furry throat, the release instantaneous. He had tried to resist the shiny saviour sitting under the seat. The presence would hang in the air of the murky interior. "Take a swig, you know you want to!"

He raised the bottle and took a sniff of the dense malt; it smelt of his father's jacket on a Sunday afternoon. Glancing over at the gated entrance to the Jolly Roger, he noticed a faint flicker of light shining through the fence gap. Jukebox selections blurted out of the distorted speakers near the back entrance: Culture Club, Ultravox, Go West songs wailing out of the speakers. Each song a reminder of a different tour serving Her Majesty, "It's my life… don't you forget… it never ends!" The heavy synthesiser tones floated over the fence, another reminder of his youth: 1984. Joel was four years old and Belinda was going through another mid-life crisis filled with cheap white wine, multi-coloured stockings and discos in crummy bars.

"A mid-life crisis in her twenties, tuh!" he muttered, remembering day after day coming home and finding his wife curled up on the couch with tears streaming from her eyes and make-up smeared all over her bony cheeks. "Always the same, always the same." He took another sip from the bottle and turned the ignition key. The Cavalier slowly chugged into life. He reluctantly grabbed the steering wheel and thought about the choices he had made. Steering on a path was always mapped out in the army. Choices and decisions were made by Whitehall and

Alfred would obey these orders inexplicably.

The path was now uncertain, unclear. Civvy Street felt like a new highway leading into unchartered territory. And for the first time in his life he was scared.

28.

Autumn was just around the corner. Leaves blew around the dewy garden, filling the border where a lone Rhododendron (the only plant not considered a weed) stood lonesome shedding pink leaves into the mud. A majesty without a kingdom. The Rhododendron had appeared out of the ground one day, growing well out of the acidic soil where the alkanets, nettles, dandelions fought for space around it.

A fence post swayed in the wind, disconnected from two panels on the damp grass. Alfred peered out of the kitchen window like the silent bird watcher he had recently become. Two magpies sat on the wooden fence opposite the post, chatting to one another, watching Reigate Terrace awaken a new dawn.

He threw two paracetamol tablets down his throat and sipped on a cup of tea. His mouth was dry, memory hazy from the previous night. It all felt too familiar. A disagreement with Belinda over a small matter which led to argument, then a little drink, then another followed by a gargantuan headache. He tried to piece together last night's friction but had long stopped taking notes. They were now daily occurrences. "You don't love me anymore, you're more interested in feeling sorry for yourself." The fragmented words felt like a jigsaw his brain was struggling to piece together.

Belinda disappeared and the front door slammed shut. The kitchen clock ticked at a quarter to nine. Today was Alfred's day off. He dragged his heels through the hallway and into the living room. A draft blew between the cracks around the front door, blowing clumps of dust around the yolk carpet. A dark patch in the wall caught his eye as he sat down on an armchair. He arose and carefully pulled away a small layer of the woodchip wallpaper. Specks of plaster flaked off the damp wall like crumbs off a cake. "For Christ's sake!" He shook his head at the wall. "Does everything have to be falling apart at the seams!"

The kitchen phone rang through the thin cavity wall. He withdrew from the damp patch, frustrated. Every day seemed like a long day, a never-ending routine waiting for something of significance to happen. He went to the corner of the kitchen and picked up the phone receiver and peered out of the window. The two magpies had gone.

"Hello?"

"Hello, is Alfie there?" a voice croaked through the crackly handset.

"This is Alfie," he replied.

"Alfie Lundy! Alright mate it's Brick. Brick Allwood."

"Brick? Bloody hell! Hello mate, how you doing? What time you call this eh?"

"It's early I know, sorry for the wake-

261

up call."

Alfred sat down at the kitchen table, fiddling with a wine cork. "Lucky I'm an early bird eh! So how you doing?"

"Doing alright, Alfie, doing alright y'know," he replied. Brick Allwood (real name Paul Allwood). He was known as Brick for the small stocky frame he had honed playing hooker in the King's Hampshire rugby team.

"So, you've been out since when was it March… April?" said Brick.

"Yeah been six months or so now, March it was… March." The receiver went silent. Alfred was afraid to break the lull; he never understood people's incessant need to talk all the time. He gazed at the fragile handset in his right hand with its tiny number buttons and useless symbols. Brick sighed at the other end. "So how you been Alfie? Up to much?"

"This and that, mate."

"Got any work yet?"

"Yeah, security."

"So, you cracking some heads then?"

"Not quite. It's a toy store over in Westhamton so don't think I'll be cracking little kids heads in."

"Yeah well kids I've seen on Civvy Street need a good crack on the head if you ask me."

Alfred's cheeks sunk into the rickety

chair with his sagging body mass. "Not now please!" he pondered. "Work-wise what you been up to?"

The silence engulfed the handset once again. "Well… started off working down this warehouse in Southampton, didn't last long then got into some security work. Shopping centres, pubs, that kind of thing," Brick replied.

"Oh… I thought you were going into some IT job?" He heard Brick licking his lips.

"That was the plan. Thought I had it worked out, y'know, get me qualification at the college and walk into something well paid. Good prospects 'n'all. Did the course but no one wanted to take me on after. Lack of experience they were saying. Tell you what I could've murdered that twat at the job centre that said I'd be suitable. Got rejection after rejection, even on junior posts."

A starling flew past the kitchen window. Alfred watched its flight over the bendy wooden fence-frames of Reigate Terrace and onto the playing fields. "So, how's Pat?"

"Ok, I think. We split up two years ago." A certain inevitability rung from Brick's charred throat.

"Oh, sorry to hear that mate. What happened?"

"Long story. Let's just say once we got out life was different. A bit too different."

"And the kids?"

"With their mum over in Redditch. See them every couple of weeks…" His voice dropped "Not easy, Alfie. Not easy y'know…" He paused. "How's thing's with you anyway? Your boy's signed up now right?"

Alfred looked around the kitchen; it felt like the walls were closing in.

"Yeah that's right," he said. This was it, the big moment. The first-time proud father gets to tell the world that his offspring is following in his proud father's footsteps and carrying on the Lundy name in the King's Hampshire Regiment.

"So?" Brick interjected.

"So?"

"You're a happy bunny then?"

A muscle in Alfred's paralysed cheek went numb; he tried to think positive thoughts. The Mediterranean sun hitting the back of his neck in '83. Playing catch with Barney the Bassett Hound on Bournemouth beach in '62 as a child. The first sight of his son lying in the hospital cot, skin bright pink and crinkled, eyelids battened down, and limbs curled up in one tight ball; helpless, innocent.

He straightened his back against the flimsy chair rest and broadened his shoulder blades. The scar on his cheek felt sore, like a ghost was prodding the flesh with a knife. "Yeah course I am. Course I am!"

"I would be too, mate; my boy won't even consider it. Reckons it's a mug's game. What does he know eh? Doesn't realise it was putting food in his mouth all those years." Brick paused and let out a dry cough. "Anyway, reason I was calling, you happen to have Colin Bell's number?"

"Colin Bell from B Company?"

"Yeah."

"Wasn't he looking at trawling up in Peterhead?"

"Apparently, so that's why I'm asking, mate."

"For work?"

"Yeah."

"Why do you want to head up to Scotland mate?"

"Need the work, Alfie, a month behind on my rent and got a load of outstanding child support to pay off. Money's supposed to be alright on the trawlers."

"But how are you going to see your kids if you're all the way up there?" His lips curled inwards, dumfounded by what he was hearing. He looked out of the window, at the white clouds slowly shimmering over the house.

"What you want me to say, Alfie? I've got to work, mate." The plea grew in desperation. Alfred felt the emotion travelling down the fibre-optic cables underground, looking for refuge in his ear.

"It's just, well…" Alfred's tongue shut down on his bottom teeth before he could carry on the inquisition. "Sorry mate I haven't got his number, no."

"Oh well it was worth a try. Listen I've got to shoot mate, look after yourself yeah."

"If you're ever around these parts give us a bell, we'll go have a few beers."

"Sure, thing, Alfie. You take care yeah."

The phone line suddenly went dead. The coarse tones of Brick Allwood, now just plain Paul Allwood, suddenly disappeared back down the phone line, out of his civilian world.

"Jesus, Brick!" he muttered. He suspected the innocent pound coins Brick had dropped down the fruit machines in the NAAFI had finally put a nail in his marriage. He knew it was the same old story. Married at eighteen just to get a pad house and escape the block. A marriage way too soon, before they had barely lost their virginity. Now he wouldn't even see his kids. He arose from the rickety chair, strolled out of the kitchen and wandered down the hallway, looking at wallpaper peeling off the walls and red wine stains in the fuzzy carpet.

Brick Allwood's predicament rung in his

ears loudly. He visualised Brick on a trawler in the North Sea, sailing away from his existence: ex-wife, children, civilian life. He pondered the fortunes of the other lifers who he served with, Chalky White, Baz Bonds, George Eccles. Men who had served twenty-plus years and were now making their way in this new unforgiving terrain. The shelter taken away from them, ripped slowly from their war-dog souls until one day they were signing discharge papers.

"Good luck," said the colonel. A pat on the back and off they go into a world of nine-to-five, rent, suits, overalls, baseball caps, EastEnders, utility bills, the local pub, the dole queue.

He sat down on the armchair in the living room but couldn't settle or get comfortable. He arose again and wandered around the empty house. Moving from the kitchen to the living room he slowly sauntered, the balls of his feet gliding against the carpet and the linoleum. For two hours he moved around the kitchen-living-room circuit, in search of some kind of answer he did not know the question to. As he sat staring out of the kitchen window, he heard a rustling of keys near the front door and poked his head into the hallway, beyond the front door into the porch. It was Belinda. He quickly ran upstairs before catching her focus, jumped onto the bed squashed into the bedroom next to the toilet and lay on the itchy blankets in a contemplative mood.

"Brick don't forget about your kids. Remember!" he muttered at the ceiling. Belinda carried on downstairs. He knew what his wife would be doing: spreading peanut butter on her sandwiches and making a mug of coffee. Alfred listened to the shuffling feet, clanging of knives and the whistling of a kettle. He then looked out of the bedroom window at the two returning magpies, arguing over a juicy worm.

29.

The front door slammed shut, creating a dust cloud outside the pre-fabricated house fronts of Reigate Terrace. The Big Dipper shone in the slate-coloured sky, peering down on the incident back on earth. Alfred rocked out of the house, voices pounding inside his head like a painful migraine.

"Why can't she understand?" Specks of dirt flicked onto his trousers as he kicked at a pile of stones piled up on the pavement.

The polished toe caps of his shoes shone off an orange glare of a lamp post as he wandered off Reigate Terrace onto the green plagued by dried dog faeces opposite his house. His mind felt twisted, convoluted. Memories of the early settling-in days sprung up… shoddy accommodation, peer pressure from the other battalion families, dislocation on tour.

"Same old arguments week in week out." His fingers trembled as he unfastened his shirt collar and stopped at a patch of dead grass in the middle of the green to stare up at the stars. A crimson sheen covered his face. "She doesn't understand. Never has. It's not easy trying to adapt. Fit in with the civvies. Never said I wanted to go back, never once did I say that!" Rage was running wildly around his body, polluting the good will he had been trying to show his wife the past few weeks. He walked in a circle around a broken Carlsberg bottle. The rage confused his senses, sending mixed messages to either side of his brain. An internal dialogue opened: Reason in the Red Corner and Rage in the Blue Corner:

"It's not her fault. She's trying to get on with life now. Like she said, for twenty-two years she couldn't be herself…"

"Bitch! You've done everything for her. Provided for her cruddy need. Got her out of that shitty town in Worcestershire. A better life. She even bloody admitted it…"

"Hang on, she was just a young girl when you whisked her off her teenage feet. Remember that, old man! She had to fit it with the army machine. For you it was already under your skin, in your blood and your soul. Selfish old man…"

"But you had some good times; the bars of Bielefeld in the late 80s, the sunshine bouncing of your skin in Cyprus, the birth of Joel. You both were close that day. Wouldn't let go of your wrist throughout the labour…"

"She should be proud of you, soldier!"

"Proud of what? Misery? You damn fool!"

His head spun and spun. Then the voices ceased bickering.

"Son!"

His tongue was dried out from the Irish whisky, his eyes heavy. It had been weeks since he had heard from Joel. The Big Dipper swayed into a murky smear as Alfred thought about Joel's entrance; a new cycle of army life, a carousel spinning. He took a piece of paper out of his trouser pocket; the number 0422 scribbled in red ink. The day Joel told him his army number he could not believe it; a divine intervention of sorts, for Alfred's and Joel's service number, the tag assigned to every soldier, had the same last four digits: 0422. Alfred 231000422, Joel 24060422.

"How's the scoff on barracks, son? Always loved a bit of that fried bread," he muttered, swaying from side to side on the dried earth.

He looked down at the Augustus badge pinned to his shirt; the silver radiated a dull shine. "A badge of honour!" He chuckled, ripping it from his shirt. His eyelids became heavier, pulling the shutters down, the pressure building. Suddenly his knees felt limp and his body toppled over onto the malnourished grass. "Was it right? This life? The next one?" he slurred as the shutters closed.

He looked around, somewhat dumbfounded. Murky clouds had appeared, blanketing the sky like a metal sheet. He had awoken in a large field of bracken and dead tree stumps, the ground a dank brown as far as the eye could see. As he wiped dried saliva from the corner of his mouth he looked to the horizon. The wind blew, whistling a song for a dead man. In the distance he saw a clump of trees on the top of a ridge. Barren wilderness filled the gaps around the small wood; an apocalyptic vision of man's last stand. His knees creaked as he gingerly got to his feet.

He wore the look of a lost child in a shopping centre, "Mummy! Mummy!" Nobody there… just faces. Featureless, unfamiliar, sinister faces. In this new nightmarish world decomposing tree stumps replaced the horrible faces. He headed for the wood on top of the ridge, the only visual reference he could see.

There was no recollection of why he was here. The past seemed like a micro-flash that had evolved quicker than the speed of light. His hands shook and body shivered while a prickly heat welled up from inside. The trees came into focus; big oak trees forty, fifty metres tall guarding and watching over the small patch of life. He groaned and spat on a large rock that appeared in front of him. The rock had an inscription carved onto its surface, squinting at the rough brown surface he made out the letters K, I and N.

A charred smell filled the air. Something was changing, quickly. He waded through wet, decomposing bracken that suddenly turned into a stinking bog. Each step his shoes got caught up in sticky peat, sludging through the thick earth like a blunt saw hacking through a thick log.

As he drew closer to the wood rumblings cut through the air, rumblings which started to sound like voices; voices that sounded like hollers, shouts, screams. He jerked his head from side to side and stopped in his tracks, lungs churning, the hairs at the back of his neck swaying in the icy wind.

"Aaaahh! Aaaahhh!" The shouts echoed around the damp, sullen landscape weaving in and out of the bracken. "Aaaaahh! Aaaaahhh!" intrigue forced him up the ridge towards the wood, his shoes grinding through the peat.

White moths, the size of blackbirds appeared, flapping around the bushes lining the perimeter of the wood in an excitable, hyperactive state. They flapped their wings faster and faster, buzzing around the lost figure. A rotten stench filled the air, déjà-vu. He knew the smell but couldn't remember where from. It was burning lead, off-beef, sickly molasses. The hairs inside his nose tingled.

He stomped through the decaying bracken, noticing crimson blotches dotted on the bracken leaves like an infection spreading fast.

The shouts grew louder, the stench stronger. He went further up the ridge, noticing red blotches spreading the further he climbed, covering the foliage like a plague of locusts multiplying, devouring and moving on. He stopped by a big boulder, panting. The entrance to the wood was approximately one hundred metres away.

The shouts began to sound like a big drone, encompassing the thin oxygen that rushed down his lungs. Alfred looked at his chest, feeling the carbon dioxide rattling through his oesophagus and forcing its way out of his mouth, leaving a charcoal taste at the back of his throat. The trees merged in the wood narrowing the vantage point as he stood on top of a boulder to survey the dark space.

The clouds grew darker as the moths buzzed around the outskirts. He felt cold and listless as his veins pumped ice-cold blood around his circulation.

Suddenly from the east he heard an enormous bang. It sounded like an explosion in the wood. Alfred instinctively ducked back under the boulder. His lips collided with a piece of brown moss. Bodies began running into the wood; bodies with helmets, camouflage clothing holding rifles. "Aaaaahhhh!" The roar was deafening. He glanced over to his right; ten, twenty, forty bodies running with pace, ducking, firing, running, screaming, rolling on the ground, firing. The wood erupted into an epicentre of explosions, gunshots and flashes. The trees took the assault like an absorbent sponge, taking hit after hit. Branches flew to the ground, a torrent of leaves and smoke billowed from either side of the wood.

Alfred grimaced, still confused by the situation he found himself in. He didn't feel frightened, just disorientated. The gunshots rang out from the east and the wasteland where he had ventured from. The soldiers were invisible to Alfred's shocked eye; all he could make out was smoke coming from the battleground ahead. The smoke raced up his nose; a concoction of wood smoke, phosphorus and death. The assault brought a sudden humidity to the bracken fields. He began to sweat profusely and loosened off his creased white shirt. He undid a couple of buttons and took a deep breath; it suddenly dawned on him that the Augustus uniform was clinging to his body.

The shouts became louder and the gunfire felt like it was getting closer, he curled up in a ball and tried to resuscitate his jaded memory. "This fucking uniform!" he shouted as the gunfire closed in, shot by shot. He peered over the big rock. A storm cloud of deathly smoke was gathering from the massacred wood, headed in his direction. He rubbed his eyes. It appeared to be a river of red liquid that was following the smoke and death out of the wood. The river's direction snaked its way towards the boulder.

He racked his brain, trying to block out the oncoming rush of smoke and blood. The smoke cloud and the red river gathered pace, an unstoppable tsunami-hurricane joined in force. Death was inevitable. The roar cracked Alfred's eardrums in two; he curled up into an even tighter ball. The men in helmets roared past the boulder. "Shout. Duck. Fire. Down! Shout. Duck. Fire. Down!"

He sunk into a small ditch next to the boulder. The soldiers rushed past, impervious to the gloopy earth on their feet as they perfumed the air with lead. One of the soldier's stopped beside the boulder. Alfred quivered in a ball on the floor, lifeless. "Dad?" the soldier said.

He awoke with a massive jolt. George Pesterton from no-10 was tapping him on the shoulder. "Your bed's over there, Alfie!" he pointed to the porch of Alfred's house.

He rolled his body through the grass as the judgemental gaze of George Pesterton followed him into the porch of his house. His head no longer spun. Instead it felt steadfast on his shoulders as he crawled into the porch and fell asleep on the yolk carpet of the hallway.

"Alfie! Alfie!" It was Belinda shouting through the upstairs corridor, trying to awaken Alfred from his intoxicated slumber. Alfred opened his eyes. He was in Joel's old room again, a welcome refuge the past couple of months.

"What?" he shouted back, rubbing the side of his throbbing head. He tried to piece together what had happened the previous night. The morning sun lit up the bedroom, distinguishing the dark in seconds. He rubbed his eyes and felt around the roof of his parched mouth with his furry tongue. His work clothes had been heaped in a messy pile at the foot of the bed: A pair of sweaty socks, muddy grey trousers and a white shirt stained green. Belinda came rushing into the bedroom in a dressing gown, where he lay comatose. "What? Is that it? What? Where the hell did you end up last night?" she pointed a finger at Alfred's forehead. "And what's that smell? Smells like shit."

Alfred looked down at his leather shoes lying near the door. Mud was smeared along the side of each shoe and a crusty dog stool had clung to one of the soles. "Aw crap, I mean literally!" he said.

She folded her arms and glared at Alfred curled up in bed. "First you hit the bottle then you end up staying out till God knows what time. What's got into you? What are you running away from, Alfie?" The blacks of her pupils began to sharpen, cutting through his weary gaze like a knife through butter.

"Nothing, nothing. Ended up on the green, I think. Had this strange dream," his voice husked.

"Strange dream?!"

"I was in this wilderness and then these squaddies…" She paced around the box room; her face looked blotchy and tired. "Doesn't matter." He turned over in bed and sat on the edge.

"What the hell you on about?"

"Like I said doesn't matter."

"Look this drinking has to stop. You're going way too far."

Alfred stared back at her like a wounded animal, ready for the fight back "Me?" he snarled. "Cheap, that's cheap. You're not exactly teetotal these days, Bel!"

"Oh, here we go again. Covering up your own insecurities by saying I'm on the booze too much. Look in the mirror, will you?."

He turned away from her. "Don't understand; you never have," he replied.

She placed her hands over her square hips. "Oh, I understand alright. We all know the real reason you've been pissing it up lately!" Her left eyebrow arched suggestively.

"Thinking about Joel recently, have we?" she insinuated.

Birds shrilled on the window ledge. The kitchen clock ticked downstairs. A car horn echoed in the distance. He heaved his stocky frame past Belinda towards the bathroom.

"Where you going now?" Her screechy tones hit a protective wall around his eardrums, distant tones that grew quieter and quieter. "I need you to go to the post office today; we're three months behind on the council tax!"

He locked the bathroom door and gawped at his reflection in the mirror; Grey hairs were sprouting from the outside of his earlobes and crease marks plagued his weathered face. Even his moustache, the pride of his face, was merging into a ragged beard.

"You're letting yourself go old man!" he murmured at the mirror.

A flannel lay at the top of the bath-tub; he glanced over at the shrivelled piece of cloth and remembered Joel washing his face for the last time before setting off for Chipping Burse. He knew she was right, and he hated her for it.

"You've got no idea!" he screamed through the door.

He sat on the toilet-seat and looked around the bathroom: a small spider creeped along the window ledge, a toothpaste lid had not been secured correctly, the hot water tap on the sink dripped. He wiped his brow and stared at the old copper tap dripping to a tight rhythm. Cigarette smoke started to find a way under the bathroom door. He could hear Belinda spluttering in the bedroom where he had not slept for weeks.

A toilet-roll holder hung off the tiled wall, limply, like a shirt flapping on a clothes line. He inspected the bracket, it had been hit hard. He recalled the night before: red wine, a documentary on the TV about Operation Desert Storm and an argument.

"I'm sick of this. Sick of it!" she screamed, rushing down the stairs, her strides sounding like a frightened horse thudding down the steps. The front door slammed shut with an almighty whack, rattling the picture frames hanging in the hallway.

It felt like glue was sticking his rear to the toilet-seat. The voices continued in his head, popping in his ears.

"No escape. This is your doing. Your wife is trapped in the cycle and your son is travelling the circumference of the cage. This retched cycle of life. What life? You are stuck. And so is she."

He smashed the toilet-roll holder to the floor.

30.

The handbrake of the old Cavalier creaked as the ignition ceased. Alfred turned his head, hearing the sizzle of burgers frying and traffic whooshing along the A346.

"She stood there laughing Ha! Ha! Ha! Felt the knife in my hand and she laughed no more," he bellowed at the top of his voice. "Why? Why? Why? Delilah!" He stared out of the windscreen, looking straight at the bear of Augustus. The bears face beamed around the car park, lighting up the early morning darkness.

"Forgive me Delilah I just cannot take any more! I just cannot take any more!" As he finished the rendition, crumbs from his creased jacket fell onto his lap.

He stepped out of the Cavalier. A breeze cut through the car park, travelling up his trouser legs. He played around with the tie hanging off his neck and moved around the back of the store. The shutters of the garage next door were locked tight. He smelt the emissions hanging in the cooling air.

As he approached the Augustus staff entrance he noticed a red glow in the lifting dawn, moving up then down. It looked familiar, like a convoy signal on night ops in Kuwait:

The pure silence of the sparse desert night punctuated by groans of APC engines and shouts from the turrets. Then suddenly a red light appearing from the back of the next vehicle, showing the way into battle, out of battle, back to camp. Even the sand-mice didn't suspect. "Follow that damn light! Even if it leads to the edge of the world follow that damn light!" Night ops always felt surreal.

The boy continued puffing on his cigarette, moving the red dot in a semi-circle motion, unaware of Alfred approaching from his right. He waltzed past the boy and entered through the door, his vision watery and lacking colour. Once inside he stumbled through the dusty corridors, knocking past silver cages and packaging lying on the floor until he reached Mr Wallace's office.

"Morning."

Alfred went to the water canister in the corner of the room. The water trickled into a plastic cup. He gulped the water down voraciously then filled another cup. "Morning."

"Thirsty today, are we?" said Mr Wallace.

Alfred nodded in the general direction of the security manager. Colour began to slowly come back to his cheeks. "Got a dry throat is all."

"Well its six minutes past, hadn't you better be on the floor?" Mr Wallace gave a discerning look.

Alfred straightened his tie before

heading onto the shop floor.

The minute hand of the corridor clock ticked eight minutes past nine. His head ached. The tips of his toes felt numb. The store felt hot and prickly. He took up a position on the shop-floor entrance and glanced over at two girls giggling at the checkouts. A voice croaked in his head: "Stop laughing. I'm the security officer here! Stop laughing!" The car park was blurry, fading images: mothers walking sideways, toddlers with extremely small heads, cars parked at peculiar angles. Sweat started to drip around his ears. He shook his head and tried to regain his arcs to the west and east.

Two uncomfortable hours passed by. His composure felt off-key, wobbling like jelly on a plate. Customers passed in and out of the store: toddler, pensioner, black, white, oriental, disabled. All blurring into one. He swayed off each foot waiting for the golden hour of eleven o'clock when he had his cup of tea and digestive biscuit.

He clenched his fists, trying to keep his mind clear, focused. Out of the corner of his eye two teenage boys loitered near the video game section; one had cropped hair with a green puffy bomber jacket that covered his body from the knees upwards. The other had a mix of European and Oriental features with a darkened leather jacket stuck to his slight frame. They both looked around the store, a jitteriness punctuating their bright eyes.

He eyeballed the two boys before looking at the reception clock: 10:59. All he wanted to do was sit down and drink a gallon of water. The boys walked down the aisle selling slides and paddling pools then headed for the tills. Alfred stood staring at the clock, waiting for the minute clock to hit the magic eleven. All he could do was stare transfixed at the clock.

"Hey!" shrieked a voice behind one of the tills "Hey!."

Alfred tore himself away from the clock.

"Hey! Stop 'em!" The woman pointed towards the gangway behind the tills to the two boys sprinting to the exit. He quickly focused on the first boy racing out; it was the one in a leather jacket, his brown eyes looking steely, determined, focused on the detection barriers ten feet from Alfred's toes. A video game case fell out of his jacket, sending a compact disc out of the case. Alfred looked down at the flashing disc, then at the thief running out of the store. He quickly dashed past Alfred. The barriers beeped a high pitch tone around the store, the tone failing to register in Alfred's ear drum. He had the next kid, loads of time.

"I'm one step ahead of you, sonny!" he nudged forward, adopting a rugby tacklers position. The boy charged forwards. Alfred tried to grab the accomplice by the puffy material sticking out his jacket, managing only to swipe at the air.

"Oi!" he shouted at the boy. "Oi! Come back here!"

Alfred leapt out of the store, the beeping now registering in his left ear. "Get him! Get him! Show the little oik who he's messing with!" He went left out of the store, following the green jacket heading towards a field adjacent to the retail park. He ran one hundred metres at full sprint, feeling good, fresh, catching the thief up slowly.

"I gotcha you little prick, gotcha!" he panted. The thief ran out of the car park with arms tucked into his thick jacket to avoid spilling his catch of video games. His accomplice trailed behind, fifty metres ahead, looking behind every few seconds in a wild panic. Alfred swung his arms up into his chest and downwards towards his hips. His legs motored along the pavement with clicking noises bouncing from the soles of his shoes. The thief in the leather jacket ran up a concrete ramp and looked around, before dropping into the field. Alfred followed, his breath wheezing. He approached the ramp and skidded down the slope into the field, nearly stumbling on a large stone.

"That's it old man, huh? Is that it? Ha ha!" the thief shouted at the top of his pubescent voice. Alfred continued into the field passing disused syringes and tatty blankets lying strewn in the grass.

The thief gained metres, shuffling along like a penguin on steroids. Alfred's panting got worse, rapid breaths gasping for air. His legs felt heavy, like he was dragging logs. A sharp pain occurred at the bottom of his rib cage, pulsing with every stride.

"Fuck!" he shouted at the criminal striding into the free world. "Fuck!" He stopped for a quick breath and put his hands on his knees, all the while looking forlorn at the assailant escaping to a row of bushes. He was nearly out of sight. Alfred tried to carry on running but his legs felt numb, pulling all his weight against the damp grass. The thief ran through a gap in the bushes and was gone. He looked at a hill in the distance, seeing two large fingers sticking out of the ground pointing in his direction.

"Pathetic! You're pathetic!" The gods above lambasted the disconsolate figure struggling for breath down below. "You let them get away. Fool! Worthless fool!"

Alfred fell on a damp patch of grass. He looked up at the white clouds shielding the sea blue sky. One cloud morphed into an old soldier's face, the face not his own: rugged, stern, weathered; a sideways profile looking to the east.

"I know, old man. I know," he said. A sweet aftertaste of whisky tingled his tongue. He trudged back to the store panting like an old hound with the face in the cloud's watching and judging the old soldier. The old Cavalier appeared to his right some fifty metres away. He opened the passenger door and sat inside. He felt safe here, protected. The face in the clouds could not see him.

31.

"What is wrong with you?" the old face said.

Alfred looked in the newsagent's shop window, recognising the face once again in the reflection. The window was blurred and smeared with a grey dust. He made out a haggard face with wispy grey hair and a high forehead. A grey moustache weaved its way around thin, waif lips; the facial hair looked mature and jaded. The reflection looked sternly back at him.

He took a step back from the glass, it wasn't his own reflection. It was him again. The face of his father; Edward Herbert Lundy. A ringer took Alfred's attention away from the shop window. A piercing shriek.

He awoke suddenly in a cold sweat. The sweat sticking to his back. He looked around the darkened room; a white handset on the dresser kept ringing. He slumped back on the bed, wishing he was somewhere else. The red LED light of the digital alarm clock flashed in rhythm with the high pitch tone. Stumbling out of the bed he wildly swung his legs, knocking over a can of lager on the carpet. The stale liquid foamed on the carpet, hissing like an excitable rattlesnake.

His hand shivered in the dark as he felt around the dresser for the handset with a photograph of Joel in school uniform following the veins of his hands.

"Hello." His hand continued to shake.

"Hello, is that Mr Lundy?"

"Yeah, who's this?"

"My name is Sergeant Willman at the Patchley Police Station."

He felt a rock drop from his throat into the lining of his stomach. The shivers gripping his hands grew in intensity. "Yes, what can I do for you?" he replied.

"There has been an accident, Mr Lundy, are you the spouse of Mrs Belinda Lundy?" the sergeant asked.

"Yes I am…" His fragmented mind raced back to when he last saw Belinda. Yesterday morning, the argument when she stormed out of the house fired up. "…What happened?" he shouted.

"There was a road traffic accident, Mr Lundy, in which your wife was involved this evening." The sergeant took a deep breath; Alfred gasped at the musty air in the darkened room.

"Unfortunately, your wife is now hospitalised in a serious condition, Mr Lundy."

"Oh." He casually placed the receiver on the dresser and looked around the small bedroom; ghosts began to appear from the window, abstract shapes hovering around his numb body.

"Mr Lundy? Mr Lundy? Are you ok?" the

sergeant asked, his tone well-schooled.

"Sorry yes fine. Where is she? Westhamton General? Westhamton you say yes?

"Westhamton general that is correct."

"What ward is that then?"

"You'll have to ask when you get there, Mr Lundy."

"Right, ok. Thanks for letting me know."

"If you need anything ask for me, Mr Lundy. An investigation will start shortly."

"Ok."

"Goodbye, Mr Lundy."

"Bye, Sergeant."

He hung the receiver on the dresser, switched on the bedroom light and felt around the wardrobe for a pair of black suit trousers and woolly jumper. He slung the clothes around his large frame. A sinking feeling pierced at his chest cavity reaching all the way to his rectum.

"I'm sick of this, sick of it!" the words floated around the bedroom like a call from the grave. He felt the knife scraping an epitaph on the soft walls of his brain.

He arrived at Westhamton General Hospital just after 5 o'clock that morning. The darkness was lifting, a tangerine hue filling half the sky as birds begun a dawn song. As the birds chirped, he looked to the sky, wondering if a god was going to help him today.

He parked the Cavalier in one of the disabled bays, swinging the Cavalier at an odd angle that made the back end stick out, then stumbled along the car park motionless. Part of him wanted to see his wife; part of him didn't want to know the extent of the damage. "A broken arm? Few broken ribs? Brain damage? Crippled? Dead?"

He passed through automatic doors at the hospital entrance with all the subtlety of a drunkard looking for his next gin. The reception area smelt of fresh coffee wafting in from a kiosk in the corner. "Coffee? Well it had to be didn't it?" He smiled briefly.

"I'm here to see my wife. She's been in an accident," he said to a black woman with sun-blushed freckles sitting behind the main reception desk.

"Get her name?" Her reply was care free in a West African tone.

Alfred looked around the hospital interior; the walls were painted in a faded light green emulsion and leaflets were pinned on boards promoting disease diagnosis and treatments. He looked up at flies buzzing around the light fittings in the ceiling, drowning out the silence that gripped the early morning shift.

"Lundy. Belinda Lundy. Was, was in a car

accident." Dread trickled into every vein upon saying her name.

"Ok let me go find the duty A&E consultant. Go and take a seat in the waiting area." She left her seat behind the desk and wandered into a swing door marked: RESTRICTED ACCESS in large red font.

He stumbled into the waiting area, shaking and breathing heavily. As he sat on an orange plastic seat, he noticed a man in a tatty raincoat with long scraggy hair, talking to himself in the corner. The look of a man who had been told bad news.

Alfred sat upright. His senses became heightened. Just like the big push into Kuwait from the Saudi border. Yesterday's lunch of soup clung to his trousers; he could smell the tomato and garlic. An ambulance siren wailed in the far distance. The waiting room temperature dropped. He looked out of the waiting room window at a shift worker smoking a cigarette, watching two pigeons pecking seeds off the ground. It felt like the Earth's magnetic fields were pulling Belinda's soul away.

A doctor dressed in hospital blues with a clipboard tucked under his arm approached Alfred. "Mr Lundy?"

"Yes."

"Come this way please." The doctor's tone lowered. He held out his hand to Alfred in a submissive gesture, like a beggar asking for a spare cigarette. He smelt chemicals, a bleach kind of smell, in the cold air of the corridor. Their marriage flashed before his very eyes as he took the long walk to the consultation room at the end of the corridor: a first encounter at the Mirage nightclub in Winchester. Whisking her off her delicate feet to Brighton. The wedding at the registry office; him in his parade no.2 dress that stuck to his puffy skin, her in her mother's frilly magnolia wedding dress… His memory flashed back to the tour of Cyprus in '84. Weekends at the beach, her hair catching the salty sea wind, cold beers in Ayia-Napa, quality time spent away from the garrison machine.

"The good memories. The good memories"

The doctor closed the door of the consultation room. The door closed with a quiet whimper and the lock deftly clicked into place. The doctor's outstretched arm pointed towards a chair lodged against a small desk.

Alfred sat down. The legs of the chair slanted to one side. Wall to wall he looked for a distraction, away from the doctor's rotten prognosis. He smelt the air; it was unsterile and clear of chemicals, now it didn't feel like a hospital. It reminded him of their first accommodation in Bulford, stuffy, warm, airless, that burning sausage smell that followed him from room to room.

"Mr Lundy…" the doctor said. Alfred

stared blankly at the yellow tiled floor and saw patterns emerging in the grout lines. "I'm afraid the news is not good."

Alfred took a deep inhalation, staring vacantly at the discs rolling inside the doctor's eyes. Two discs purring, rolling with life. "Your wife died this morning from her injuries. I am deeply sorry."

Alfred waited. The dagger that was supposed to rip his chest open did not arrive. He tried to muster a response to the doctor: nothing, blank, a void. With a limp nod of his head he withdrew from the chair and gazed at the patterns in the tile grout.

"Mr Lundy?" said the doctor.

Five minutes of an explanation and Alfred had heard enough. He nodded at the doctor again and unlocked the door. The sterile, cold corridor appeared before him.

The doctor arose from the desk. "We will contact you with the report. Would you like phone numbers for bereavement counselling?"

"No. Thank you, doctor," he replied hazily and closed the door.

He stared at the ground as he left the hospital where pigeons and wheelchairs and paramedics carried on like nothing had happened. His emotions felt twisted, convoluted. "Why?" he kept thinking. "Why?"

He arrived at the very spot where

fifteen, twenty minutes previous his life felt different, before the news. He dropped the car keys on the floor and felt the texture of tarmac melting into the skin of his hands, then retrieved the keys and unlocked the car door. As he manoeuvred the Cavalier from the tight spot the wing scraped against a BMW in the bay next to his; the scrape of the metal barely registering. The outside world seemed somewhat irrelevant right now.

He drove along the back streets of Westhamton looking up at smiley faces advertising toothpaste and mothers washing their laundry with the latest in smooth conditioner. He looked to the heavens.

"A fatal collision in a taxi coming home from the George," the doctor's exact words.

"Course the driver was ok…" he thought. "He was wearing a seat belt. Belinda didn't bother and went through the windscreen. Stupid woman! Why?"

He didn't feel angry. Mustering the energy was hard.

"You are condemned. It was your fault, Alfred Lundy!" His father's voice cut through the dirty windscreen of the Cavalier. "She wouldn't have gone on a binge after work if you'd have treated her a bit better. She would have been more with it. Put a seat belt on. Alive now."

The Cavalier passed the retail park on the A346. The Augustus bear beamed at him through the windscreen, mockingly. He drove down the A346 past Patchley town, heading north until traffic lights appeared and scraggy-looking men emerged selling wilted carnations through the side window. He rolled down the window and bought six of the faded pink variety, having no idea why or where he was going. The Cavalier went through the green light and Alfred placed the carnations on the passenger seat, musing.

"I did love you, Bel, well I thought I did. Loving you was part of the wheel of trust. I did love you back in '76 I know I did. But you were so different then: carefree, flared trousers, broken necklaces and purple headbands, sexy, au fait and risky. You looked at me with that sparkle in your fresh young eyes: trust, ultimate trust.

"Whisk me away, soldier!" Soldier takes you away. To a better place, my dear. A place of liberation, freedom, a wild adventure romping around the world, a passport to a life away from the grey skies and the gossip mongers. A safe place. A place to raise a family."

Joel's innocent face abruptly appeared in the rear-view mirror. "Son!" Alfred cried out. The realisation dawned. A son had lost his mother. A son who was in another country trying to make his father proud. He thought about Joel's whereabouts in Germany: shooting at metal targets on the ranges, stumbling out of squaddie bars and spewing vomit on the Ziegborn streets. Chatting the local girls up at the bus garages and bonding at the NAAFI with the platoon.

Kinship. Solidarity. A band of brothers ready to take on the world.

The numbness floating around his body turned into a sudden angst. The angst tightened his heart strings and restricted his airway and he gasped and felt a symphony being composed out of his own soul. Violin and cello strings drifting out of Westhamton towards the English Channel. The steering wheel of the old Cavalier creaked as the tyres burned rubber on the tarmac. He steered in the opposite direction of the road. He thought about hitting play on the CD player but hesitated and glanced out of the rear-view mirror:

Birmingham 110 miles

As the Cavalier headed back towards the tragic scene.

32.

"I aaaam sooory, Mr Luuundy, weee haaave been trying to contaaact you," said the officer.

"Had no idea. I really didn't. I do apologise, sir," Alfred replied. Ice was starting to melt in his glass, diluting the whisky smell. 'Sir'. He didn't need to use that term anymore.

"Sooo our protocol now. Mr Luuundy, is for you to tell us the last time you saw your son."

Alfred took a deep breath. He felt his forehead, the migraine was getting worse. His gaze diverted to a chair in the corner of the bedroom, focusing on the winding pattern running vertical along the chair's dark green fabric. The bows in the pattern started baggy and loose then seemed to pull tighter as the bows became smaller the further up the chair the pattern went.

"Was a couple of months ago he was getting ready to go to Ziegborn. Excited he was. Least I think he was."

Alfred could hear the pen scribbling frantically on a piece of paper at the other end of the line. "So, this is Westhaaamton, correct?" the officer asked.

"Yeah he came here for his leave, then left to go to Ziegborn."

"And how long ago was this precisely?"

"I dunno four, five months."

"So, you have not heaaard from your son?"

"No, like I said."

"Are you sure, Mr Lundy?" An uneasy silence developed. Alfred thought he could hear ghosts chattering in the silence. He sat uneasily in bed; upright, tense.

"Yes sir," he scoffed back.

"We have to ask the questiooonnns, Mr Lundy, as there have been occasions when parents have tried hiding their children."

He took a deep breath and looked around at the piles of dirty bowls and the empty baked bean cans littering the carpet. "So where am I going to hide him? The kitchen sink? The broom cupboard? Maybe under the bed?" He took another deep breath and smacked his right cheek. "I'm sorry, sir. it's just… well… I would never help my son go AWOL. It's not the right thing to do.".

"I understand, Mr Lundy." The officer paused and cleared his throat. "Woooould you have any ideaaaa where your son would have gone to?"

Alfred imagined the young second lieutenant sat in his poky little office, twirling his red cap and reading the questions off a laminated card. "Wish I did. He doesn't have loads of friends.

He probably wouldn't want to come back here when he finds out…"

"Finds out what, Mr Lundy?" the officer asked, scenting an opportunity.

"Oh nothing."

"If it has an impact on the investigation, I urge yoooou to tell me, Mr Lundy."

He smirked into the receiver knowing all too well there would be no investigation, or man-hunt or sniffer dogs at the house. Just a few phone-calls and a record on a database.

"Well his mum she… she… died a few days ago." He still couldn't quite believe what he was saying, like he was stuck in a dream and couldn't wake up. Pinching his left forearm, he felt nothing. He pinched harder, squeezing the flesh until a pink rash appeared. Still nothing.

"Oh, I am sorry to heaaaar that, Mr Lundy. Please accept my condolences, was it a sudden death?"

Alfred put the rectangular receiver on the dresser and sat back. Condolence. What does it really mean? Did you know her? Are you sorry or is that another fancy word you've got scribbled on your laminated card?"

"Mr Luuundy, Hello? Mr Luuundy?"

He thrust his legs forward and picked up the receiver, the phone wire missing the whisky tumbler by millimetres.

"Thank you. I was miles away. Was a car crash."

"Does Private Lundy know about the accident?"

"No he does not, so I need to get hold of him quick. When I do will be in touch. Now if you don't mind."

"Of couuurse, Mr Luuundy. We will send round local arrangements."

"Ok bye, sir."

"Goodbye, Mr Luuundy."

He hung the receiver back on the handset. "Local arrangements?" It did not sound right.

He sat back among the un-made bed and reached out for an Irish whisky bottle sitting on the window ledge. As he took a hit from the bottle he dwelled on the implication, like there was a surveillance happening right now on Reigate Terrace: spies dressed in black hanging off the rooftops, covert police cars patrolling the area, dog handlers scouring the bushes in the park.

He smirked, knowing it was just hot air. The only way they would find Joel was if the police arrested him and found some dirt on his record. He tried to picture his son in the present, running around Germany jumping from train to train. As free as a soldier AWOL could be. The thought was supposed to make him disappointed, livid, spitting mad. But all he wanted to do was hold Joel tight to his chest, stroke his hair and tell him no matter what life throws at you and how caged you feel inside this tiny world it will eventually be alright.

"Hello son..."

33.

A stream of muffled tweets groaned around Joel's ears like gulls hovering around a hungry nest. With a subdued lethargy he opened his eyes to the Westhamton station sign, shining in the afternoon sun. The sign had been freshly painted, with a sharp white glistening against the red background.

WESTHAMTON. It felt eerie. A homecoming of sorts. He imagined his mother looking down at his stained clothes, trainers with a brown sheen and his chin sprouting a fine patch of stubble.

He collected his rucksack and limped towards the train door, the dream still alive in his memory of the dark abyss and his father shouting. He lumbered off the train, passing the old key-maker and the kiosk where the Pakistani man sat, eating syrup-coated sweets. "Can of Fanta, please," he said.

The vendor handed over the can and inspected the pound coin. "Not seen you round here for a while, boss."

Joel opened the can of Fanta. "Been away."

"Holiday?"

"Not exactly."

"Well good to see you back, boss."

Joel shrugged. "Thanks."

He turned away from the kiosk and looked around. Not much had changed in the station: The same rusty Coke cans and crinkled crisp packets cluttered around the rail buffers. The same pigeons congregated around the sharp nails above the Edwardian clock. Diesel still hung in the air from the maintenance depot next to the station. He looked at the Edwardian clock: 1:16 PM. A sense of anticipation took hold of his body, like a soldier returning to a hero's welcome only to find a muted response.

HOMETOWN ARREST OF AWOL SOLDIER AFTER SEVEN HOUR SIEGE

He envisaged the headlines of the Southern Herald, exacerbating the story beyond recognition. Sorrow battled with relief in his conscience thinking the reaction from his parents. He'd let them down, there was no getting away from the dread of disappointment about to be carved deep into the tissue of their eyes. Well, his father's anyway. He strolled into the smoggy Westhamton air with the whiff of burning oil from the power station punctuating his nostrils. He took a deep breath and looked around, feeling liberated.

The bike racks outside the station were still there, corroded steel racks with many locks and chains still attached. He remembered the day he forgot the combination on his chain lock and phoned home for help.

His parents turned up ten minutes later, father fuming mad while his mother remarked: "These things happen. Just make sure you memorise it next time, you hear?" and she rubbed his floppy fringe like the soppy old bird she always was.

The memory was still vivid of that day. Of the ten minutes it took his father to break the lock. Ten minutes when his father could have been down the pub sipping his whisky and snacking on salty nuts. Something still did not feel right. That same niggly dread from Germany, still there, malignant. He lit a cigarette, dusted down his denim jacket and headed down the slope which bowed into the town centre.

The body of the renegade soldier floated down the hill taking in the sights and sounds of the past; the lush green hills either side of the Westhamton basin, seagulls screeching on their way to the south coast, children chasing grey squirrels down the hill.

Soppy old bird he thought. It had only been a matter of months but the town's inner beauty seemed to sparkle in the sunshine. He walked for half a mile when the power plant's booming towers suddenly came into sight, the gigantic chimneys towering over the Westhamton skyline like two monoliths.

"Lundy? Joel Lundy?" a voice shouted from a bus stop on the other side of the road.

"Oi! Joel! Joel!" He turned around, scanning the improvised shelter made from corrugated iron on the other side of the road. The tall slender figure of Max Harlington waved at Joel, his leather jacket flashing against the glass. He crossed the road, attempting to broaden his shoulders and arch his eyebrows.

He stroked the neatly trimmed stubble growth around his jaw. "How you doing, Lundy boy, haven't seen you in ages."

"Max, how you been?" Joel replied hesitantly, he wasn't sure what to say.

"Alright yeah how long has it been?" Max asked.

"Since we left high? '95 wasn't it?" He was unsure why the mighty Max Harlington was talking to him.

Both he and Joel were in completely different social standings at school: Joel in the lower leagues, Max in the Premier League. "Three years. Time flies eh?" Max tapped the base of a plastic bench with his foot.

"Listen Joel, I'm sorry to hear your news, mate. Wouldn't want that to happen to me so sudden. I'd be proper gutted." Max looked into the brown richness of Joel's eyes with a calm sincerity.

"What news? What do you mean, Max?" Joel's heart thumped an extra beat. Max veered from Joel's perplexed gaze, focusing ahead towards a block of flats: left towards the top of the hill, right down the hill; as if he had a guilty secret.

"You know?" Max's tongue paused.

"Sorry you lost me. What do you mean?"

Max's face went pale. He fidgeted with his hair, pretending to pull the hairs from their roots. "Oh it's nothing mate must have got it wrong."

He gesticulated to a group of boys further up the hill. "Listen Joel, I've probably got it wrong I'll catch up with you later all the best yeah!" He darted up the hill towards the group of teenage boys loitering around a corner shop.

Joel looked at the athletic figure of the immaculate Max Harlington running up the hill, the guilty one with a secret regarding his own private life. Max was hiding something. He feared the worst.

He ran. As fast as his legs would carry him down the hill into the town and past the parade of shops where kids would hang out after school, drinking stale lager and sniffing glue. He dashed off the road into the park where he would walk with his mother around the green space, trying to cool off after another family disagreement.

He ran at full pace "I love you, Mum. Love you," he stuttered. The wind rushed past his ears. He hadn't run this fast since the ill-fated CFT in Ziegborn. The red and grey townhouses that greeted the entrance to Reigate Terrace suddenly

307

appeared. The loose stones on the pavement clung to his muddy trainers as he slowed down to a fast walk. A black cat darted past his feet in a rush to climb the neighbour's fence. He looked around, not a soul stirred in the afternoon breeze.

As he approached the porch door a foul stench rose up from a torn bin bag strewn across the drive; beer cans, cereal boxes and discarded food covered the paving slabs, scattered slapdash like a grenade had exploded in the bag.

He felt around in his jacket pocket, breathing still heavy, the urge to see his mother prevalent.

"Damnit!" he cried, realising the house-key was still in a locker at Gallipoli barracks. The quintessential Hollywood burning house scene. He imagined breaking down the front door and rescuing his mum from a smoke-filled room. Taking a deep breath he walked up to the porch step, coughing up tobacco spittle and wheezing. The tips of his fingers felt cold.

He went to knock on the door but could not. He tried again, but a cowardly instinct kept him at bay. He didn't want to face the music, but knew he had to.

The afternoon sun picked up a shine near a milk bottle sitting on the edge of the front-step. He turned his head. It was a spare key carelessly tossed to the side. He grabbed the key and unlocked the front door.

"Mum!"

"Mum? Dad? Anyone home?"

The foul smell from outside lingered in the house. He got inside the porch and kicked away pamphlets and unopened mail stacked up by the letterbox.

"Hello! Hello!" Slinging the rucksack to one side of the porch he entered through the hall. The yellow carpets were stained with mud. He frantically went into the living room. An eerie suffocating silence gripped the living room; as if a vortex had swallowed up all the oxygen.

The carpet was littered with beer cans piled ankle high around the scratched leather sofa. Some of the cans had spilt onto the carpet, leaving a musty aroma like the floor of an old saloon bar. Polystyrene shreds were spread around the sofa from where the cushions had been slashed. Rotting food was strewn across the table: chips, noodles, slimy vegetables, baked beans. The living room he knew resembled the filter of a sewer.

"Mum? Dad? Anyone?" He proceeded to the kitchen where a stench of stagnant water was being emitted. Dirty cutlery was piled high over the sink, over-spilling onto the laminate worktop and smashed bottles covered the linoleum floor. He looked down and saw a red stain on the floor; Blood or red wine? He couldn't tell.

"What the fuck is all this?" he screamed, unaware of the horrors his eyes were relaying to his brain. By the washing machine a puddle of brown water sat idly, the smell engulfing the whole kitchen. He kicked away a broken wine bottle and timidly made his way upstairs with dust blowing into his lungs, all the while his conscience procrastinating between finding out and walking away. He looked down at the smashed photograph of 1 PLATOON – C COMPANY – 1ST BATTALION KINGS HAMPHSHIRE REGIMENT lying on the landing. Alfred's face in the second row had a black mark through it.

The devil jumped in front of him, laughing, waving a suggestive finger. As he stepped off the last two steps he noticed bits of plaster scattered across the carpet.

Malt fumes filled the fetid air. He looked up at the light fixture hanging by a bare thread from the ceiling. Next to the wire a hole had been punched into the plaster. He edged closer to the gaping hole and saw a leather strap tied to a ceiling joist tucked away in the plaster.

He tried the handle on his old bedroom. It was locked. He then barged at the door with all his strength. No luck. The door stood firm on its hinges. He tried again, then ran downstairs and pulled out a jack hammer from under the sink. An instinct took hold; he ran back up the stairs and smashed at the brown door. A hole immediately appeared from the impact. He pushed his hand through the hole and managed to unlock the catch from the other side and burst through the door:

Clothes and underwear covered the carpet and photographs were strewn across his old bed. In the corner by the window was his father, sat in a bundle rocking back and forth wearing stained jogging trousers and a vest where an oval sag was dripping onto his lap. Joel leapt over the bed and shook his father by the shoulder.

"Dad! Dad! It's me! What the hell's going on?"

Alfred was unrecognisable, whiskers of facial hair sprouted out from his cheeks and his face was purple, blotchy. His eyes appeared inconsolable and his breath smelt of stale alcohol.

Alfred buried his head in his hands, trying to avoid the incoming inquisition.

"Dad!"

Alfred rocked back and forth with a strict rhythm.

"Dad!"

Joel gazed at his father's ruby red cracked lips.

A red eye peeked out from under an armpit. "It wasn't my fault, son," he murmured under his breath.

"What's that?"

"Wasn't my fault. Please believe me, son!" Tears flowed from his bloodshot eyes as banks formed in his withered cheeks, ready to irrigate the salty drops from his face.

"Wasn't what, Dad? WHAT IS GOING ON? WHERE'S MUM?"

Time stood still for both father and son as they looked into each other's eyes. A telepathic feeling connected the two lost souls trying to make sense of a horrible event. Alfred swallowed and closed his eyes.

He wiped his eyes with the fabric of his dirty vest. "She's gone. Dead. I'm sorry I have to tell you, my boy."

Joel took a step away from his father. Staring at him. All he surveyed was a jabbering podgy wreck, cowering on the floor. A pale shadow of the tough old soldier he knew.

"What? Can't be. What you saying?"

Alfred nodded.

"But… but what happened?" He felt angry, confused. Unsure which door he had walked through between reality and nightmare.

"Accident. Car accident in a taxi. She was gone before I got to the hospital."

Joel took a further few steps away and slumped to the carpet by the wardrobe. A piece of aluminium can pierced his thigh as he hit the carpet. The numbness kicked in, fighting off the thumping pain as blood began to flow steadily on the mucky carpet. His face went the colour of a swan's feathers. His heart dropped from his chest into his gut. "No! No! Can't be, Dad. Can't be. Tell me it's not real, you old fool! Tell me!"

Joel dragged his body onto the bed with blood dripping and looked out of the window. All he could see was a hill full of red colours; trickling out from every artery. Everything else erased. No pigeons flying from tree to tree, no kids playing football on the field, no sky, no sun or any hope.

"Tell me, Dad!" He shook Alfred vigorously. "Tell me it's not true!"

34.

A German Shepherd barked at a Jack Russell across the muddy field, the look on the dog's face eager for a chase.

The owner of the German Shepherd pulled on the harness, making the dog recoil back while the Jack Russell continued to agitate the German Shepherd. Yapping fervently, the Jack Russell eyeballed the larger dog then suddenly chased after a tennis ball. The dog's legs scurried quickly after the yellow dot in the sky, without noticing a slumped body on a park bench. A man casually strolled towards the Jack Russell, his green waterproof jacket crackling with each step. The man's face was well kempt, a rogue colour around his cheeks blending seamlessly into olive skin. "Go, Jackie, go!" he said.

A cloud of smoke rose from the park bench. The body lay like damp dead wood, covered in a soggy denim jacket and black corduroy jeans. A pair of worn, sunken eyes poked out from under the jacket, the eyes resembling tiny scuffed marbles staring up at the grey sheet blanketing the sky.

"Hello? Hello? You okay in there?" The dog walker shook the body by the shoulder. The eyes of the vagrant shifted towards a row of trees in the near distance, downcast.

"Hello! Hello!" the dog walker's boots

squelched in the mud. A sudden look of panic hit the man's face. It was Joel.

Joel pushed off one side of his jacket, uncovering one side of his face; clumps of hair growing around the cheeks and a jet-black colour running through his hair. His face was thin, malnourished, looking as dry as burned toast.

"What?" he sulked at the dog walker.

"Oh… just checking you were ok in there."

"Why wouldn't I be ok?"

"Well you weren't exactly moving a lot on the bench, was a bit suspicious!" The man looked around the field. "Jackie, here please!"

"Well don't worry, friend, I am fine. Was watching the clouds go past, marvelling nature and all that."

The man's mouth scrunched up irritably. "No need for that, mate, I was just seeing that you were alright."

"Well I'm ok, alright?"

He looked at Joel with a slight contempt "Well… what would you do if you saw a body lying on a bench dead to the world?"

Joel pulled the damp jacket down away from his face, sat up and took out a pack of Golden Virginia. "Hmmm what would I do…" he tested his dexterity on a rolling paper. "Three options I reckon, pal. One, let him become worm-food. Two, save his poor sorry soul from death's door with a miraculous piece of CPR. Or three, become God and… well… the options are endless…!" He sat back on the rickety bench feeling smug.

The dog walker took a step back away from the bench. "Jackie!" he shouted into the air.

"No need for that, mate. People like me are just looking out for less fortunate folk like you. It's not my fault you're in whatever place you've found yourself in."

"And what place would that be?"

"Sitting around… homeless… broken life. I don't know your circumstances, mate. But all I am doing is trying to help. Remember that."

Joel laughed out loud, loud like an evil sorcerer hatching a plan to take over the world. He felt his rib cage. "That's a good one that. Nice of you to judge me, pal."

"Well my obvious thought was that you were a homeless. Have you looked in the mirror?"

"Not one to make presumptions then?" The laughter faded. "You don't know me. What if I was sitting here in this public space gathering my thoughts and trying not to hate the human race?"

"Well…" The man walked towards the Jack Russell. "You started this argument, mate. I was just looking out for you."

With a nonchalant stomp he squelched his boots in the mud and walked away from the bench. Joel looked at the back of the retreating foe, noticing a tail pinned between his buttocks.

"You don't know anything about me, pal!" Joel shouted at the man.

The animosity he was trying to quell built up in his lungs: the hate, the pure hate, the disregard for humanity. No amount of tobacco could stop the poison swishing around his body. He picked up a clump of muddy grass and blew the blades into the wind.

"Fucking arsehole!" he shouted as he walked on the waterlogged field. "People just want to help don't they? Be the Good Samaritan. Just to stroke their own precious ego. Be the better man, love thy neighbour and all that shit. What do they know about me? Where I came from? Everyone's the bloody judge!"

The rain started to fall in heavy bursts. Joel carried on regardless, shaking off the excess raindrops from his jacket. He ran over to a small playground, into a child's playhouse, and sat in a tiny chair. He looked around the interior of the playhouse. The chair smelt of fresh paint, shiny Smurf drawings beamed out of the table with harmless glee. Papa Smurf looked directly at him, beard fully intact with a red hat flopping over his wise old face. The drawing looked suggestively; a subliminal message buried underneath the make-up of glee.

He grinned.

His father had bought him a cuddly Papa Smurf for his sixth birthday. He remembered it fondly. Unwrapping the wrapping paper Papa Smurf crawled out smiling at him; the look on his father's face a rare picture of joy when he saw his son laughing and smiling in genuine gratitude. Joel knew then that Papa Smurf would look over him like an extension of his real father, a guardian of sorts. His father's face was a funny thing back then, twisting between sad, indifferent and happy. Before the accident that had scared him with a permanent scowl. He remembered looking at his father; the young soldier on that day with a full head of hair and optimistic zest in his muddy eyes, remembering a moment of genuine empathy between father and son.

The drawing on the chair had been distorted; his head out of proportion to his body and white beard an off-orange colour. Joel took out a notepad from his jacket pocket and started sketching the real Papa Smurf. The one he knew and loved from his childhood. The wise old man always there to defend his innocence. To snuggle up to on cold nights in Londonderry away from the wind and the rain lashing against the bedroom window, away from the bullies at school and the muffled arguments downstairs.

35.

A sticky salty sensation rolled around the inside of Alfred's mouth until a ball of phlegm dribbled onto the filthy linen.

Crack! A sudden thump hit the bedroom window. He awoke with a sudden jerk and rolled off the dirty mattress. His hand wiped dew from the window. A bunch of kids ran across the green kicking a football, shrieking.

On the carpet a sheet of paper lay amongst a pile of clothes and beer cans. He picked it up:

Dear Joel,

I am writing to you as your father but I would like to think you are adult enough to digest my thoughts now that you are nineteen years and a soldier.

I recall my early squaddie days. The shock of basic training, the adjustment of battalion life, beers and girls every weekend (before your mother of course) and stinking hangovers on the parade square. Then the loneliness, the despair and the boredom lying on a bed ticking off a calendar, waiting. Maybe sooner than you think the waiting will lead to deployment, but well, we can talk about that another time.

As you probably know, your grandfather also spent many years treading the army road and kicking up a filthy dust that clung to his combats, and then his civvy clothes. The dust was always there, in everything he did. Proud he was, always proud to wear the cap badge, "be somebody".

I too felt like 'somebody' in the early years. Trips around the local hangouts of my youth felt like a royal parade when I was home on leave, and I felt like the king. "Infantry soldier" I'd tell anyone who'd listen. Mr Average I was no longer.

The thing is the army provides a lot for a young family son: a roof, money in your pocket, job security. It's an inducing sell. Only now do I realise it's not as black and white as that. I know the dislocation that comes with the constant tours and battalion moves have not been beneficial to your upbringing, son. I now realise that as I sit here in the kitchen writing this, staring out of a window that is blank, cold and unrecognisable. A voice talks to me every day…

I don't know why I'm telling you all this, son, it's just my mind has taken a new direction since departing the army. I guess all I'm trying to say to you is its ok to think about the other side and Civvy Street, to dream. Just do what you think is right for you. I followed your granddad because I had to. The time is right for you to decide your destiny. I won't be disappointed.

Dad

"A ghost? Was it? Was it him?" His neck creaked like a rusty machine part as he turned and surveyed the bedroom scene:

Walls specked with mould that were rising towards the ceiling. Crisp packets, milk cartons, cans strewn across the buttercup carpet. The cartons had spilled dregs of milk on the carpet making the room smell sour.

He moved to one side of the bed and rummaged amongst a pile of photographs and condolence cards. "Bel. Bel. It was him. I know it was him. I'm not dreaming am I? He's come back."

He took a swig out of one of the beer cans on the carpet, then looked into a mirror on the dresser, at his receding scalp getting longer around the edges like one of those American detectives on an 80's cop show. He stroked his moustache, noticing the lack of shape. He then slapped himself on the cheek, putting the can down beside the bed.

Rushing down the stairs he entered the toilet, slapping white soap under his armpits and gurgling emerald mouthwash. The sting of the chemical wash hit the sides of his teeth for a few seconds then subsided.

"Was him. I know it's him, Bel!"

He sprinted down the lime green sidewalk of Reigate Terrace and onto the playing field that backed onto the gardens. The mud on the grass hampered his run in a straight line towards a gap in the hedge row leading to the A314.

He ran purposefully down the busy A road, past the parade of shops where old Jimbo Gadge would always greet him outside the off-licence and ask for a swig of the whisky bottle he was holding. The Crow's Nest, the Duke of Cornwall, the Pike's Head. Pubs with accounts yet to be settled.

A solitary figure raised a hand to him in the street before disappearing through the swing doors of the Pike's Head. Alfred ignored the salutation and continued with his stomp. Lungs grinding, heart thumping, leg's motoring. He hadn't run like this since his last CFT in Bulford. He thought of one thing and one thing only: seeing the ghost, the ghost that had entered through hell's gates with a simple message: hope.

Arms threw across his chest as he started the slow climb uphill towards the new housing estates on the edge of town. A Bull Terrier barked from the other side of the road. The noise didn't even register. He had a goal; the other distractions in the town could not pull him away from his rendezvous with the ghost.

For two miles he ran until he could see the elevation of the road plateauing. He carried on for another two hundred metres and with a flick of his left ankle he turned off the A314 into a cul-de-sac. Just past the glistened sign of the cul-de-sac rectangular lawns were yellowing to the autumn. Next to the lawns were estate cars parked on wide driveways.

Alfred looked at overhanging shrubs beginning to wither in polished ceramic pots and moss patches forming in the gaps of newly laid driveways. Cooking aromas delicately drifted from kitchen extractor fans: roast chicken, lamb hotpot, curry spices, stewed apples. The aromas made the juices in his stomach swirl.

Ivan peeped from behind a net curtain with a worried look in his eye.

The hunched, bloated figure of Alfred Lundy limped down the cul-de-sac, nodding his head to a broken beat and coughing viciously. The knock on the door came instantaneously, reverberating around the foundations of the new built house.

Ivan opened the front door.

Alfred locked his hands into a nervous embrace. "Ivan. How you doing, mate?"

Ivan gawped at the unrecognisable figure standing on the porch: gone were the broad athletic shoulders, replaced by a sloped, sunken muscle mass that ran all the way to his expanded waistline. Gone was the vibrant colour from his face, the sharp look in his brown eyes and the confidence that radiated from his military persona.

"Mr Lundy. How are you?"

"Yeah, not bad thanks." Alfred looked from side to side, shifty. "Listen, Ivan."

"What can I do for you?"

"I'm looking for Joel, you seen him around?"

Ivan could smell the digested alcohol coming out of the old soldier's mouth. "Haven't seen him for a while to be honest."

"Oh…" Alfred's shoulders slumped.

"Have you tried the playground on St Anne's park? Heard he was over there quite a lot nowadays."

Alfred cupped his mouth with his hand. "St Anne's Park? What… what's he doing over there?"

"I don't know to be honest, Mr Lundy. Listen do you want to come in? It's getting a bit cool."

"No thanks. I'm going to try and find him. St Anne's Park. But thanks, Ivan… thanks."

Alfred turned away from the polished PVC door frame. "Listen, Alfie," Ivan interrupted.

"Yeah."

"I'm sorry to hear about Belinda. Tragic. Real tragic."

Alfred turned and acknowledged the condolence mechanically; he had been through it so many times that the words were beginning to sound empty. "I am too, Ivan. Anyway, I'll see you around yeah?" A glint re-appeared in his left eye and he turned away.

"If you need anything, you or Joel, please let me know."

Alfred marched down the newly built cul-de-sac with a new turn of pace, left after right, knees at the correct angle, feet set to the exact rhythm of his heartbeat. Passing the swanky new Vauxhalls, Fords and Volkswagens parked on the road he caught a glimpse of his own reflection in the car windows. The reflection didn't matter anymore; it was superfluous. The extension of him and who he was could be in trouble. A reflection hanging off the precipice unsure, confused, in no-man's land.

The figure of a woman dressed in a jumper and a pair of stonewashed jeans watched the old soldier, perched on a static cloud. And he marched on.

36.

Hours slowly moulded into days. Days turned into weeks and all Joel did was stroll briskly. A continual motion facing the winds and the rain that bounced off his face to drown out the tears.

He wandered through Westhamton like a ghost. Derelict buildings, garden sheds, pieces of disused cardboard a makeshift shelter away from the prying eyes, his face covered by a darkness resembling a black hole that had swallowed his face whole.

His mother was cremated three weeks ago. A simple thirty-minute service from a minister dressed in white who had a resemblance to Des Lynam. He sat through the service a few metres from Alfred, keeping an eye out for the RMPs who never came. He stared blankly at the minister through the service, chewing on a piece of gum until 'Sittin' On The Dock Of The Bay' led her coffin away from the final curtain.

He had not seen him since. The hate, anguish and the grief all pointed towards Alfred Charlton Lundy. How could he have not stopped her being slain behind the wheel? How was she driven to such despair?

He shimmered past a news kiosk next at the Westhamton bus station:

1st November 1998 – Two men found guilty of armed robbery of jewellers in Southampton

The grey clouds which had hovered over autumnal Westhamton were beginning to subside into a sea of blue, refreshing the damp air and cooling the tips of his fingers. A bus pulled out of the station throwing up a black cloud that clung to Joel's denim jacket as he headed for the refuse bins at the back of the station.

As he arrived at the bins he felt his teeth with his tongue. They felt fragile, almost hollow. Soft drink cans, tuna sandwiches, wrinkly apples and black bananas were piled high in the one bin. He buried through the metal bin like a worm burying into fresh soil, managing to find a packet of ready salted crisps and half a bottle of mineral water. He stuffed the goodies into his jacket pocket.

As he passed the side of the station a man with charred grey skin and a black eye scuffled past him. Joel steered clear of the stranger, carefully hiding the goodies in his jacket. The tramp shuffled his scuffed boots towards the bins. Once he had passed Joel, he took the bag of crisps out and ate them cautiously. A group of bus drivers congregated by the station entrance glared at Joel as he moved past. "Get a job!" one of the drivers said under his breath.

The Westhamton High Street was a hive of activity with street lights and placards advertising bonfire night adorning the busy street. Joel could see mothers walking frantically between the stationery stores and the card shops to find fireworks while pushing buggies and carrying heavy loads of shopping bags.

He sat on a brick wall overlooking the Jolly Roger pub and lit a cigarette. Smoke circles appeared in the air. He then scoured the pavement for used cigarette butts before the others gathered by the off-licence could get a chance.

The shoppers kept coming, darting in and out of the shops with lightning speed. A mass of bodies swarming the shops. Something suddenly caught his eye. A flash of red, similar to the sudden flash a robin gives off in quick flight. He rubbed his eyes and wiped his damp, congealed hair. It was a burgundy red slowly walking amongst the shoppers. He rubbed his eyes again. "Can't be!" he muttered.

A green woven jacket broke up wavy red locks with the jacket falling to a pair of small legs. Covering the legs was a long, bohemian style dress dragging on the floor. It was Julie Jay.

Joel ducked under a bin but soon realised his current state would make him unrecognisable to anyone he knew. Julie strolled with the forceful elegance she had adopted at school; a lioness strolling through the Hampshire Savannah, afraid of nobody. Seeing Julie

brought a wry smile to his face and for
one moment he forgot about everything and
marvelled at his old friend. He rose off
the wall and walked after her. For the
first time as long as he could remember
he felt warmth. It felt peculiar. His
greasy locks blew into his line of
vision; he quickly attempted to comb his
hair into a side parting with his jagged
fingernails.

She turned a corner towards a
supermarket. He kept behind her, nerves
pulsating with trepidation. Passing a
phone box, he caught a glimpse of his
reflection, for now he didn't care.

He turned another corner and followed her
trail only to find an empty street where
an old lady was sitting on a bench
caressing a walking stick. He looked from
side to side.

"Was it her or a figment?" he had heard
about hallucinations happening to the
malnourished. He paced back towards the
supermarket and glanced through the
entrance; trying to avoid the burly
bouncer he had a confrontation with last
week.

"Can't be, can it?"

He turned around to the voice. Julie
stood ten metres away with a perplexed
expression.

He smirked. "Hey Jules."

"Mr Joel Lundy. My God I thought it was
you!" She beamed and ran over to him.

"How are you Joel?" She hugged him, and Joel embraced her, holding her tight while the velvet of her jacket rubbed on his dry hands. He could smell honey in her hair and rosemary in her dress.

"I'm ok…" He bashfully looked at the pavement. "It's good to see you. Really good to see you."

"When was the last time I saw you? Last summer?" she asked.

Joel fiddled with the buttons on his jacket. His hands suddenly became cumbersome, useless tools. "Reckon so, yep reckon so."

"So?" she said.

"So?"

"So why are you not away with the army somewhere?"

"On a bit of leave. Just hanging out." The weeks sleeping rough made the lie fall out of his mouth with considerable ease. She gave him a discerning look. "What?" he said.

She gleamed. "Oh, nothing you just sound just like your dad."

His cheeks turned the colour of Julie's locks. "My dad? Please tell me you're joking?" The image of the old man curled up in the bedroom hit him, whimpering and cowering and helpless.

"Relax will you? Is that such a bad association?" she said. He looked away from the paving slabs into her serene rich blue eyes. He could feel his heart starting to race away.

"So, what are you doing right now apart from the usual hide n' seek from your dad?"

The redness in his cheeks began to subside. "Not much. I was just going to… never mind."

"You busy? Fancy going for a coffee somewhere? I know this great organic place round the corner. Does cappuccinos, pastries that kind of thing."

"Sure. That thing I was going to do can wait a while," he stuttered, knowing his story had fallen apart two minutes ago.

"Damn right it can wait a while, soldier. I can borrow HM's finest for the morning, can't I?" the gentle facetious expressions floated in the air like tones from a harp, putting him at ease.

"So where is this new world haven at?" he replied.

"Follow me," she grabbed his hand and they walked past the supermarket, avoiding the rush of frantic mothers and screeching children.

"We'll find some big fireworks! Ones that have a big bang don't worry! Don't worry!" A look of worry furrowed across every mother's face.

"We have to, Mummy, have to. Big bangs!

Lots of colours!"

"What's with all the mad mums today?" Julie said.

"They've been getting worse over the week. Taking over the town centre." said Joel.

"No shit. Invasion of the firework snatchers! I mean so what if you can't get the best fireworks? Is the world going to end?"

A smile leapt out from his cracked lips, nearly cutting the dry tissue. "See you haven't forgotten what to say, Jules."

They washed through the paved street with Joel hanging onto Julie's velvet jacket like a sick child. Julie looked at Joel. She could see a wry smile hid underneath the charred skin of antipathy.

They passed an eagle sculpture in the middle of the walkway. Joel noticed the ugly piece of metal for the first time, particularly the corrosion seeping through the soap green paint.

"Spare change?" A tramp held out his hand as they turned into an alleyway littered with flattened cardboard boxes. Joel caught a glimpse of a tattoo on his right forearm: wings of the Parachute regiment.

They carried on down the alleyway away from the marauding masses, their shoes crunching on broken glass. He could smell the coffee wafting out of Daphne's coffee shop. The smell reminded him of the coffee vendor in Hannover station which led to his mother; he caught nutmeg, cinnamon, fresh muffins baking.

They entered the shop through a small glass door. "What do you want?" Julie asked.

"Just get me a coffee," he replied.

Julie looked at him blankly. "White coffee, one sugar?"

The attendant behind the counter gave him an icy glare "Hmm… yeah," he replied.

His knees creaked as he wearily sat on a wooden stool by a window and looked to the alleyway outside, his apathetic stare transfixed on an imaginary object in the small cobbled walkway; he didn't know what it was or why he was staring at it.

"Here you go, mister," Julie placed two mugs on the oak table.

"Thanks, Jules."

They both slurped from the mugs: Joel looking at the floor, Julie looking straight at Joel. He felt her warm breath coasting across the small table. It was something he had missed. The buzz from the coffee percolators suddenly became mute and he waited for the inevitable questions to come.

"You going to tell me what's going on then?" He moved his eye-line away from the dusty beech floor and towards the frothy milk sitting in the coffee mug.

"Don't know what you mean."

She stirred her black coffee with a miniature silver spoon, focusing on him maternally, like a school teacher trying to reveal domestic violence from a beaten down kid. "C'mon Joel, you don't exactly look a million dollars. Where you been sleeping?"

"Sleeping? What's that got to do with anything? You know where I've been… Abroad… Germany in fact."

"Ok so you've been living in Germany. Inside or outside the barracks?"

"Inside."

"I think you're lying."

"What do you mean?"

Her expression turned stern in a blink. "It's all over your face. I know when you're telling a porky pie."

He looked her dead in the eye. A duel, a tussle, was about to start but he had no energy to fight it. Her serene blue eyes radiated calmness, benevolence. An imaginary hand broke through the clouds offering a hand through the road to hell.

"I'm just tired, Jules. Just tired is all." He saw the hand slipping back into the clouds. The conversation halted and the percolators started to buzz and shoo again.

He picked out dirt from his overgrown fingernails. "Ok ok you got me."

"You've been sleeping rough, haven't you?"

He nodded reluctantly. The shame dropping into his bowels.

"How long?"

"Three weeks, four, five? Lost count."

"But why leave the army? Get kicked out? What happened? You were adamant it was going to work."

"Tuh!" he exhaled. "You believe it?"

She took another sip of the coffee, looking around the shop like a naughty schoolgirl about to tell their parents of a school detention. "Not for one minute. I could tell you were joining for all the wrong reasons, could see it a mile off."

"There's something…"

"Something?"

Blue shades appeared on his cheeks. He placed his hands out front on the table and stretched out his fingers.

"It's about Mum."

"Oh dear… what?"

He took a deep breath and reached for an imaginary pack of Golden Virginia on the table. It felt strange, the first notification he had to deal with. He almost felt guilty dropping the news on her. "She's gone. Dead."

Julie put her hands in front of her

mouth. "What no! How? God… I'm… I'm so sorry, Joel."

He hadn't heard the 'sorry' word in a few weeks, from the incessant compassion shown by distant relatives to the dead sorrow that hung around the streets. This was different; he looked into the ocean colour filling her eyes and saw compassion, empathy, a sincere sorrow.

"How? What happened to old Bel? God I can't believe it!" her serenity turned aghast, fearful like a lightning bolt had struck her on the forehead.

"Car accident. Was dead when she got to the hospital. Internal head injuries they said." His expression was vacuous, as if he were the police officer reeling off the statement to close relatives.

She gulped her coffee down. "I only saw her a few months ago, down in the library. Said she was thinking about starting a fine art course again. Damn!"

"What she always wanted to do, go to art school." He looked away towards the window. A fair-haired toddler was sucking on a lollypop, the look on the little girl's face calmness personified, not a care in the world. The only care or thought how to extract the sweet juices from the purple sweet. Joel looked at the little girl and wished he was a three year old again, innocent, chaste, incorrupt of life.

"So have you been on the streets since the funeral?" she asked.

He nodded and stirred the coffee.

"But why? Why are you not at home? What about your dad?"

His pupils dilated and bottom lip protruded. "He's at home I guess."

Julie looked at the wreck sat opposite, stern. "Joel, why are you not at home with your dad? Was there an argument?" She leant forward on her stool.

"Why don't you go round there and ask the old man?" He looked her in the eye then quickly focused on the floor.

"So what happened?" she asked.

"What happened?" The expression on his face laid bare more cracks, more blackheads manifesting on his dry, milky skin. "I need some water, could you?" Julie leapt off her stool and fetched a glass of tap water from the counter.

"It's ok you know. You can tell me." She grabbed his left hand and cupped it in her hands. Her grip felt warm, her delicate hands acting like a log fire on a cold winter's day. He bit at his little finger nail until a shard of calcium came tearing off.

"I came home weeks ago from… oh that's another thing I didn't tell you anyway doesn't matter, they can do one. Anyway, I came home to find the house in a complete state, rubbish everywhere, all over the floor. Thought we had been burgled or some squatters had had a wild party. So I go upstairs and there he is, reeking of booze and cowering in a ball. Just cowering!"

"What he'd...?"

"Think he tried."

"Oh. Was he ok?"

"Curling up on the floor tuh! Who did he think he was?"

"So he'd let himself go?"

"Let himself go!" The tension in his cheeks wound up. "He was a quivering wreck! But the worst thing about it was that he wanted all the pity! He looked at me all dole-eyed telling me my mum was dead but he didn't give a shit about my feelings he'd made no attempt to get in touch with me!" He brushed his eyebrows and his beaten eyes began to well up.

"It's just I don't know... I never expected to find out a death like that. Especially not my dear old mum." The tears steadily rolled down the cracks in his dried-out cheeks. They flowed through the nearly formed tributaries, smooth, sleek, fresh.

He tried to fight it. The emotional black hole engulfing him began to open. And with it came a bursting catharsis.

"I... It's juuuust... I..." The viscera gripped his entire face, the muscles in his cheeks became numb, his nose turned a darkened red, lips formed a tight cap around his mouth.

"Hey it's ok. It's ok," Julie repeated. "Sounds like you've been through hell."

"I… I still feel like I am." He took a napkin from the table and dried his eyes. "When I found out I had all sorts of shit go through my head and it all leads to him. First I even thought he had a part to play in it."

"You really think that?"

"I don't know anymore!" He lifted the glass from the table, his fingers gripping it tightly. Julie looked down at his trembling grip, the colour of his fingertips a darkened purple.

"Listen, I know you've been grieving. But I very much doubt he would have done something terrible to his wife. Your mother."

He looked at Julie. Her wavy red hair, the small dimple on her chin. "I don't know any more, Jules."

Julie took a brief glance out of the window. "What is with you and your dad?"

The black hole widened, filling his neurons with a massive urge to tell the truth. "Do it!" they shouted through his skull. "Do it!"

"Nothing really. We've just always been at opposite ends."

This was now unchartered territory for Joel. He had never talked about his father. Not to anyone in barracks, Ivan, Julie, even his mother. A wry smile leapt out from his lips like a raconteur about to tell the killer joke. "Old man, old man!"

"Go on," she said.

"You got any rollies?" he asked.

Julie placed a blue packet on the table. "Here."

"He'd always sit there in his armchair telling me about this tour and that tour, this squaddie pal and that one like it was his life or something."

"Well it was wasn't it? He did spend twenty odd years in. That's a heck of a long time."

"He didn't have to. He could have said to Granddad: No thanks! I'll try something else. Anything! Building houses, pig farming, delivering beer barrels, molecular scientist… I don't know. But no, he had to follow granddad's orders and join the Kings. 'Best infantry for the job,' Granddad would always preach when he was recounting his war stories. Was amusing as a kid, it's only now I realise it's been the poison that's run through our families blood for many, many generations, Jules."

He fiddled around with his jacket pocket until a card dropped onto the table. "See this?" he thrust the card towards her.

"What is it?"

"Read it."

"It's a picture of you with some numbers, some kind of ID?"

"Just read it."

She took the card, squinting at the small font.

HM ARMED FORCES

PTE J LUNDY KINGS HAMPSHIRE

24060422

"What about it?" She asked.

"The number at the bottom."

"Is it some kind of number tag?"

He nodded. "Just a number is all you are. But this number, the last four digits are the same as Dad's. 0422"

"That is some coincidence."

"Is it?"

"Of course, it is."

"I saw it as some weird fate, when the recruiting officer told me my number. Like this was my destiny, Dad's destiny. There was no point resisting it. A curse, a cage that could not be broken. Even now as I sit here, on the run, I feel trapped. And now it has caught up with Mum too."

As he dried the last teardrop from his cheeks it felt like the shackles had lifted slightly. He took a deep breath and looked out of the window; the little girl with the lollipop had disappeared.

Julie fiddled with her hair, weaving loops with her fingers then untying the knots, carefree. "This may sound crazy to you but do you think he had a choice? Sounds like your granddad may have coerced him."

"Of course he had a choice! Everyone's got a choice haven't they?" the china mug wobbled as he slammed his fist on the table. Julie sat back in her chair, surprised.

"I'm sorry," he said.

"Never seen you so worked up!" Her red eyebrows parted sideways. "I'm not going to keep telling you I'm sorry, it will be ok et cetera et cetera. Because to be honest you've probably heard it so much it feels empty."

He looked from side to side, feeling awkward, embarrassed with the outburst.

"All I can say is that I'm here for you." She took his hand and rubbed his arid, raggedy fingers against her plum clasp. He looked into her eyes and felt safe, wanted.

"Do you remember that night after our English Lit exams?" he said.

"English lit exams? Oh you mean our rendition of Macbeth after downing that nasty Drambuie you found," she replied.

"Yeah that's it. After I left you I ended up falling asleep in those bushes at the back of the football club…" He again felt around the air for rolling paper. "That was the first time I didn't arrive home. Remember it well considering I was pretty drunk. Sitting there in the bushes looking up at the full moon all I could think about was this destiny I had inherited, a divine right to follow in his footsteps, to not let the family down, to serve this country blah blah. Stand on my own two feet, start on this cursed journey that clings like a parasite to every male in the Lundy clan…"

Julie passed him a rolled cigarette. He lit the cigarette and exhaled a big smoke cloud into the bare ceiling joists.

"It was freezing that night. I remember shivering away next to a thick hedgerow but feeling unperturbed by the cold. I don't know, Jules, it felt like an in-grown toughness was starting to blossom, but not for anything the army was to throw at me. More like life in general."

He took a drag on the cigarette and brushed his hair from his forehead.

"It felt like I was on a ship sailing to a faraway place with only one captain steering; my destiny, my future." He paused and contemplated, gazing out of the window.

"What do you mean?"

His contemplative gaze moved away from the window and slewed towards a fair-haired man emptying coffee filters into a large bin.

"He's the one responsible! Responsible for everything, everything!" the anger returned in his eyes. "But hey it was for my own good eh?"

He felt the pores in his armpits moistening; the sweat filled his nostrils with an intense hit. The last time he had smelt the harsh whiff was standing in front of a sandbag.

"Listen I know you're angry it's ok to be. There are a lot of bad things that have happened. But it can get better, Joel."

"Anger. What defines anger? Irrational rage? Or a life of bitterness?"

He butted the cigarette out on the floor. "Mum followed him, just like I have. Down the path into the cage and then that's it, we were trapped; trapped in a machine that swallows up personalities and churns them into one. Squaddie or not. Conform or end up ostracised. Like a black swan circling the lake never knowing if he wants to join the flock or not." He exhaled and sat back on his stool, his cheeks rouge and the whites in his eyes incandescent.

Julie ceased playing with the fine strands of hair in her palm. "I never realised you hated it so much, why did you not mention it before?"

"Scared I guess. I always imagined someone was looking over my shoulder, waiting to try me for espionage or treason or something."

"That's ridiculous!"

"I know. But all the time I heard Dad banging on about the army made me feel even more unsecure, unconfident. I was a quivering wreck."

"Why what did he say?"

"All the usual rhetoric which I heard from the guys I was in with. King's Regiment being the best infantry in the army and how it flowed through the family's bloodline, right back to the 1800s!" He coughed. "Then it was the whole army encompassing family idea. Houses we lived in, the food on our plates, the air we were breathing. Whether that was in Cyprus or Northern bloody Ireland."

"Do you reckon he REALLY believed all that?" she interjected.

He wiped his forehead and rubbed his tired eyes. "I don't know, at first I would have said yes but there were moments when I saw fear in his eyes. A kind of fear in his face like he didn't quite know where his life was going, as if the years were catching up with him."

"Did Belinda ever say anything to you?"

"About what?"

"Just general stuff. How she felt."

"Not really. Think she was scared."

"Of what, your dad?"

"And the system, she was so scared of

going back to her life in Worcester."

Julie signalled to the man behind the counter for the bill, then turned towards Joel. "I never told you this but I spoke to her a few years back on the high street. She seemed different, like she wanted to tell me something. Think she was ready to put the army behind her and was ready to move on."

His brow arched. "Go on."

"Let's walk." she grabbed her satchel.

"I'm sorry, Jules, was there somewhere else you had to be today? There's me venting."

"It's fine, c'mon. Let's walk." They dragged the short stools along the wooden floor and tucked them under the round table. As they headed for the door Joel stumbled on a doorstop jutting out next to a brush mat. "Ow!" he yelled. Julie smirked like a giddy schoolgirl.

The wind rushed down the alleyway, lifting Joel's short fringe into the air. His hair hung stuck in time for a few seconds while the shoppers rushed past the diminutive figure of Julie Jay. Julie ignored the oncoming buzz of hurried consumers, gently gliding along the pavement, angelic. He took a quick peep out of the corner of his eye while her dress dragged along the dirty pavement. He took another look but could not find a micro-spec of dirt on the beige cotton.

"Let's head over to Copthorne Park. This

lot are already annoying me." She gestured at a middle-aged woman with heavy shopping bags barging against a sea of legs.

"Oh, and by the way, Joel." She grabbed the sleeve of his jacket and pointed her nose into his chest.

Lethargically he turned towards her.

"You know you stink right?"

37.

A mist hovered over the playground, clutching at rusty swing bars and the handles of a see-saw painted red. With the mist a chill grew in the air, a sharp chill that cut like a spear through the air and rattled Joel's bones to the core.

He buttoned up his jacket and looked down at the small rectangular table lodged between his knees with marker pens strewn over the surface. He spread his elbows towards the tight walls of the hut, looking outside at a group of children who stared dumfounded at the grown man squashed into the playhouse. But they were now used to the site of this eccentric man in a tatty denim jacket, scribbling away on his canvas, ignoring the outside world.

He looked down at the family of creatures sketched into the table, then reached for a Rizla packet and tobacco pouch nestled in his jacket pocket. He emptied some tobacco onto the table with his free hand. A few brown crumbs fell out of the packet. He picked up the tobacco with the edges of his fingertips, carefully placing them in the paper and lit the limp cigarette. All he could taste was wet paper at the back of his throat.

He buttoned up his jacket and left the playhouse with the wind chilling his bones and a dampness hanging in the autumnal air. He had done this routine many times, scouring the pavements around the playground for cigarette butts, discarded tobacco packets or if he was lucky a whole cigarette.

The chill blew straight at his cheeks, penetrating deep into the stubble forest occupying his face. He rubbed his hands together and looked up at the sky at a small white dot passing overhead. He gazed at the dot, wondering if it was a missile on its way to the Middle East or a chartered flight to Tenerife. Rubbing his eyes he slowly walked along the path; dizzy, dehydrated and starved of nicotine. He approached a gate at the end of the playground path. It blew open from a big gust of wind and he slipped through, each time managing to get through a tighter gap between gate and post as the weeks had gone by. A sharp pain struck the back of his head as he closed the gate. A sudden pain, like he was being watched. The same feeling from Hannover.

"Go on, just take me. Get it over and done with!" His time on the street had heightened his senses, increasing his paranoid delusions. A crosshair on a rifle, a pair of beady eyes, a lion in a zoo. He felt it. Like a cancer clinging to a dying body. The pair of eyes beamed straight into the marrow of his skull, locking him into place. No escape.

He panicked, thinking of the RMPs set to drag him back to battalion, dead mum or not.

No great escape, just hard time in

Colchester and a reputation for being a deserter, a coward. With the sudden thought of incarceration, he turned on his ankles and moved his head back towards the playground, ready to confront the intruder hunting him down.

The figure, just about visible in the mist raised its hand and the hand hung in the air, steady and upright. He made out a tatty black leather jacket hanging off the stranger's sloping shoulders, and a pair of dirty white jogging bottoms.

"Joel!" the stranger shouted. "Joel!"

The stranger waved again.

"Joel, it's me, son!" the stranger shouted. Joel focused on the stranger. He could make out the tired lines on his face and the body frame once solid as a rock, now beginning to droop.

Alfred walked towards the gate. A shadow following behind.

Joel's lips veered halfway towards a smile, a smile that had been impossible for many weeks, months. He unlocked the gate and slowly trudged towards the old man. He stopped ten metres from his father and dolefully scanned the bark chips that were sprawled across the playground track. "My son. It's good to see you, Joel!" Alfred's hands were shaking incessantly. "Been trying to find you for days."

Joel wiped his forehead with the sleeve

of his jacket. "Alright, Dad…" his brain froze, cutting off his vocal chords. "I… I…"

Alfred took a few more steps forward. He reciprocated, trotting forwards.

Alfred's eyes appeared sharp, focused. As if the fog had been lifted. Joel noticed a similar expression on his face to when he was home after the gruelling deployment to the Gulf War.

In a sudden rush of emotion Alfred charged forward, grabbing his son by the shoulders, squeezing him, holding the thin bones in his clubby hands. Joel froze, unable to reciprocate the embrace, standing like a corpse frozen in time with mouth wide open and eyes glued together.

"Where have you been? Look at you!" he whispered into Joel's ear.

Joel tried to move his feet. The soles were rooted to the pavement. He tried again, it felt like the ground was swallowing up his body into a pit located underneath the Westhamton sewer, reserved only for the damned, the nihilists, the infidels, the ones who hated the family structure and its poisonous loyalties. He looked straight ahead into the field where he had spent many nights wandering, looking for answers. Suddenly she appeared out of the mist: a blurry epiphany, her mousey hair blowing in the wind. It was his mother, kitted out in a chequered shirt and stonewash jeans. He smiled at her. "No need for white gowns in heaven. Wouldn't have been your style eh, Mum?"

Belinda gazed at Joel, hands in her pockets, a serene look on her face. She then turned around and walked across the field in the opposite direction, strutting purposefully into the mist.

A sour drop left his eye. As the tear rolled down his cheek he grabbed the old man's stale-smelling jacket and held it close to his face; it smelt stale and worn, of hope crushed, dreams shattered and of a life that had taken a sharp turn into the unknown.

38.

Sun rays peeped through the net curtains, warming the side of Joel's cheek. He could see the waves of orange in his dream as he awoke slowly and stayed in the same position on the bed; basking in the warm rays. A chirp from a sparrow outside his window opened his eyes.

Another day was beginning. But this day felt different. It didn't feel like he had to exist. He felt like he could live today, be hopeful. He tossed away the duvet and headed for the bathroom.

"Eggs? Want some eggs?" Alfred shouted up the stairs.

"Sounds good," Joel replied.

He showered and began hacking away at the fierce stubble occupying his face. Once his skin was sheening and smooth, he wrapped a towel around his body and sat on the toilet-seat. He could still smell it somewhere on his body, the smell of the street lurking under a hidden pore. All the soap and shampoo and conditioner could not erase those weeks spent sleeping on urine-stained cardboard and eating a putrid diet.

He arose from the toilet-seat, went back into the bedroom searching in a chest of drawers for a pair a trousers and white shirt. With a thrust of a steam iron he pressed the clothes, hurriedly put them on and ran down the stairs. A framed photo of his mother hung in the hallway as he passed.

Alfred waved a spatula in the air. "C'mon then, sit down."

Joel went up to the mirror in the kitchen and fiddled with his hair, combing it into a side parting. Alfred finished frying the last egg and joined him at the table while the oven hummed in the background. Father and son broke open the yolks on their plates and dipped brown bread into it.

"What time's your train?" Alfred asked.

"Nine twenty. Need to get my skates on."

"Sure you don't want a lift?"

"No it's alright. Could do with the fresh air."

"Well don't say I didn't offer!"

Joel wiped crumbs from his chin and mockingly glared at his father. "That's the only time you'll be offering!"

Joel wiped his mouth, searching for a packet of Golden Virginia on the table and glanced at his father. "I know, I know. Clean turkey not easy you know."

"You'll thank me someday."

Joel placed his knife and fork on his plate. "Right, that's me."

They both slowly moved towards the front door. Joel grabbed a rucksack and threw a black denim jacket over his shoulders.

A sudden silence gripped the thin passageway as Joel felt his father's heartbeat pumping through the air. Alfred stared at a small crack appearing on the side of the yellow wall.

"Really need to start looking at these cracks that keep appearing," said Alfred.

Joel nodded his head politely and closed his lips. "Well I'll be seeing you soon then, Dad."

Alfred's bottom lip quivered. "I know I will. Your mum would be proud y'know."

Without parting his lips Joel reciprocated with a grin. Alfred moved into the porch, opened the latch on the front door and stood silent.

"Don't let those screws give you too much shit, son." He waved his son towards the door, his countenance downbeat yet calm as he ushered his son back into the wild world of reality. Joel shuffled into the porch and caught the first nip of the frosty morning air. The Westhamton air tasted good today.

He took two steps out of the door then turned around and grabbed his father by the shoulders. The muscle had become squidgy and flabby. He squeezed hard, glancing at the old soldier from the side: his nostril hair turning grey, circles forming under the eyes. Alfred stared straight ahead towards the Pritchards' front door across the Terrace. A dog barked. A sweet wrapper blew past. A car engine sparked into life.

Joel broke the embrace and took a final look at the old man standing in his grey jogging bottoms and oversized cotton shirt. Radiance was forming in his cheeks as the shell-shocked look departed. In its place was a vacant look, akin to a farm animal accepting it's lot; nonplussed, indifferent, c'est la vie.

For the first time in his life he felt sorrow for the old man. But he also knew the old man was tough; he'd get through it and he knew he would see him again. He may have lost his wife and his instruction on how to live but he was not going to lose his son. Alfred Lundy was not a perfect husband, soldier, father. All along he was just trying to make the best of his lot. Maybe now he could experience something else, a new direction away.

Joel waved his right arm and lifted his rucksack over his shoulder. "Bye Dad."

He strolled down Reigate Terrace and caught a glimpse of curtains twitching and eyeballs shining. The playing field appeared and his shoes squelched in the mud as an imaginary football was kicked into the sky. Something inside felt peculiar, like a force was killing all the negativity in his head. As he took a deep breath, his spine tingled; levity wrapped itself around his legs. It felt spiritual, like his soul was being nudged into the heavens.

He approached the gap in the bush, slid through and joined the A314. He walked for half a mile down the A314, marching in a straight line with intent.

"Oi!" His clarity ignored the familiar voice. "Oi! Joel Lundy!" He turned around.

There she stood in the middle of the pavement, all five feet four inches, wrapped up in sheep-skin jacket and red trousers, oblivious to two boys loitering past, eavesdropping. He loosened the grip on his rucksack and gazed at the pavement. "Going to leave without saying goodbye, were we?"

"Not as simple as that, Jules."

She stood rooted to the spot. "You're off to hand yourself in, aren't you Jesse James?" A chortle left his lungs, laughing at her way with words. Here he was about to plead guilty to an AWOL charge and he was being compared to an outlaw from the wild-west.

"It's for the best. Can't start afresh without getting this monkey off my back."

She released her hands from her jacket. "What you reckon they'll give you?"

"Not sure, could end up in the garrison nick. They'll give me what they give me."

"Well let's hope for the best eh?"

He curled his lips together. "My only crime is wanting to be free, free. That's all, Jules, escape this bloody cage that's been locked. Locked for so long…" His brow lifted in a triumphant pose. "I'm going back without a conscience."

Julie looked at the confident figure stood in front of her, hair tidily combed, clothes neatly ironed, shoes tied in nice neat bows, the muddy colour in his eyes turning light, hazel. A self-assurance beaming.

"So what about your dad?

"What about him?"

"You getting on better?"

He smirked like he was in on the funniest joke and swapped his rucksack onto the other shoulder. He then looked up at the sun breaking through a cloud; angels dancing, the devil doing the tango with God. The cage doors were creaking.

"Mum, Dad, me. I think we're in a better place now. I mean I still want her to be back with us badly. But things have to move on." His attention turned to Julie's red locks. "Thanks, Jules, for everything. I can't thank you enough."

"Well I can't say I did an awful lot, you just needed some ears." She nodded at him pensively. "Look after yourself, Joel, you hear me." She walked up to him and kissed him on the cheek. He took a step back.

"Be seeing you soon."

He left Julie on the pavement. As he crossed the road he turned around for one final glance. She was gone. Just like that.

Stretching out of Westhamton from Londonderry to Limassol he felt the force of the cage. The big rusty old cage was starting to crumble all around him in a silent collapse. It creaked and groaned in the cool, windy morning. As he approached Station Road, a flicker appeared before his eyes; bright yellow specks that flashed and pulsed against his retinas. The specks whizzed past him like fireworks in the night.

The last time he had seen the yellow flashes darting above the grey buildings seemed an age ago. They were muted then. He now heard a melodic chirp, bringing the train station to life. The high pitch tones drowned out the car engines on the road and the tannoy of the station. 'Chirp! Chirp!'

The canaries did a loop of the station then flew within inches of his nose, quickly changing the angle of their flight path to avoid the Westhamton station sign.

The flashes pulsed in mid-air, hovered for a few seconds, then disappeared beyond the station perimeter. The chirping blew in the wind, lingering in his conscious; unhindered, jovial, free.

As he walked into the station, he overheard the vendor talking Urdu down a mobile phone. The key cutter was shredding pieces of steel on a cutting machine, humming a Shadows song. They carried on regardless, without noticing the convict ready to board a train back to the real world.

He boarded the next train headed for London and looked at the palms of his hands. The jitters had gone. He took a blue biro pen out of his rucksack and drew the numbers on his palm… 0 4 2 2. He then licked his finger and scrubbed until all that was left was a faint smudge on his palm.

He looked to the sky as the train rattled through the villages of Hampshire, passing cottage gardens whose flowers had now set seed, pubs with Labradors laying on the grass and trees of the woods shedding the last of their leaves. Christmas was not far away.

The great blue sprawling sky floated above his head: a cauldron of optimism and hope laying in front of him. Maybe anything was possible.

39.

The guardroom of Gallipoli barracks. A hollow transitory room, full of echoing voices, none staying for very long. He picked out a rectangular battalion photograph hanging off an indigo wall. Some four hundred soldiers packed onto the parade square on benches, seven rows tall. He picked out a few faces in the front row looking stern, purposeful. He now recognised something in their young, fresh faces not seen before. The same look on his father's face back in the days when Joel was just a toddler: stoic, purposeful, of life having meaning.

"Right then, Lundy. Need you to sign these forms here," said the guard commander.

"Here?"

"Yeah that'll do."

Joel put pen to paper and with a stroke of the ink his life was signed back. It took seconds. He had expected a drawn-out sentence in the pits of the barracks, mopping a cold floor everyday with only a hairy assed provost sergeant for company and a routine of hard, punishing exercise. It didn't happen. The medical officer had deemed Private Joel Lundy 'eligible for early release due to family circumstances' and he was given two weeks incarceration in the guard room.

"What you got up your sleeve now then?"

the guard commander seemed curious.

Joel finished packing some clothing and a drawing pad into the same rucksack he had left Westhamton with weeks ago. "Haven't figured it out to be honest, take it day by day."

"Well good luck anyway, Lundy, if it's all it's cracked up to be. Give us a shout yeah? Name's Finchton, B Company." The guard commander looked Joel in the eye like he meant it; intrigue and fascination, a curious envy of the ex-squaddie ready to take the next step in life.

"Finchton? What's your Christian name?"

"Christian," he replied.

"Yeah, Christian name?"

"That's it."

"What… Christian?"

The guard commander nodded.

"So long then Christian, you seem like a good guy. All the best!" Joel slung the rucksack on his shoulder and vacated the guard room.

The steps out of the guard room were icy, glistening against a mirror on the steel gate. He slowly made his way down the steps, exhaling a triumphant sigh into the fresh morning air. He looked back at the parade square, to the giant Christmas tree in the middle of the square adorned in the shiniest of silver tinsel. In the fading light of morning the lights on the tree flashed; reds, yellows, greens, blues. Pulsing with the excitement that Christmas was coming.

The guard at the gate signalled to Joel. No need for words. The steel gate opened, and a wash of bright heavenly light poured in from the Ziegborn main straße.

A figure appeared out of the light, sat on the bonnet of a car with a UK registration.

"You ready?" Alfred signalled to his son, tactically avoiding the glare of the 1st Battalion Kings Hampshire Regiment plaque. The yearning on his face had gone, the subtle looks craving for some semblance of routine in the military machine. Instead, his face, now crisply shaved with pink cheeks, focused solely on Joel.

Joel turned around to look one last time at Gallipoli barracks. The large steel gate closed tight. The machine carrying on regardless, waiting for the next big deployment from Westminster. A blackbird sat on the edge of the gate with a small worm squirming in its beak. Joel glanced at the King's Regimental plaque. "Maybe that's just the way it is," he whispered to the blackbird.

Alfred winked at his son. Joel smiled back at his father as he turned his back for the final time, feeling the creaking carousel grinding to a halt before his very eyes. He then nodded at the two figures sitting on a brick wall on the other side of the street; one looked like his mother, the other more of a faded image, half in this world, half fading into another realm. He squinted and recognised the mysterious, blurred figure sat next to his mother, wrapped in a patchwork jacket.

A beaming smile, full of unbridled hope, leapt towards her. "Don't worry. I had that shower in the end!"

Alex Conway was born in 1978 in Luton, Bedfordshire. He served in the 2nd Battalion Royal Green Jackets between 1997-2000 and was based in Paderborn, Germany. During his service he was involved in two tours of the Balkans region, serving in Bosnia-Herzegovina and Kosovo.

He now lives in London having worked for many media broadcast companies. He also works part time as a copywriter.